CATRINA WHITEHEAD

LEGAL INSANITY: THE CAVIAR CAPER

Catrina Whitehead

LEGAL INSANITY

CHAPTER 1

DISORIENTATION DAY

I walked into the firm of Wagner, Tibbs, and Cobbs on my first day as a new associate, continued past the receptionist's desk, and down a short hallway that led to the attorney's offices. My high heels echoed loudly on the marble floor. The stern visages of named partners, some now dead, peered sternly down at me from their photographs hung on wood-paneled walls on either side of the entryway into the inner sanctum. Even as I promised myself I would exceed all expectations, I felt their imaginary disapproval.

After three grueling years at a top-tier law school, this was an enviable position according to my classmates. Wagner, Tibbs and Cobbs was high on the list of the most prestigious law firms in the area although known for chewing up and spitting out at least one new hire every year. There was definitely an air of something to prove. I was girded to devote everything I had gained in earning my legal license to the task of proving my place. While other law students had spent leisure time at the local bar or attending concerts, I'd been almost bereft of close friendships and completely devoted to my end goal. *Now, it's all going to pay off. Right?*

Exiting the short corridor, I found the glass-enclosed main conference room in front of me. They said my office would be to the left and my name would be outside the door. I turned to that direction, peering at names on office doors until I found my own on a gold engraved tag outside a door. As I entered, I discovered my assigned partner, Thomas Carbone, already waited in my yet-decorated office, sitting in a guest chair and drinking a cup of coffee from a large mug bearing the firm's logo. I was early, but it felt like I was late.

He didn't waste time with a welcome or hello. "Ms. Ashford, I have a research project I want you to get right on. Black market caviar sales. They're ruining our client's aquaculture business."

I dropped my purse behind the prominent, wooden associate's desk and sat down. The chair looked like it had been borrowed from a conference room. I glanced around frantically for a pen or paper to take notes, to no avail. Mr. Carbone looked at me expectantly. I met his gaze as he resumed with a sigh. "As I started to explain, I have a new case concerning a caviar farm. Our client raises California sturgeon for their roe. He believes there are illegal sales of wild caviar in direct competition with his business. We need to find out who, where, and how, and stop it."

It was too early in the morning. I hadn't been adequately caffeinated. "Caviar farm? They farm fish eggs in California?"

Mr. Carbone shot me a look of disgust as if I were the lowest form of intelligence on the planet. "Yes. You'd better get educated about California caviar quickly. We're meeting with the client, Ben Akers, tomorrow afternoon." He abruptly stood, turned with military precision, and left.

I breathed out a sigh and looked around. A large, empty bookcase on the wall in front of me spanned nearly the entire length of my relatively compact office from the doorway to the next wall. Two uncomfortable-looking, black faux-leather guest chairs, one previously occupied by Mr. Carbone, sat between the bookcase and my desk. My generic associate's desk was empty except for an office-style phone with rows of unlabeled buttons and a large, outdated desktop computer. Behind me, immense windows spanned the length of the back wall, providing a view of the parking lot and an abundance of glare on the computer screen.

A four-year degree followed by a two-year M.B.A. and then three years of law school got me to this point where I was fresh meat and staring down more than a quarter million in debt of student loans. I paid my first set of dues in law school but now there were clearly new dues to pay. I could expect to make partner in about four years if I played my cards right, but it meant figuring out the way big law works and devoting myself to the firm. Until then, my personal life was on hold. It wasn't like I had a personal life anyway. New city. New apartment. New professional wardrobe. At least a small assortment that I could afford before my first paycheck.

My thoughts were interrupted. A woman appeared at my doorway. Sixties, slightly plump, but well-kept, she wore dark gray slacks and a tucked-in white button-down shirt. Her short gray hair and black glasses could have looked stern but for her pink complexion and understanding smile. "Good morning, Ms. Ashford. I'm Felicity Banks, your secretary. Or at least partly your secretary. You share me with Mr. Compton."

Felicity. Old-fashioned name, but it suits her. "Good morning, Ms. Banks. Skyler Ashford. New here. But then, you knew that."

"Just Felicity, please. Yes, they briefed me regarding your arrival. I'm here to get you settled. First, we need to get you some office supplies and a tour. Oh, and do you have your diplomas with you?"

"Uh, no…was I supposed to?"

"Just bring them in tomorrow. Let me show you around." She looked at me expectantly.

I stood, following Felicity down the hall past dozens of attorney's offices, each with a secretary's station on the opposite side of the hall. As we passed a kitchenette break room, Felicity gestured at the open doorway. "Coffee brewer with pods available at all times. Feel free to put perishables in the refrigerator, but make sure they are clearly labeled. We clean things out on Fridays, so if you leave anything past then, it won't be here when you return on Monday." I nodded even though she wasn't paying any attention to me as she quickly marched on.

Felicity turned abruptly into a large side room, and I followed as she rattled on. "Copying. I'll give you a code. You'll need to enter your personal code and a client number each time you use one of the machines." The place looked like a copy-n-ship store. Three huge machines lined one wall. A large worktable sat at the center. Shelves against the back wall held reams of various papers, envelopes, labeled dividers, boxes of paper clips, and assorted binder clips. Another table against the side wall housed both standard and high-capacity staplers, as well as hole punches and binding machines.

A sturdy and muscular young man wearing khakis and a red polo shirt emblazoned with the firm's logo looked up from multiple stacks of papers at the center table. Felicity smiled at him. "Gabe, meet Ms. Ashford. New associate. Ms. Ashford, Gabe is here for any document preparation needs you might require. He's also a new hire. Just yesterday." I smiled at Gabe and started to say hello, but Felicity was already out the door and looking back at me. Gabe shot me a strange look. I shrugged before exiting to catch up with my tour guide. I felt his eyes continue to stare at me intently like he was studying a bug under a magnifying glass as I left.

We walked past another room with row upon row of filing cabinets. Felicity paused at the doorway before moving on. "File room." As we proceeded past the vast records storage space, she pointed to a closed door. "Restrooms are in the outer hallway. You can access them through here."

Walking through the next door, we entered another room with rows of industrial shelving. "Supplies. Call if you need them. Don't walk down here and waste time. I'll bring them to you." Felicity efficiently gathered pens, yellow legal pads of paper, and other basics as I contemplated her meaning. Meanwhile, I observed a shelf filled with an assortment of over-the-counter medications—pain relief, Band-Aids, cold and flu remedies, cough syrup, antidiarrheal, and pink bismuth syrup. It looked like a miniature pharmacy, clearly insinuating how sick you had to be to stay home.

Arriving at my office, Felicity deposited the office supplies on my desk. "Grab a pen so you can take down some numbers."

I dutifully grabbed a pen and legal pad. "42685 is your personal code to operate the copiers. You will also need to enter a client code for each use. Use 9999 if you use the copier for personal use. They will keep track. The access code for the front door security panel is 5834. It gets changed monthly. You'll get an email when it's been changed. Your computer login has been set to 'associate' and '$password!' but you need to change that right away. I.T. has made sure it's only good for today since it's not a strong password. They're careful about security. Is there anything else I can do for you?"

I was still stunned by the whirlwind tour, hoping I could find my way back to the bathroom when necessity called. "No. Thank you."

"I'll email you a phone directory. In the meantime, if you need me, just dial my extension on the intercom. Human Resources will send you all the forms you need to fill out for tax withholdings, insurance, and such. After you fill them out, you can return them to Annette in HR down the hall to the right. If you don't get those done by the end of the day, she'll come look in after you."

I nodded. Felicity looked at me like she was dropping off a child on the first day of kindergarten before exiting my office, leaving me to navigate my new world.

It was only nine o`clock, and my senses felt like they'd been assaulted—no gradual entry into this job. I stashed the office supplies in a drawer, turned on the antiquated desktop, and logged into the firm's software portal. There was a client directory. I scrolled through the As but didn't find a file labeled "Akers." I buzzed Felicity. Thankfully, her name was next to one of the intercom buttons on the phone.

"How can I help you, Ms. Ashford?"

"I was looking for the file for Ben Akers, but I don't see it in the client files."

"Oh, that would be under Chairo Caviars."

"Huh? How do you spell that? Is that like the Egyptian city?"

"No, not Cairo. C-H-A-I-R-O. Something about a Greek word for cheerful, I recall hearing."

"Thanks, Felicity." I hung up the phone, then scrolled down to the Cs in the client file directory until I found Chairo Caviar and a client number. Clicking on the file, I found no documents. It must have been newly opened.

About the only thing I knew about fish eggs was putting salmon roe on a hook as bait to fish for lake trout with my dad—the fishy smell of the eggs, the bright red color, and the slightly sticky feel as I put them on the hook. I'd never thought of them as food, although I now found several websites were selling them as a type of caviar.

I'd always thought of caviar as the tiny, black pearls from Russia portrayed in some movie where they wanted to impress you with how much money the high roller had. It was always Beluga and served in tiny bowls with tiny mother-of-pearl spoons. Growing up poor and then eking my way through law school on an inadequate student budget, I had no personal experience with such a product. No real interest in something sometimes described as salty and fishy. No need to show off to my friends. I'd spent the last few years as a starving student, grateful to find a hard pack of ramen noodles that wasn't expired lurking in my cupboard. I'd struggled, not wanting to call my folks to ask for money.

This was going to be my first client encounter with Mr. Carbone watching. I needed to become informed and sophisticated concerning caviar before that meeting. I logged onto the antiquated computer and began the learning curve to navigate the firm's software and then start some research.

When the lunch hour arrived, I felt awkward. I didn't have any friends yet. I hated the thought of eating alone in my office almost as much as I dreaded the potential of an unintentional foray into office politics in the lunchroom. Fortunately (or not), Mr. Carbone stuck his head in my doorway. "Firms taking you to lunch for your first day. We're going to Brookside. Do you want me to drive, or do you want to meet us there?"

"Uh. If you don't mind driving, I'm not familiar with this part of the city yet." *Hmmm...Brookside's a nice place.*

Carbone started walking without another word. I hastily grabbed my purse and followed like a servant walking five steps behind. He didn't slow and didn't seem to have a problem with it. We went to the elevator, rode down five levels to the main lobby, then turned down a long hallway leading to the back lot where employees parked. Carbone showed me to a high-end sports car and unlocked the door. This year's model. Back-up video, built-in computer with voice commands, supple leather, burled wood dash. It smelled of money and potential, if one applied themselves and paid heavy dues to make partner.

The restaurant was not far away—a gathering place for the lawyers, accountants, and other professionals who lived to network. Carbone was silent the entire drive. He held the door open as we entered the restaurant, and I wasn't sure if it was gentlemanly or obligatory and condescending. The hostess showed us to a table toward the back set for twenty. Most of the chairs were already filled by other attorneys from the firm. One in particular, a man in his late forties with graying hair and a shiny light gray suit, rose as we approached. "Carbone, good to see you. I see you have your new associate."

"Yes. This is Skyler Ashford. Ms. Ashford, this is Daniel Tellis, senior litigation partner."

I shook his hand, making sure to provide a reasonably firm grip back and providing good eye contact. "Good to meet you, sir."

Carbone indicated two seats toward the middle of the table, apparently saved for us. "Ms. Ashford, these are our other new associates, Carly Jeffries and Peter Mand." He indicated two young lawyers across the table from us. A young woman with short, dark hair, and hazel eyes, wearing a serious navy-blue skirt suit. A young East Indian man with dark eyes and hair, wearing a cheap but professional black suit, white shirt, and non-descript tie. Both looked like they faced an inquisition, body language stiff and voices quiet.

As I sat, Carbone nodded toward another man who appeared to be Armenian, mid-forties, slightly balding, with glasses perched on a diminutive nose. "This is Theodore Melikian, head of our transactional department." Melikian looked up briefly from his menu, gave me a nod, and got right back to deciding on his meal. Melikian was sitting next to Peter Mand. I wondered if he was Mand's assigned partner like I had been assigned to Carbone.

The woman seated next to me was in her mid-thirties, with short, blonde hair and blue-green eyes. She wore white slacks, with a white silk short-sleeved blouse covered by a flowing long-sleeved silk jacket in multiple shades of green. I was surprised she wasn't wearing a suit and wondered if she was also a lawyer. She looked over and quietly said, "Welcome. Skyler, is it? I'm Diane Walden. I'm a junior partner working primarily in trusts and estates, but I also do some real estate law. Do you know what kind of cases you want to work on?"

"Not really. Not yet. This is my first position other than clerking. I clerked last year for Delaney, Gerber, and Martens. They had me do a lot of corporate drafting. I also got to work on a banking law litigation case."

"Good firm. I'm sure you gained some valuable experience with corporate transactions and the litigation process generally." She smiled congenially.

I hated to tell her how little I felt like I'd learned. I realized how much law school had not prepared me for the actual practice of law. After figuring out that plagiarism is encouraged in the legal profession, I'd started keeping a personal computer file of every good contract provision, discovery response, motion argument, and contract I could get my hands on. I'd also learned that the other attorneys you work with can make or break you. Even crush you until you run crying to the ladies' room no matter how tough you think you are. This was especially true of the women toward their own kind—either your best friend or watch for a knife in your back. After a particularly ego-shattering encounter, leaving scorched earth behind, I was wary.

I looked down at the menu the waitress had left at my place. First firm luncheon death traps. I imagined that menu was screaming out silent first impressions. The burger says you're unsophisticated. The lobster says you're a leech. The spaghetti is messy. The salad says you're a little lady at a table of almost all male senior partners. And that doesn't even get to the booze. Half of the partners had a gin and tonic or a dirty olive martini they were nursing, but that would be a label of irresponsibility for a mere associate. On the other hand, there was definitely a Good Ole Boys Club feel, even as a few stray female partners were given an equipment waiver to join that insider group. When the waitress returned and asked for my order, it was nothing about what I wanted to eat and all about avoiding all the labels my brain was attaching to the food options. "The Chicken Masala and an iced tea, please. The mashed potato and seasonal vegetable side options." *Whew! If cases took this much mental energy, I was going to be completely knackered by three o'clock.*

Luckily, the polite conversation around the table took little effort. Virtually ignored by the veterans, my best bet was just not to say something stupid. It was a great time to listen and observe. The other new associates eyed me. It seemed obvious we'd all come to the same conclusion. We'd talk later, but not in front of this crowd.

We didn't get back from lunch until one-thirty. I wasn't stupid enough to think I could get away with that on my own any other day, but today I was with Carbone. It was turning into a nice, leisurely first day. That is, as long as I had enough information on aquaculture by the end of the day to hold my own at tomorrow's client meeting. Aquaculture. Yeah, that was the correct term. Not fish farming. I'd learned that much.

Back at my desk, Felicity looked in on me. "How'd the firm's new associate lunch go?"

I took a hard look at her. *Another woman. Best friend or staunch enemy? There's been no in-between in the legal world. At least not any exception that I'd met yet. Did I want to trust her on my first day? Secretary, not attorney. Informant?* I decided to play it safe. We could be chummy later—or not. "It was very kind of the partners to take the new associates to such a nice lunch."

She chuckled. "Have you sized them up yet? I've seen associates come and go. They give you an impossible billable-hours minimum, and you have to scare up your own work."

"What do you mean? I work for Mr. Carbone on his cases."

She smirked. "Until he doesn't have casework that

suits you or decides he likes one of the other associates better or something else."

"Then what?"

"You'd better make other friends. Check with other senior partners to see if they need help. It's also a good way to figure out what type of legal work suits you."

Rats! She had a point. "Thanks for the tip."

"Oh, and that's before they tell you to bring in new business."

"How am I supposed to do that and still make billable hour minimums?"

She gave me a knowing smile. "It's the way to move up the ladder or become irrelevant and replaceable. You're going to hear it soon… You eat what you kill."

With that picture of the jungle I'd just been air-dropped into, Felicity left. I wasn't sure if that made her a doomsayer or a mentor, but I figured I'd better start logging those hours like every second counted. I'd already whiled away a whole morning.

When I logged back into the computer, there were several emails from HR with a stack of forms attached—tax withholdings, insurance options, malpractice insurance application questions, an employee handbook. By the time I'd finished with them and hunted down the human resources department after a couple of wrong turns, it was already four o'clock. I took the last hour of the working day for some rudimentary Google searches about caviar production in California. Relieved when the clock indicated five, I gathered my things and left, exhausted. Walking past the (all-male) partner photographs down the hallway, they seemed to sneer. They were not impressed…yet.

CHAPTER 2
BEN AKERS

Second day at the new firm. I took the elevator to the fifth floor, walked through the lobby, greeted Cammie, the receptionist, and headed for my office carrying my diplomas. Felicity jumped up from her desk as I approached. "Those the diplomas?"

"As requested." I took a sip of my Grande Latte with an extra espresso shot. Caffeine coursed through my veins, making me feel like I was ready to kill it today.

Felicity spread the framed documents out on her desk, frowning. "We're having these re-framed."

I blinked a couple of times. "Uh, okay, I guess."

"It's on the firm. We want them to look their best. I'll have it taken care of and have maintenance hang them when they're done."

I guess there's a particular way of doing everything around here.

She stacked the diplomas with pursed lips, then looked back at me as if she were wondering why I was still standing there, wasting time. *Why was I still standing there wasting time? Billable time.*

"Don't forget your one o'clock meeting with Mr. Akers. I'll let you know as soon as he arrives."

How could I forget?

I dumped my purse in my office then headed back down the mysterious hallway to see if I could find the lunchroom to deposit my salad with grilled chicken strips I'd brought from home. After peering through every door, I finally found it. Entering the lunchroom, I found Carly and Peter huddled over the coffee pod brewer. They looked up simultaneously. We were alone. I suspected they were as anxious to drill me as I was them. Carly's suit skirt was halfway up her thigh today, displaying her long legs ending in a pair of patent stilettos. Not my style. I wanted to be taken seriously, not looked at like a poster girl.

I stuck my salad in the refrigerator before walking over. As I approached, Peter asked, "So, you're Carbone's fresh meat?"

"Guess so. I saw you with Melikian yesterday. He's your assigned partner?" I looked at him pointedly.

"Yeah. And Carly here is with Tripper in litigation. That's Grayson Oliver Tripper III. Third-generation lawyer. Grandfather was a founding partner." His eyes rolled slightly.

One of those good ole boys in the portrait hallway.

I asked, "Was Tripper at the lunch? I don't recall being introduced."

Carly's look turned sour. "He's in trial this week. I'm

stuck without enough to do until it's finished. Running around like a crazy person trying to find work to make billables. He didn't leave me any instructions or assign me to work with anyone else."

I turned toward Peter. "What about you? Do you have assignments?"

His lips pursed, and one eyebrow climbed upward. "A ton of corporate busywork. A client who didn't do his annual minutes for like a decade. Now he's getting sued. We're playing catch-up on the records before the discovery starts rolling in. The opposing attorney will probably be asking for answers to a million questions and requesting boxes of documents, including those corporate minutes that don't exist yet. We're backdating them as effective dates. Oh, and I'm reviewing force majeure clauses in some agricultural leases because a well collapsed. We're trying to attribute it all to an Act of God. The client hopes to get out of paying to drill a new well for six figures when he's only got a couple of years left on the deal. What about you?"

"They have me on some case about caviar poaching. I'm meeting with the client in a few hours along with Carbone."

They both looked at me with astonishment. Carly blew out a long breath. "He's letting you near a client already?"

I figured that didn't need a response, and I'd gathered about as much intel as was reasonable for this morning. I changed the subject. "Did you see the wall of meds in the supply room? Not so subtle hint we're supposed to be billing right through pneumonia."

It was like I'd set off a bomb. Peter stopped leaning against the counter and went to full attention. Carly hissed,

"Yeah, I don't know how I can make my billables goal unless I set up a cot. There have to be tricks to it." With slight panic in their eyes, they grabbed their coffee cups and made for the door.

They were right. Every second counted. It was signaled at every turn, from the wall of meds to the instruction to make Felicity go fetch if I needed a paperclip. My attention needed to be laser-focused on one thing—making the firm money. My job would depend on it. I clearly wasn't a valued employee–I was a profit center.

I arrived back at my office. Felicity had deposited a thick stack of billing tracker sheets on my desk. Old school paper. Columns for client, matter, work description, start time, and stop time. Documentation down to the minute. I buzzed Felicity.

"How can I help you, Ms. Ashford?"

"Thank you for the time sheets. At least, I think that was probably you. But why paper? Why not a computer system?"

"Oh, I do that for you. I enter all your time into the system daily, so you need to turn them in to me at the end of the day. The forms keep a reminder in front of you to build the habit. You need to make sure you're recording all of your time."

"About that. You said you'd seen a bunch of associates come and go. How did they complete the expected billable hours? Were they here until really late every night? Work weekends?"

"Some of that, yes. Associates are basically indentured servants to the firm. You pay your dues until you make junior partner. But you can also find ways to pad the bill."

I repeated, "Pad the bill? That sounds immoral." *I cringed at the accusation.*

"No, I didn't mean it that way. It would be wrong if you are fraudulent about the time that should be charged to a client, but let's say you're waiting in court for your case to be called and you know you're trailed on the docket, meaning your case will be heard at the end. In that case, you can bill both clients if you're also reading some research or writing a letter. You have to wait, so it's appropriate to bill the client with the hearing. You're also doing something productive for the other client you're writing the letter for."

"I see."

"You will also always bill at least six minutes for a phone call. That's our billing minimum increment. But if you make two phone calls in ten minutes, each client is billed the minimum time. It all adds up."

"Anything else?"

"Talk to your partner, but most will tell you to charge a forms fee if you use a form already in our documents database."

"Forms fee?"

"Oh, my goodness, you *are* green. That's when you bill... say a half an hour for using a form that would take you half an hour to generate."

"Even if I'm using something already in the computer?" I was feeling a little greasy at this point.

"Exactly. Just add a bit of extra time to the task. It's

done all the time, so we're not reinventing the wheel."

"I don't know how I feel about it."

"Ms. Ashford, you're thinking small firm or solo. This is a big firm with a lot of overhead. Some of that overhead is you. You have a significant expectation placed on you to earn your keep and pay some of that overhead, as expressed by the minimum billables you agreed to when you signed on. I guarantee you'll get over yourself when you see how easy it is to get behind on that expectation. They hire several associates at a time. They always lose one or two within six months. You'd better get ready for that meeting. Good-bye."

As she hung up the phone, I began to get a sick feeling in my stomach. *Was that Felicity's idea of tough love? What the heck had I signed myself up for? Indentured servant. Billing bloat. A cutthroat competition to be the associate they keep. You eat what you kill. Not to mention the total jettison of any prospect of a social life... for years. Was it this way at all law firms?*

But I didn't have time to think about it. I had billables to create and a meeting to attend. And a lot to learn about caviar produced in California.

The intercom buzzed precisely at one o'clock. "Mr. Akers is here for his meeting. Mr. Carbone has requested you join them in Conference Room B. Cammie will show Mr. Akers back as soon as Mr. Carbone has arrived."

Where was Conference Room B? I grabbed a yellow pad and pen before exiting my office, frantically looking for

Felicity, who glanced up from her desk across the hall with a knowing expression. "Would you like me to show you to Conference Room B?"

I shot her an ever-so-grateful look. "Yes, if you would, please."

It was just off the hall of portraits. When I entered, Mr. Carbone was already there with Ben Akers, who was much younger than I expected. Close to my age and easy on the eyes. Rather than the stuffy businessman I'd expected, he was wearing jeans and a V-neck nylon sports top in a shade of dusky blue that brought out his eyes. I found myself slightly slack-jawed, which must have been apparent because Mr. Carbone nearly rolled his eyes as he said, "Ms. Ashford, have a seat."

He turned to Mr. Akers. "This is Skyler Ashford. New associate." He looked away from me dismissively.

Mr. Akers stood. With a warm smile, he extended his hand across the table. "Ms. Ashford, Ben Akers. I'm the guy with the caviar company. You're welcome just to call me Ben." As I shook his hand, his eyes met mine. I instantly liked him. Wanted to do a good job for him.

Ignoring the paper file beside him, Carbone opened his laptop to take notes. "Ben, can you tell us a little about what's been happening at the company?"

I took up my pen, ready to scribble notes on my simple legal pad of yellow, lined paper.

"Before the 1970s, caviar was obtained in the wild, but sturgeon population was threatened by overfishing, poaching, and pollution. A worldwide ban went into effect, leaving fish farming, or more properly aquaculture, as the only means of producing sturgeon caviar. Russia was known for having the best caviar in the world. Still, a couple of immigrants who relocated to California believed that local sturgeon could produce a superior roe able to compete with the Russians in quality. They were right. A Russian fish research biologist also defected from the Soviet Union. He helped jump-start the industry. Now, California produces about eighty percent of the caviar produced in the United States. That was around twelve to thirteen tons a few years ago. By now, my company alone produces that much.

"In the last six months, our production has dropped. The market for sales of our caviar has also dipped. We're investigating our facilities to determine why some females are reabsorbing their eggs. While that can be natural, it's unprecedented at this level in our stock. Additionally, the change in demand leads us to believe that a substantial amount of black-market caviar is being dumped on the market."

I was caught up in the story. So much so that I forgot that I was a lowly first-year associate who should be seen but not heard. "Isn't that a criminal matter?"

Carbone scowled. "There are both criminal and civil aspects."

Ben nodded, "The police have been investigating, but with everything else on their plates—murders, kidnappings, hate crimes—fish eggs are pretty low on their list of priorities. It's of more interest to Fish and Game, but they're understaffed. Aquaculture is an expensive business. We consume almost as much electricity as a small city in a year. If we don't find out who's behind this and shut them down soon, my business could go under. Fish and Game catches poachers all the time, but we've never felt this kind of effect on our business. That's why I'm turning to you as a last resort."

Carbone was dutifully taking notes on his computer. "Have you talked to Fish and Game?"

"Yeah. Bob Colburn. He's a fish biologist."

"And the police?"

"I called, but they said there was nothing they could do unless I was reporting a crime, like a theft at our facilities. As far as a general poaching ring, they said they'd look into it, but I don't have much confidence in any real action. They mentioned it's Fish and Game's investigation until there's proof of criminal activity."

"Do you think the decrease in production at your facility is somehow related to illegal fishing?"

"I'm not sure. Many animals can delay giving birth if they perceive their environment as unsafe. In the case of the mature female sturgeon, they can reabsorb eggs when they feel the conditions are not favorable for their future young. When we took samples recently, we found an unusual number of females that should be ready for harvest, but with no eggs. I've got my team on it, monitoring water conditions closely and watching for signs of stress. I don't know how that could possibly be related to poaching, but the timing feels suspicious. Maybe I'm just being paranoid, but I figured I should mention it."

"I have a retainer agreement for you to sign." Carbone withdrew a document from the file and slid it toward Ben.

Ben thumbed through the three-page document. His face grew stony. "Geez, Carbone, you serious about this retainer? That's a steep sum."

"We've got to hire a private investigator, pay the

associate here, and dog Fish and Game. We'll want more if we find something actionable and file litigation."

Ben raised an eyebrow, staring down Carbone with a stern gaze. "Give me a pen and get me some results...fast."

Carbone smiled and slid a blue ink pen across the table.

Ben signed the document and rose. Carbone stood. That was my signal to do likewise. We exited the conference room. Carbone accompanied Ben toward the receptionist's desk. I hesitated. Carbone looked back and barked, "You heard the client. Get some results."

It was already nearly three o'clock. I wasn't sure what to do next. I gave it a few minutes for Carbone to walk Ben out and then wandered down to Carbone's office. His secretary, a thin and graying old biddy with a sour expression, gave me the once over. I didn't feel like I'd passed her litmus test, but she didn't stop me from sticking my head in the door. Carbone was at his desk.

"Mr. Carbone, I wanted to follow up after the meeting. What are you handling, and what do you want me to handle on the caviar case?"

Carbone shot me a look like I was an idiot. I was getting used to it. I stepped the rest of the way into his office but decided that sitting would be too familiar. It felt like an undue amount of decorum would keep me in his best standing. He didn't even stop typing on his laptop to speak to me. "Ms. Ashford, I'm frankly on overload right now. I'm getting ready for a three-week-long fraud trial. I don't have any margin. When I said to get results, that's what I meant. Do whatever is necessary."

"Like hire a private investigator as you suggested?"

His fingers stopped tapping the computer keys. He met my eyes. "Like that, and interview Fish and Game, visit the site with the client, and get your rear in gear on becoming an expert not only on California caviar but on the black market for it. Am I going to have to spell things out, or can you handle it?"

"I...uh....um..." *Good grief, now I'm sounding like I really am an idiot.* "No, sir, you don't need to spell things out. Just give me some guidelines. I'm unfamiliar with the office protocols. Spending money to hire an investigator, for instance."

"For that kind of question, you have Felicity."

His fingers went back to typing, his eyes back to the computer screen.

"Yes, sir."

There was nothing further from Carbone. Clearly, I was dismissed, so I left. As I exited his office, I nearly ran into Gabe loitering just outside the door, narrowly missing a collision. He hurried away, trying to contain the condescending smile teasing one side of his mouth. Carbone's secretary across the hall looked down, a slight sneer on her face like she'd seen associates come and go, and this was entertainment to see me flustered.

I stopped at Felicity's desk on my walk of shame back

to my office. "Just talked to Carbone. I'm pretty much on my own on this caviar case. It's clear you know your way around here much better than I do. I was hoping for some guidance."

She gave me a knowing, motherly smile. "I'm not trained to do legal research, Ms. Ashford. What is it specifically that you need?"

"Just Skyler, please."

"Maybe out of the office. I prefer Felicity, but it's not appropriate for me to call you by your first name when we're at the firm."

I let out a sigh, probably more audible than I intended. "Mr. Carbone indicated I should tour the client's facilities, talk to Fish and Game, and hire a private investigator. I'm unsure I know how to get started on any of that."

I could see her lips purse ever so slightly, but Felicity kept her outward expressions to a minimum. I couldn't tell what she thought of me just yet.

"I'll call Mr. Akers to set up an on-site meeting and call in a private investigator. I'm assuming you'll want to meet with her also?" It wasn't really a question.

"Her?"

"Yes. One of the best. Victoria Delaney. I know the legal profession is still male-dominated, and there's a stereotype of male private investigators, but a woman can get information a man never could."

"I didn't mean to imply…"

"Of course, you didn't. Did you get the name of the Fish and Game rep?"

"Yeah, uh… I have it in my notes."

"Email it to me. I'll send back a contact number. Oh, and do you have the firm's calendaring app on your phone?"

I unintentionally gave her my best impression of a toddler in trouble. Didn't mean to. It just felt it overtake my face. She took in a breath like she was going to sigh, then swallowed it, letting the air out ever so slowly as she reached for the phone I held out. "I'll take care of this too if you just unlock it for me."

I swiped the screen and the device's facial recognition feature opened the phone to my home page. Felicity took the phone, quickly and efficiently adding the law firm's proprietary app before handing it back to me. "Anything else? I'm here to help, but I'm on a rush for Mr. Compton."

"No. No…and thank you, Felicity."

I went into my office, closed the door, and sat, resting my face on my hands, eyes closed for a few minutes. Before I normalized, my brain started screeching, *Billable hours. Every second counts. You can't double bill for waiting for yourself to reboot. It's already three-thirty. What's on your timesheet?*

I looked at the blank page, blinking. *You can't do this. You have to keep track. If you don't do it in the moment, you're going to lose time. Think, Skyler, think. What have you been doing all day?*

I thought back on the day. I had a meeting with the client that was supposed to start at one o'clock, but what time did it really start? He was prompt, so I wrote down "1:00 p.m.," but when did it end? Estimation was not my strong suit. Underestimate, and I'd be cheating myself of precious minutes of billable time. Overestimate, and I'd look like I was padding my time, plus it would be unfair to the client. Ask Carbone? Hell, no. I put down thirty minutes. I knew I was skinning myself. I'd just have to do a better job of keeping my time and make up for today's complacency later.

What else had I done? *C'mon, Skyler, think. You didn't just twiddle your thumbs and wake up with the clock magically ticking its way steadily toward the end of the day.* I'd done a little background research on caviar. That should count. I put down an hour. I'd talked to Carbone after the meeting. I didn't dare clock that fiasco. I'd spoken to Felicity about billing practices and making appointments. What the heck is billable and not? I was getting desperate. Everything I'd done today except gossiping with the other new recruits was for the firm's business, but it didn't translate to client billings. The sparseness of the timekeeping sheet entries mocked me.

Okay, today was a near total write-off. I decided that the firm's old-fashioned timesheet was a dinosaur. I knew the protocol was for the secretaries to enter the time into the firm's computer system, but that wasn't working for me. *Why don't they just let the associates enter time on their phones through an app? Cheap or old-fashioned?* I needed to have some better way to keep myself from a surprise at the end of the month. I opened up an Excel worksheet on my desktop and saved it as "Billables." First column, Client. Second column, Case/Matter. Third Column, description of what I'd done. Fourth column, time billed. That was going to be a pain because the firm wanted one-tenth increments of an hour when they added up my billable time. I decided to add two columns for start and stop time like the timekeeping form and create a formula that would automatically do the calculation for me for the "Time Billed" result. I added a total at the top and then a place to enter how many days were left in the month. With that information, I created a worksheet cell that indicated how many hours I needed to bill each day to reach my billing minimum.

Pleased with my efforts, I entered my hours for today into the new worksheet. It recalculated how much time I would need to bill each subsequent day to meet the goal. That's when my brain started saying all the words Mamma told me never to use. I might not say them—I even tried not to think them—but they bubbled right out into my consciousness in a stream like a drunken sailor when I saw *that* number. Well, that, and I started hyperventilating and had to tell myself that getting caught crying would be the only thing worse than facing that number again tomorrow.

My phone beeped. The notification screen for the firm's app advised me of an off-site appointment scheduled with Ben Akers tomorrow morning at nine o'clock. It went off again. Appointment scheduled with Bob Colburn, Fish and Game, at one o'clock. Doggone it, I'd forgotten to give Felicity his name. I could just hope she hadn't asked Carbone for it. Probably his secretary, but I could already tell from my earlier encounter that sneering biddy would not be my friend. Well, it couldn't be helped now. And God bless Felicity, I had something to do to get billables tomorrow.

A knock at my door. "Enter."

Felicity cautiously opened the door as if she knew I'd been having a mental meltdown. "It's five o'clock. I'm heading home. I just wanted to check if you needed anything before I leave."

"No. All good, Felicity, but thank you for checking. Thank you for getting my phone calendar set up. I just got several helpful notifications. Oh, and thank you for the advice today."

"No problem. I'm on your team. Good night, Ms. Ashford."

I waved. She left the door open as she exited. It was good to hear that someone was on my team. It felt like my team was very small.

CHAPTER 3
THE TIME THIEF

Arriving at the office at seven in the morning, I noticed that more than half of the employee parking lot was already full. When I'd left last night and looked up, most of the lights had been blaring. Were there no business hours for this place? Of course not. I knew that coming in. Law firms are notorious for their grind, primarily on new associates. As a first-year, I was the lowest of the low, unless you counted summer clerks, and there weren't any of those around in February.

I entered the rear entrance from the back parking lot, making my way up a narrow tunnel of a hallway to the cavernous main lobby and the bay of elevators. Exiting on my floor, I could see through the glass doors that the law firm's lobby was dark even though office lights were on in the inner offices. I entered my electronic door code to let myself in. As I walked through the yet-unlit corridor of past and present partner photos, they seemed especially disgruntled this morning. I tried to pad softly so my heels wouldn't echo against the marble floor, waking their disdain and announcing my arrival to others. I felt like I was sneaking to my office despite the unavoidable *click, click, click* my steps made, betraying me. Wasn't this early? Why did I feel I needed to be covertly at my desk as if I'd just materialized there?

Bright overhead lights fully lit the inner sanctum. None of the secretaries would arrive for an hour, but many attorney offices had lights on, streaming into the hallway and joining its luminescence. I flipped on my office light. My diplomas and court admittance certificates had been framed and hung, precisely organized on the wall to the left of my desk, in prominent view for anyone sitting in my client chairs. Nicely framed, I noticed. Expensive looking.

I threw my purse behind my desk and logged into the computer. I brought the Excel timesheet onto the screen but then deferred work to browse online for a briefcase. Every lawyer needs one. I didn't want to be carrying a file into court like a high school sophomore carrying a load of books. Within thirty minutes, I'd purchased two. One slim in two shades of brown with a fold-over flap. Fashionable and functional. It'd look good with my suits. Another sturdy, hard leather one, about seven inches across, that had wheels and a retractable handle for trials and heavy-duty motions. I entered the address to have them delivered to the office. Done. Now I had to complete how many billables today to keep on track? I was gonna need Felicity to fetch one of those OTC headache pills.

As if she could hear my thoughts, Felicity appeared at my office door. "Did you fill out your timesheet yesterday?"

"Yeah. It was on my desk. Did you take it last night?"

"Remember, I left before you. It's supposed to be put in the 'in' box on my desk at the end of the day. Very important. You need to find it."

I looked around for the mysteriously missing timesheet, then decided it was a waste of time. I had my electronic version. I copied my hours from yesterday onto a new sheet and took it to Felicity.

At already almost eight o'clock, I hadn't logged any billables yet, but at least I had a solid set of meetings lined up thanks to Felicity's organizational skills.

I entered the address for Chairo Caviar into my phone. Driving time with traffic was about an hour. I needed to leave soon for my meeting with Ben Akers to give myself sufficient travel time. I logged onto a search engine to do some quick research on the background of caviar in California.

It turns out this Russian fish research biologist by the name of Sergei Doroshov defected from the Soviet Union in the late seventies and got a job at U.C. Davis. Local Sacramento farmers wanted to set up a sturgeon hatchery in 1978. It was fate that they found Doroshov to help them. The Sacramento River had a population of wild, white sturgeon. There were enough of them for a breeding program that lasted until 1987, with the first farmed caviar ready for harvest in 1994.

It seemed that the Caspian Sea Beluga caviar I always saw in the movies had become more of a Hollywood myth than a reality. With overfishing and pollution, Russian production had plummeted while California's caviar production had been on a steady growth streak. Who knew? California produced nearly eighty percent of American caviar. Most restaurants hadn't sold Beluga caviar in nearly a decade. The restaurants were instead stocking American caviar because it was less salty and fishy. It also looked better with larger, firmer eggs. The only thing Russian about most caviar was the name. American caviar companies chose Russian-sounding names because of customer appeal, so many people just assumed the origin of what they ate was foreign and exotic.

I looked at the clock at the top of my computer screen. Eight fifteen. I'd better leave if I wanted to make my meeting with Akers on time. I threw a couple of pens in my purse, grabbed a yellow pad, and checked out with Felicity. I'm not sure why I perceived she needed to keep tabs on me, but it instinctively felt like that was the way of things.

GPS took me from the city into a suburb, then to the countryside. Out where they grew rice in the Delta. When the phone was telling me I was close, the location wasn't at all what I expected. There was nothing else around except weedy, dry grass. The road led past two enormous holding ponds with gigantic pipes pumping water into them. I wondered if that's where the fish were. I pulled into a parking lot in front of very unimpressive offices. I'd seen cow sheds that were fancier. I parked, got out, and walked up to the entry door. Or at least I was hoping it was the right door. Walking in, a couple of folding chairs and a well-worn metal receptionist desk, unmanned, greeted me. I wasn't sure what to do. Sit and wait? Call out? Go poke around?

"Hullo? Hullo?" No answer. I waited a moment then started slowly toward the door leading to a hallway. Just then, Ben Akers popped out wearing what appeared to be a black rain jacket, yellow waterproof pants, and black rubber boots. Sort of a giant plastic bumblebee effect. We nearly collided. He stopped abruptly, his eyes momentarily going wide.

"Ms. Ashford, thank you for coming out to meet with me. I hope I didn't keep you waiting."

"Not at all."

He looked at my slacks, jacket, and heels. His brow crinkled. "They should have at least told you to wear jeans and sneakers." He frowned harder. "Um... I think we have an extra pair of waterproof boots in the office. You're going to need them."

He took off the black raincoat, revealing a plain white shirt underneath. He looked a little less like a giant bumblebee. Possibly a firefighter. After disappearing down the hallway, he emerged again a few minutes later with a pair of rubber boots close to my size. He thrust them toward me. "Put these on."

I could feel my cheeks turn bright pink. I started to protest, but I didn't see any way out of wearing them, so I sat down on one of the metal chairs, pulled off my heels, and put the ugly rubber rainboots on, tucking my dress slacks into the tops.

He nodded his approval. "That's better. You wanted a tour, they said."

"Yes, Mr. Akers, that would be helpful. I'd like to understand your business."

"Ben, please. Let me stow your purse in my office. It'll be safe there. You won't want to cart it around."

"Thank you, Ben. It's Skyler, by the way."

"I remember." He smiled and opened the door leading back out toward the parking lot.

We walked around the corner, where two rows of massive metal tanks with black tarp tops shaped like circus tents loomed like a field of giant, black metal and plastic mushrooms. Ben gestured toward them. "These are tanks for juveniles. Mostly three and four-year-olds."

"Those are the ones that produce caviar?"

Ben turned his head as we walked, giving me a wide smile. "No. They aren't ready for roe harvesting until they're about seven or eight years old."

My eyebrows shot up. "So, you have to take care of them for seven years before you get the first eggs from the fish?"

"The first and the last. We have to remove the ovaries to harvest the roe."

"You kill them?" Oh, I know I shouldn't have squeaked like he was a puppy killer, but it came out before my filter took hold. Good thing he seemed understanding. His pace slowed as he peered over at me.

"There are ways of removing the roe by massage without killing the fish, but they're extremely expensive. It's slow, and specially trained handlers are required. Not economically feasible under almost any business model. If the fish spawns the eggs on its own, a protective membrane on the egg is removed during ovulation. The caviar would be substandard. So, yes, we have to kill them. We do it very humanely. There's a secondary market for the meat. We even process the other parts into fertilizer, so every part of the fish is used."

We stopped near one of the tanks. I nodded, trying to

redeem myself. "I guess it's like raising cattle you know will go to slaughter."

Ben walked over to the edge of the tank. A gap between the top of the metal pool and the circus top revealed swirls everywhere in the water—a massive biomass of fish for the size of the tank, all circling.

"Ben, how big is this tank? How many fish?"

"About seventy thousand gallons. There may be up to a thousand fish in any one tank."

We continued our stroll. As we reached the end of these tanks, we came across even larger tanks toward the back of the property. I pointed. "Bigger ones?"

"Correct. But we don't use those anymore. The tanks you saw outside are for overflow. We will be demolishing them soon and using this area for a building to smoke meat."

We turned to the right and entered a vast building that resembled an airplane hangar, big enough for a couple of 747s. Workers inside wore blue jumpers and thin, yellow food service head coverings reminiscent of ugly shower caps. There were tanks full of fish everywhere. The lighting dim, the building was nearly silent except for the sound of falling water. Ben pointed to tanks on the left side of the building that looked like above-ground pools with numerous plastic pipes pumping water in and out of them. His quiet voice reminded me of the tone people use in libraries or sacred spaces.

"When we allow the fish to spawn and we hatch eggs, the hatchlings are minuscule, but they eat voraciously. We constantly feed them high-protein food pellets. We have to filter the water carefully to remove the resulting waste. After about a year, they're moved into the nursery tanks. At that point, they weigh a little more than a pound. They remain there until they are big enough to sex them so we can separate the caviar-producing females from the males."

"How can you tell?" *Oh great, I'm not sure I wanted to know about that part of fish anatomy with someone I'd just met. What was I thinking?*

Thankfully, Ben didn't flinch. "We have an ultrasound for that. The males are sold for their meat. Once we separate the females, we move them to the production tanks." He pointed to larger tanks on the other side of the building.

We walked over to a tank where a worker in waterproof overalls stood in the water. Ben addressed him. "Trevor, bring one of your pets over here. We have a visitor."

The man in the water leaned down, grabbed a fish about four feet in length, and walked it over to the edge of the tank where we stood. It was ugly—dang ugly. The sturgeon looked like some prehistoric leftover with flat, bony plates on its back and four feelers coming out of its mouth like a catfish.

Ben motioned with his head, a twinkle in his eyes. "Give it a pat."

"Seriously?" I gave him a stink eye. "Do they bite?"

He broke out in a full-blown grin. When I looked over at Trevor, he seemed to suppress a smirk. Sort of like when the boys in biology dared me to let the tarantula crawl up my arm. I didn't freak out then, and I didn't intend to now. I reached over and touched the cold, wet creature.

"It feels like sharkskin."

Ben nodded toward Trevor, and he returned the sturgeon to its habitat.

"Yes, they do feel like a shark, but they're bottom-feeders like a catfish. They don't have any teeth." He shot me a closed-mouth smile, a good-natured gleam in his eyes.

I tilted my head and raised an eyebrow accusatorily. "You could have told me that sooner. How do you get more fish if you kill them to collect their eggs?"

"Good question. The roe we collect from the segregated females for caviar are unfertilized, but we keep breeding stock. Prime females we select. They grow even larger—up to two hundred pounds—and we breed them. Not only do we not collect sturgeon from the wild, but our operation replaces the population in the local rivers."

I heard a large splash behind me from the tank and turned. "What was that?"

"They jump. In fact, we have to keep a close eye on them. Kind of like babysitting. They've occasionally been known to try to jump out of the tanks. If they aren't put right back and we lose the fish, we've lost seven years of what we've put into that fish, as well as all of the caviar inside her, at more than a hundred dollars an ounce. The eggs can be up to fifteen percent of the fish's weight."

"Does that happen often?"

"Not too often, and we usually find them in time, but we lost three this last month found on the floor by the day shift." His expression looked troubled.

Could an insider be causing these kinds of problems? Was it possible the fish had some help out of the tanks?

We slowly walked toward even larger tanks that looked like sunken pools with edges about two feet above the floor. I followed Ben over to one. "These are harvest tanks. The eight-year-old females average sixty to one hundred pounds. Harvest season typically lasts a few months, starting in February, so you're here at a good time to see that operation. This year we'll be harvesting around six thousand fish to produce around thirteen tons of caviar."

I asked, "I thought you said the water has to be kept clean. The water in these tanks seems cloudy. Is that one of the problems you've been having?"

"Good observation, but no, not at all. We keep the fish waste cleaned from the water, but we're very purposeful about what's in the water. Minerals are added, and we allow the water to appear cloudy because these fish are bottom feeders. If the water is too clear, it makes them nervous."

As we walked back out of the building, I assumed the tour was over, but Ben led on toward another industrial-looking building. As we entered a lobby-like area in this building, I could see inside through a doorway. Workers inside also wore blue jumpers with hair covers like we saw in the last building, but they also had surgical face masks, sleeve protectors, and fabric booties over their shoes. They looked like they worked in a computer clean room or a surgical amphitheater.

Ben handed me a hair cover, a face mask, and a pair of booties. "We need to wear these going into the caviar production building."

We entered the first part of the building, where the clean room people monitored huge tanks of fish. Ben pointed. "Females ready to be harvested are moved here."

We watched as a man in a tank caught a huge sturgeon and handed it to another worker, who transferred it to a large table where he held the fish down for a worker there. The man at the table laid the fish out, used a small scalpel to quickly make a tiny incision, then bent down with what looked like a drinking straw. Ben whispered reverently, "He's checking if she's ready to be harvested. It takes years of training for that position. A wrong assessment can cost the company a lot of money. He's trained to make the tiniest incision necessary and to avoid cutting any organs. He will suck out a small sample of the roe to judge it for maturity. If she's ready, the fish will be moved into these special tanks." He pointed to yet another row of tanks. "These are purge tanks where the fish remain for about a week in extremely clean water to ensure there are no off-tastes to the eggs. If the fish isn't ready, she'll be taken back to the production tanks, and we'll recheck her next year. Only about twenty percent of the fish tested in any year will be ready for production."

The tester waved to yet another worker, who took the fish to the purging tanks. We followed. I watched the same scene repeated at various other tanks with other employees, moving fish toward the caviar room like a production line. As we went through the next set of doors, work was at a steady, quiet, and purposeful pace. On several tables, fish that had finished their time in the purging tanks were being humanely killed with a lightning-quick electric stun. Afterward, a quick cut was made to retrieve the ovaries whole, like a C-section. I was shocked to see the entire insides of the fish seemed to be eggs embedded in fleshy tissue like seeds in a pomegranate.

Ben said, "The females produce about twenty-five hundred eggs per pound of their weight, so a typical fish at caviar harvest will produce around two hundred thousand eggs."

As we walked closer to one of the tables, I watched as a woman in a hair cap, surgical gown, and gloves massaged the roe free of the tissue of the ovaries through a sieve.

Ben explained, "The goal at this point is to preserve flavor. We try to have the caviar from the fish to a sealed tin within thirty minutes to avoid oxygen exposure. Everything is precisely measured on a scale. Salt is added as the only preservative. The brined roe is allowed to drain, then it's spread for grading."

I watched as a woman carefully observed, tasted, and graded the caviar, then other workers, using spatulas and scales, carefully weighed it and enclosed it in enamel-lined tins. Ben led me to one of the tables where the caviar was spread out. From a table nearby, he produced several small plastic spoons. He scooped a small portion of caviar onto each and handed one to me. "Have you had caviar before?"

As he met my gaze, I felt a slight color rise in my cheeks. "No."

A gratified smile emerged that rose to his blue eyes. "Then I'm pleased to give you a first taste." He looked at me expectantly.

I didn't want to tell him that I was imagining both the sticky, red salmon eggs from the fishing trips with my father and the slimy, black frog eggs from a National Geographic show. I swallowed a mouthful of nervous spit before I could put the spoon in my mouth. I was prepared to control my reaction and sing its delights no matter what.

Ben instructed, "Don't chew. Allow the caviar to explode using your tongue."

Not fishy. Not overly salty. Buttery. Quite amazing.

"Oh, wow, that wasn't what I expected. It's

wonderful." I caught myself still licking my lips unconsciously.

Ben grinned. "The caviar is typically aged up to three months to come to full flavor before being exported to restaurants and distributors worldwide, but I'm partial to the fresh taste you just experienced."

A blue-jumper-clad worker came through the door and bee-lined straight to Ben with a look of concern. He whispered something I couldn't hear. Ben's face transformed—all-business, brows knit with concern.

The tone of his voice echoed the worry on his face. "Sorry, but we need to cut this short. You've seen most of the facility except the hatching building. We've got a problem with one of the main pumps. I've got to get to the bottom of it straight away. Water quality control is critical, especially for the females close to harvest. It's been a stressful month. First the night staff missing the jumpers, now the pumps."

Jumpers, females with eggs being reabsorbed, faulty pumps. There are a lot of problems "coincidentally" arising in a short period at Chairo Caviar.

As we removed the clean-room booties and walked quickly back up to the main offices, I was glad Ben had insisted on the rubber boots. My shoes would have been a muddy mess by the end of our tour. Ben retrieved my purse, setting it down next to me. He shot me an expectant look as I put my high heels back on. "What next, counselor?"

Totally clueless, I wasn't sure what to say. I threw out the only bone I had. "I have a meeting with Fish and Game this afternoon." I tried to say it authoritatively. I hoped he was more convinced by the effort than I was.

He smiled like he had confidence in me. He oozed something appealingly down-to-earth without being overly countrified. A crossover between the sophistication of caviar and the comfort of a long sip of cold iced tea on a hot summer day. I smiled back as I picked up my purse. "I'll let you know if I find any leads."

I think I started breathing again when I exited the facility gates.

Returning to the office, I passed Carbone's secretary in the hallway. She gave me a look like she could smell the fish farm on me. That was unlikely since the fish farm didn't smell nearly as fishy as I had thought it would, but her look made me do a quick pit check nevertheless as soon as I got back to the solitude of my office. Reconsidering, I figured she was more like a vampire who could smell the fear coming off all of the first-year associates.

Felicity walked in. "How was the tour?"

"It was really interesting. More so than I thought it would be. I got to taste the caviar."

"Well, well, I'd like to have your job. I just got to make about a thousand copies of exhibits to a brief for Mr. Compton."

I searched her face to see if she was having fun with me or if there was something more sinister behind the sarcasm. It was unreadable. She'd already gone back into her professional shell but looked a little tired. I chalked it up to a day standing by a copier.

Felicity asked, "Did you get the notification of the meeting with the P.I.?"

My eyes widened slightly as I quickly retrieved my phone from my purse. There was a pop-up notification on the lock screen. Meeting with Victoria Delaney at three o'clock—today. I looked up. "I didn't hear it go off. I left my purse in the main office when I went on the tour with Ben. Thank you for letting me know."

She turned with a saucy smile and a raised eyebrow. "Somebody's got to herd the new kittens."

I walked into my office, settled at my desk, and logged onto the computer. The computer clock read noon. As in lunchtime. And that teensy spoonful of caviar was not going to hold me over, but I had the one o'clock meeting with Fish and Game. I needed to be prepared.

I buzzed Felicity.

"Missed me already?"

"You know it. If I ordered a lunch delivered, is that okay? Will they be able to find me?"

"Just instruct them to deliver to Cammie at the front desk. She'll let you know when it's here."

"Right. Thanks… Bye."

I pulled out my phone, checking the "Fastest Close By" menu on the food delivery app. A deli sandwich didn't sound too unhealthy. They could get it to me in an estimated twenty-five minutes. Sold. I punched in an order for a basic turkey and cheese five-incher and a diet cola, then filled out the delivery instructions, including a request to have Cammie notify me upon arrival.

Waiting for sustenance, I wandered down the hallway to the break room to see if anyone else was around. Peter was at the break table, tucked into a homemade sandwich, chips, and a canned soda. No one else was around. I figured with that cheap suit, Peter was trying to mind his money by bringing a brown bag lunch like I had yesterday.

"Hey there, Peter. Mind if I hang out with you for a few minutes?"

"Nah. I'd actually like some normal company." He took another bite of his sandwich. I put my smartphone on the table with the delivery app's map showing me my order was still being prepared. He glanced at it. "Ordered in?"

"Yeah. I've got a meeting. Didn't want to risk going out and being late for it."

"I think half the people here eat at their desk while doing something else. They'd probably sue some other business for violating the labor code, but it's just talk for a law firm and deemed our discretion when we don't take our breaks. That is, except for the partners. I think they all go out at lunch. Probably schmoozing new business or something on the firm's credit card."

"Kind of what I'm planning. Not the schmoozing, but the researching while eating at my desk, except I'm not sure what I'm supposed to research."

"What's the deal?"

I briefly explained the caviar case to him as he systematically downed his sandwich. When I finished, he gave a slow nod. "Man, I wish I got something half as interesting to work on. Did Carbone just throw you out there with no instruction on this?"

"Says he's got too much on his plate to babysit me. And I need to get results."

"Okay, so you got a little background on the client's operations, and you'll get a download from Fish and Game. What about motive?"

"What do you mean?"

"Duh. What's the motive for selling black market caviar?"

My turn to say duh. "Money, obviously."

"But you said it was enough product to affect the bottom line of your client's company. That's moving a lot of perishable product. That makes things complicated."

"Good point, but how does that help me?"

He crumpled his sandwich bag, made a "basket" into the trash can behind me, then stood up to leave. "Who's got the know-how and the motivation to do something like that? And you're not just looking to do the police's job; you're looking for someone to sue, right? By the way, your lunch is here."

I looked down at my phone. He was right. The notification said, "Delivery Completed." I looked up. Peter was gone.

Gabe walked in and started a coffee pod brewing. "Hey…Skyler, isn't it?"

"Yeah. Sorry to be so unfriendly yesterday. Felicity had me on the speed tour of the office. Are you stuck in the copy room all day?"

"My very own little cave." The coffee pod made its last little farting gasps, signaling the cup was complete. Gabe removed the little plastic cup of spent grounds and threw it hard into the trash. "You're Carbone's new associate working on that caviar case, right?"

He gave me a strange look. *Maybe he's heard about how many associates get fired. Maybe there's an office pool on which one of us will get ousted.*

Gabe leaned toward me. "Sounds unusual. Anything interesting?"

"Uh, my lunch just got delivered. I've got to get it from Cammie. Nice to meet you more properly, Gabe."

He gave me a perfunctory nod before I walked out.

My brain hurt. I had a meeting to prepare for. I didn't have time to ruminate on Peter's comments. I hated to admit he had a point about looking at motives. One that I didn't have time to ponder before talking to this guy from Fish and Game.

I grabbed my lunch order from Cammie before heading back down the long hallway. Entering my office, I shut the door. I always thought open office doors were the best policy, but I didn't need everyone walking past gawking at me chowing down. I took a bite of turkey and cheddar then realized how hungry I was as I woke up the computer screen. Between less than ladylike bites, I surfed the web. I discovered there were more caviar companies in California than I could have imagined. Competition. Now that's motivation and enough quantity to explain the dip in Chairo Caviar's sales. So, was it a bunch of black-market garage operations or something more significant? Black market or could it be corporate interference from the competition?

I slurped the last of my soda just as the phone rang. First time, so it startled me. Why was I so jumpy today? I picked up the receiver. How was I supposed to answer? "Good afternoon. Wagner, Tibbs, and Cobbs. Skyler Ashford speaking." I heard what I thought was suppressed laughter on the other end of the line. Felicity's voice. "It's just me, dear. If you look, it's one of the intercom lines." A pause. "But you'd make an excellent receptionist." I could hear the amusement in her voice, but it sounded good-natured, so I decided not to take offense. I was glad the door was closed so she couldn't see my hot face from her desk across the way.

"Sorry, you caught me off guard."

"Bob Colburn from Fish and Game is here. Conference Room A."

"Thank you, Felicity." I hung up. Before I gathered my notepad and pen, I took a few breaths to try to wash off the feeling of foolishness and breathe in an air of professional competence.

The door to Conference Room A hung open. Inside, a man wearing a Fish and Game uniform—brown slacks and a tan shirt with the agency insignia on the sleeve—sat at the table. I figured him to be in his late thirties, with sandy brown hair, a slightly receding hairline, serious, black-rimmed glasses, and a tan, presumably from being outdoors to do his job. He looked up as I entered, then stood.

"Mr. Colburn?" He nodded slightly. "Skyler Ashford. I've been assigned to work on the case for Chairo Caviar." I walked to the other side of the table and sat. He resumed his seat and looked silently at me as I searched my brain for how to take the lead. "I understand you talked previously with Ben Akers?"

"Yes."

Oh, my goodness. This is going to be more of a deposition than a conversation with those kinds of succinct answers. Try again. "Can you tell me about your conversations with Ben... I mean, Mr. Akers?"

"Oh, sure. I've known Ben Akers for years. Good guy. When the caviar industry started in California, they were taking wild fish. The same thing that got Russian caviar into trouble. The difference is that these guys worked with the university biologist and with us at Fish and Game. They knew that wasn't a sustainable plan. Soon as they got breeding stock going. Chairo became one of the leaders to help replenish the sturgeon back to the natural rivers. They help make sure the population is doing okay to help us keep them off the endangered species list."

He paused.

Okay, that was his area of interest. Glad people are watching out for the fish, but that doesn't help me with this case. Let's try another prompt. "Ben talked to you about his concerns about the dip in sales?"

"Oh, uh, yeah. Weird. We haven't been aware of any recent black-market activity, but it sounds suspicious. I have seen an uptick in fishing violations on the Sacramento River. White Sturgeon aren't illegal to fish like the Green Sturgeon on the endangered species list, but the White Sturgeon are on a list of concern. We have our eye on them, especially as recent droughts have made it more difficult for the fish to travel to their spawning grounds."

"Has the department done anything about these suspicions concerning black market poaching?"

The fish biologist shrugged, took a deep breath in, then let it out slowly. "We try, although Fish and Game covers an enormous amount of territory, and we're woefully understaffed. We only have a couple hundred officers patrolling. They don't just cover sturgeon. Poachers take deer, abalone, Dungeness crab, and other species illegally. We're talking every hill, mountain, stream, river, and nook and cranny for two hundred miles until you reach the ocean. Makes it easier for criminals and near impossible for us." The tension matched the palpable disdain in his voice in his posture. "Aside from that, we have access to technology to help. We've traced wire transactions, placed GPS trackers on cars, and conducted nighttime stakeouts. Stuff normally reserved for drug trafficking, but it's been necessary for this caviar crime. It's another type of black-market gold that's gotten outta hand."

"Sounds like a police operation."

His chin lifted and his voice animated. "Pretty much. We work in cooperation with local law enforcement. We have the ability to take action like we were the police. If we find criminal activity, there's an arrest. The District Attorney's office then prosecutes the case. Several cases went to trial this last year."

"That's a lot of public resources devoted to illegal fishing."

That remark was rewarded with a *humph* from Bob.

"That's just the start of it. Garage caviar pirates process the roe, which then goes to middlemen before being sold to restaurants at a deep discount."

"How deep of a discount?"

"The black market sells a pound for what a properly sourced ounce would cost." Bob's hands had made a fist on the table. I could see his muscles tense with the thought.

"That's such a big difference in price! The restaurants should know better."

"Far as I'm concerned, the restaurants that buy at prices too good to be true are criminal too." His fist lightly pounded the table, then he caught himself, quickly shifting back into a more relaxed posture.

"What's the penalty? How can so much risk be worth it?"

He scowled. "That's another thing that just gets me mad. Poaching will land you a thousand-dollar fine and up to six months in jail for each infraction, plus we can take their fishing license away. But the business can be pretty lucrative with an average illegally-caught female yielding around thirty pounds of roe. Heck-, if we don't catch 'em, they could be pulling down thirty thousand bucks a month. That's a significant incentive."

"But that's also a lot of risk."

"I dunno. If they're caught with, say, three fish for a night's fishing, that would be a maximum fine of three thousand dollars and eighteen months in jail with a chance of earlier parole. Not a sufficient penalty if you ask me. And the last guy we took to court got off with a five thousand dollar fine, two months in county jail, and an order to stay away from the river. You know he's not gonna. After all our work—all those hours and public resources—he just got a slap on the wrist."

"What about these middlemen you were talking about before?"

"There's a little know-how involved. Illegal fishermen aren't exactly the type to know much about a sophisticated product like caviar. The middlemen who buy the unprocessed roe from the garage poachers at about seventy bucks a pound convert it into caviar that they sell for a hundred and fifty bucks a pound. The fish eggs aren't caviar until they've been sorted and salted."

"Got it. I saw a little of that when I visited Ben's facilities. Any current leads?"

"The middlemen we used to keep an eye on have been pretty quiet, but it feels like there's something up. We just have to get a lead to investigate. I'll be watching the Sacramento River as closely as I can with the limited personnel I've got available."

"I'd appreciate if you kept me updated."

"Likewise." Bob handed me a card with his direct dial number on it.

I nodded and rose. "Thank you for coming in today."

Bob stood and shook my hand. "Anything for Ben. He's a good guy. I'd hate to see a legitimate operation that cares for the environment take a hit from scumbag poachers."

I walked Bob to the reception lobby, then headed back to my office with more to think about. I didn't have much time to process since my meeting with the P.I. started in twenty minutes. As I passed the main conference room with its all-glass front walls, I saw about a dozen lawyers convened for a deposition. A witness sat in the hot seat with a court reporter typing away as he spoke. Carbone was seated next to the witness. He looked up, saw me passing by, and shot me a questioning look as if my presence in a hallway meant I was not billing. I gave him a serious nod then looked away, sure that I'd be the next person deposed by him soon.

Twenty minutes until my next meeting. *I should be billing. Do I have anyone I need to call? I can't think of anyone at the moment. What I could use is a shot of caffeine. Wait. Shucks, that would mean walking past that glass conference room again to get to the break room. Fat chance. Could I ask Felicity to bring me a cup? She probably would, but I don't want to treat her in a demeaning way. I could update my timesheet.* In fact, I'd put down my start and stop times on my notepad when I'd met with Bob. I was learning.

I was overjoyed when my phone rang at two forty-five. Intercom. The P.I. arrived early? I answered cheerily, "Hey, Felicity."

A booming voice. "Tom Carbone."

Had to engage my thought purity filter. Hard.

He asked, "What have you found?"

I gulped. "I took a tour of the caviar production facility. Learned a lot there. I also spoke with Bob Colburn from Fish and Game. He updated me on their activity pursuing the black market. I've got the personal investigator coming in any minute now."

I hoped that also signaled the phone call needed to end.

"Keep working on it. And keep me updated."

No attaboy for all that work. *He didn't sound pleased, but he didn't sound displeased. Maybe that was approval from Carbone?* Anyhow, he'd hung up abruptly. I could stop worrying about him for a bit.

The next time the phone rang on intercom mode, I was more professional. "This is Skyler."

Felicity's voice. "Victoria Delaney in Conference Room A. Can I bring you both some coffee?"

"Coffee? You're a lifesaver. Conference Room A?"

"Other side of the hallway from B"

"Gotcha." I hung up.

Conference Room B was a mirror image of Conference Room A, with its long faux burlwood table to seat a dozen on cushy, dark tan executive chairs, big screen television on one wall, glassy whiteboard on the next for presentations, and a countertop kept stocked with water bottles, cans of soda, and ice buckets that magically replenished. It had better chairs than the one they scrounged for my desk. It felt professional to the point of being sterile.

Victoria Delaney was nothing close to how I'd imagined her. A tall woman with long, wavy black hair and dark brown eyes, she wore bright red lipstick and was impeccably dressed in flowy black pants and a tight-fitting black jacket with a blush-beige silk camisole underneath. Her four-inch black patent stilettos didn't seem like the proper attire for either a night stakeout or a run after a criminal. She looked up at me under long, black eyelashes. "You must be Ms. Ashford. I understand Tom wants me to help with a black-market caviar case." Her voice was velvety smooth, calm, and confident.

I bristled at her familiar use of Carbone's first name. I leaned toward her. Already not liking her, I took a seat, sitting tall in the chair like a toad puffing in front of a threat. "Yes, he's put me in charge of getting fast answers. The firm recommended you."

"Yes." She met my eyes and pinned them. I felt challenged. Like I wanted to strike back.

Breaking the silence, Felicity walked in, bearing a tray with two cups of coffee, some individual packets of creamer and sugar, and black plastic stirrers. She asked cheerfully, "Coffee, anyone?" before setting the tray on the edge of the table and exiting, shutting the door.

I gratefully grabbed a mug bearing the firm logo and emptied two creamers in before stirring vigorously. Victoria gently reached for the other cup and took a sip—black and unadulterated. I asked, "What have you been told about the case?"

She raised an arched eyebrow as she took another languid sip of the dark, bitter brew. "I thought you were here to brief *me*, but what I understand is that caviar poaching has been going on in the Sacramento Delta for at least a decade. The change is that, recently, Chairo Caviar has been feeling enough of a market hit to suspect something more organized may be commencing. There's also the mystery of fewer mature females at Chairo reabsorbing roe."

"Fish and Game wonders the same but doesn't have

any leads."

"And do you?"

Isn't that your job? My filter kept it from coming out of my mouth for once. "Working on it, but I've only been assigned to the case for a couple of days. I understand you're the big guns when it comes to finding leads."

She gave me a slow smile. I could tell she was still sizing me up. "Don't let Tom give you too much garbage. He likes to intimidate the young female associates, but he knows you're a smart one, or he wouldn't have given you so much leash."

Okay, so maybe she wasn't so bad.

She picked up her purse from beside her chair, opened it, and took out a card. She pushed it across the table to me. "My direct line is on here. If I get any leads, you'll be my first call."

I took the card. "I'm looking into competitors."

She didn't remark. The look that crossed her face was indiscernible, but I could tell her brain was processing. She asked, "Anything else?"

"Unfortunately, no."

As she stood. "Have Chairo give you an employee list. Run the names through the court system. See if any have a criminal background."

"Good idea." We shook hands, and she left.

Checking the employees was a great idea and provided a few more hours of billables to churn out. I took my half-finished coffee with me as I scurried back to my office. After logging our meeting on my paper timesheet, I duplicated the entries on my computer spreadsheet to see how I was doing. Hmm…holding my own but not gaining any ground. *Should I have kept her talking longer?*

I dialed Ben's number. No answer. It went to voicemail. "Leave a message after the beep."

"Ben, it's Skyler. Can you email me a list of your employees? Part of our investigation. Thanks."

As I hung up, I realized that call equaled a minimum billing of .2 hours. I logged it and my time starting the next task. The cursor blinked. I didn't know what the next task was. So much for gaining on my billables. My brain blinked along with the cursor, then I remembered I should do some background on competitors. I adjusted the start time. *Rats.*

By five o'clock, I'd made a list of competitors and their principals, along with some notes detailing their business operations. Felicity waved from the doorway to let me know she was leaving. I looked at the clock longingly. Quitting time for most of the world, but not necessarily for law firm associates. Definitely not for first-year associates behind on their billables. But I was starving, so I decided my best strategy was to be well-fed and well-rested for a hard start tomorrow. Checking my email one last time before leaving, I found the employee list from Ben at the top of my inbox.

I put my timesheet on Felicity's desk and logged off the computer. Walking out, I noted that many of the partners' office lights were off while the associates still put in time. I needed a strategy tomorrow so I didn't end up sleeping here to keep up.

CHAPTER 4
COMPETITORS

The next morning, I walked in, waved at Cammie, walked through the hallway of Ghosts of Past and Present Partners, and turned left toward my office. It was seven forty-five. Felicity was not at her desk yet. In the "in" box at the corner of her desk sat my timesheet from yesterday, perched on the edge, in danger of falling to the floor. I moved it back securely to the inbox then noticed... *That's not my writing.* I stopped and picked up the paper. *A good impression, but not me. And the numbers have been altered. Someone is screwing with me. The question is why.*

I took the paper back to my desk, pulled out a fresh timesheet, entered the correct numbers from my Excel spreadsheet, and replaced the corrected document on Felicity's desk. I tucked the forgery into a bottom desk drawer.

Who would do such a thing? I know the competition between associates for recognition can be fierce, but could either Peter or Carly be so cutthroat and low? Clearly, I needed to watch my back. And my Excel spreadsheet needed to stay secret and password-protected.

There might be rivalry within the law firm, but the first order of business in the caviar case was to check out the competition further. Czar Alexander Co., Rusal Caviar, Inc., Tashir Caviar, LLC, and Caviars of California, Inc. were at the top of the list. I entered each into the Business Search feature on the California Secretary of State's website and downloaded the available information.

Next, I searched for all companies with "caviar" in their names registered to do business in California. More than a hundred. I drew a deep breath. Was there anything that could narrow down the companies I should focus on? I scanned the list. Cat Caviar Pet Food caught my attention. I breathed a sigh of relief. Some of these weren't fish caviar at all.

Many of the companies were incorporated in Delaware and registered as a foreign company in California—a common practice that didn't warrant undue attention. Another group had been forfeited or suspended, most for non-payment of minimum Franchise Tax Board taxes— another common demise of companies that enthusiastic founders created then never nurtured. Among them was Czar Alexander, formed in 2002, but now FTB forfeited with a primary mailing address in Montana. The founder seemed to actually be a Russian guy by the name of Sergei Chesnokov.

I created a sub-file on my computer desktop and named it "Skyler's Research." I printed the page about Czar Alexander to PDF and deposited it into my research file. The same with a list of all companies with "caviar" in their name and the files I'd already downloaded from the Secretary of State's office.

Rusal Caviar, Inc. was still active and in good standing. Incorporated in 1998, the founder's name sounded French—Jacques Baudelaire. It made a weird kind of sense to me. The French guy was probably a foodie but wanted a Russian-sounding name for his caviar company.

Caviars of California, Inc. was formed in 2018 by a woman—Marla Fortner. As opposed to the usual corporate-formation documents, clearly drafted by attorneys as organizers or by professional corporate-formation companies, it was apparent from the online records that Marla Fortner had completed the documents herself. It spoke of a strong leader...or lack of funds for legal counsel. Intriguing.

Tashir Caviar, LLC was originally named Black Gold Caviar, LLC. The company, filed in 1997, filed a change of name statement in 2008. Strangely, the name had been changed back again in 2018. They must be marketing under a fictitious business name, but that wasn't unusual on its own. There was nothing in the Secretary of State filings to indicate the names of any individuals owning membership interests. Everything was done through a professional corporate formation company, but again, that wasn't unusual. It just made it more difficult to find out the names of the owners.

It took me the better part of two hours to pull all of the documents for each of the companies, print them to PDF, and put them in my desktop research file. By then, my eyes felt the strain of the computer screen. I decided to grab a coffee.

As I reached the break room doorway, I spotted Felicity talking fairly loudly with Carbone's secretary. I'm not sure why, but I positioned myself just outside the door, making it look like I was busy on my mobile phone while my ears strained to overhear the conversation.

Felicity's voice. "How's Carbone's trial going, Joan?"

Ah, Joan was her name. Like Joan Crawford with a metal coat hanger, maybe?

"Seems like he's winning. The judge granted most of his Motions in Limine—the motions heard before the trial starts—and that hamstrung the plaintiff by disallowing evidence relating to the bank records. How's it going with your green associate?"

"*Our* green associate, don't you mean?"

"I don't get maternal over them. They come and they go. You know how it is. One out of three will be here after a year or two. No need to make friends. They're mostly either entertainment or drama and headaches."

"Skyler seems like a smart one, and she's been easy to work with. I'm hoping she can make it in this shark tank."

"My bets on Carly. She's the one who can swim with the sharks. As for Skyler, I'm waiting for the teary breakdown. But the one thing I'm not putting up with is her making my world hell, like when the newbies give the documents to Carbone the night before a deadline and don't consider they need to be copied, punched, stapled, labeled, and all. And that's if the court clerk's office doesn't give us conniptions and kick back the filing for some technicality."

"I get it, Joan. They're lawyers, but newly minted ones. They don't know even their way around a case as well as us lowly secretaries, yet they can throw their weight around."

"But we know who really runs the firm, don't we, Felicity? Without us getting the documents filed properly with the court, making sure their calendars are updated, scheduling deadlines, and handling all the clients' nonsense, they'd be in deep trouble."

I could hear Felicity's soft laugh. "Yeah, we rule the world, don't we? And do it for a mere pittance."

I tried to walk in loudly. "Hey, Felicity." I looked over at the cranky woman casually. "Joan, is it? Got a recommendation on the best coffee pods in this selection?" I watched their faces as they evaluated whether I'd heard anything. No response. I got my coffee quickly and left.

What did Felicity privately think about me? Was I too nice to make the cut? What did Carly do that made Joan believe she was equipped to swim with the sharks?

I had to pull myself back together and get back on task. There was that email from Ben Akers with the list of employees. I was grateful for a directed task to hunker down into. I opened it up—nearly sixty employees. I hadn't imagined his operation was that large.

I emailed Ben back. "Looking into the employees. I'll search the local court for any criminal records, but that won't pick up anything out of state. The law firm has software that could do a more comprehensive search, but there would be a per-person charge. It may not be worth it unless you have someone specific you want us to look into. If so, let me know."

I hit send.

A few minutes later, Felicity buzzed me. "Mr. Akers on Line 12 for you."

I punched Line 12, not knowing what to expect. *Does he have a suspect?* "Skyler Ashford."

"Skyler, it's Ben. I got your email. No one in particular comes to mind, but if you want to meet some employees and check out more about our products, we're hosting a fundraiser dinner tonight at the company. There's a sturgeon barbeque, various caviar tastings, and a live band. We've been selling tickets to raise community awareness of our brand, but the profits go into preservation of the species."

Okay, this was awkward. *Does he want to spend time with me, or is this part of the job? Would it be billable?* I cursed myself for even thinking it. "Uh, sure. What time? Do I owe you something for the ticket?"

"Six, and no, you're my special guest."

Special guest, huh?

"Okay, see you then."

I hung up the phone, and then it hit. What did I just do? I'd have to leave work early to get ready and make the hour-long drive to the non-billable party. *Is it non-billable? I don't think I can risk billing it, and I don't want to ask Carbone. I guess this is what they call pro bono.*

I ran home to change. *What should I wear?* The tour had been muddy, but the dinner sounded upscale, and the evening was chilly. I finally decided on a pair of black slacks, a dressy, cream cashmere sweater, a simple gold necklace, and a classy pair of gold dangle earrings. I skipped the heels and opted for black patent flats, ready for any terrain.

On the hour drive out to Chairo Caviar, my thoughts wandered from caviar poaching and demanding partners to the dreamy blue of Ben Akers' eyes. I scolded myself for that thought. *He's a client, Skyler. Just a client. And this is just information gathering and client schmoozing.*

Pulling up to Chairo's facility, I found the gravel parking lot full. I located an empty spot at the far end of the lot. When I got out, I followed the sounds of a live band to find the party. Behind the unimpressive office, there was a relatively large area covered in gravel and set with rented chairs and tables. Hundreds of lights were strung from trees overhead. Near the building, I spotted several commercial-size barbeques manned by professional chefs in neat, white jackets. The band played county music, but not the nasal, whiny stuff that grated my soul like nails on a chalkboard. There was a folksy vibe, perfect for this night under the stars.

There must have been more than a hundred guests seated at the tables, milling about, or trying to dance. I looked for anyone I might know. Quite a few people wore bright blue polo shirts with the Chairo insignia. I figured they were employees, but the only ones I had met during my tour had been wearing face masks so I couldn't recognize anyone. Debating where to sit, I caught a wave on the far side of the area, near the cooking—Ben. I waved back before heading over.

"Glad you made it, Skyler."

"I didn't see this area yesterday. Do you do this sort of thing often?

"Couple times a year. As I said, it helps promote the brand and also the plight of the sturgeon."

I giggled before I could stop myself. "The ones I saw on the barbeque?"

He chuckled. "They led a cushy life before their sacrifice. And they're pretty tasty."

A server came around bearing trays loaded with tiny blinis with a dollop of crème Fraiche and a topping of caviar. Ben took one. I followed suit and took a bite. "Delicious."

"That's the traditional way many people serve caviar, but I suspect the true connoisseurs are more like me, preferring the unadulterated caviar straight from the tin."

He looked nice. No bumblebee yellow or rubber waders tonight. Navy slacks, white shirt, unbuttoned slightly, and a hint of sophisticated cologne. He was a perfect mix of a farm boy and elegant entrepreneur. I tried to ignore how that made me feel.

I asked, "Are all the employees wearing company shirts?"

"Should be. See the guy over by the band?" He pointed to a muscular young man with blond hair. "That's Trevor— your fish wrangler from our tour." He pointed to another man I recognized as the unmasked caviar tester. "You might remember Andre. He's been with me nearly since the start. Knows his stuff."

I noticed two employees who seemed to be arguing. A burly man with a beard and mustache and an Asian woman with long hair in a ponytail. I asked Ben, "What about them?"

"Demetri and Brittany. They both work with the maturing females and manage the water systems."

"It looks like they disagree about something."

"Don't know if it's work-related, but things around here have been tense lately. If we don't turn things around soon, I might have to let some people go. I haven't said anything, but I think they can sense it. Rumors have a way of traveling fast. The water systems are our most vulnerable point for tampering, so I've asked Demetri and Brittany to keep a sharp eye."

"I see."

The music stopped. A beautiful woman stepped up to the microphone. Tight faux leather pants, sky-high heels, and a minky vest over a cream silk blouse. Ben whispered, "That's Laurel—my right-hand man." His broad, delighted smile as he watched her unnerved me.

I bristled as she spoke into the microphone. "The chefs have announced that dinner will be served now. If you take your seats, we have servers that will bring plates around. I want to thank my brother for hosting this brilliant event to benefit the River Conservancy, making it possible for Chairo Caviar to release hundreds of fish back into the wild to protect the species."

There was applause. I glanced over at Ben, tilting my head. "Your sister, huh?"

"Yeah, she's about the only person that could put up with me as a business partner."

As we took our seats, white apron-clad servers brought us plates of barbequed fish, delicate and expertly prepared. The music started up again. The night sky was exceptionally clear with the slightest Delta breeze. I took a deep breath and savored the moment.

CHAPTER 5
EMPLOYEES OR SUSPECTS?

I arrived at the office early the day after the party to make up for leaving early the night before. Plus, I'd gotten suspicious about the timesheet shenanigans, so my first stop was at Felicity's desk to see if the forger had made more alterations. I took the document back and compared it to my Excel spreadsheet. The changes were subtle—just a .1 here and a .2 there being deducted, but they added up. Maybe it was time to let Felicity know what was going on. I didn't think it could be her, but I was growing paranoid about everyone at the firm. For now, I just referred back to the electronic version then filled it out a new sheet correctly before replacing it on Felicity's desk. I'd have to ask around and find out who was staying late after Felicity and I were both gone.

This morning, I needed to set aside the timesheet tampering and concentrate on banking some billables. I had that employee list to work through. I guess I could have pushed it off to a paralegal, but I felt it was okay for me to take the reins. I punched in the first of sixty names into the Superior Court's case search interface one at a time. Henry

Nottingham. "No search results." Cleared. Next name. Danica Morrison. Cleared. Jose Martinez. Cuss word filter. Eighteen cases pulled up, but were any of these hits "my" Jose Martinez? After all, it was a common name. I would have to open every single electronic case docket to see the case details. If it were just a traffic infraction, it wouldn't matter, but if there was something more suspicious like fraud or a judgment, that would demonstrate motive to seek illegal ways of getting money and warrant further investigation. I might even need to go to the courthouse to match the file to a social security number, address, or other identifying information to confirm a match. Unfortunately, Jose's name wasn't the only one with complications. This was California. There were a lot of Hispanic names like Garcia, Ramirez, and Hernandez. There were also Sikhs and many Singhs and Kaurs along with the cliché Smiths and Joneses.

After three hours, I was only halfway through the list. On one hand, my billables total for the day was doing a happy dance. On the other hand, that fast progress Carbone expected was not happening. I figured this was another eat-at-your-desk day. I kept grinding through the lunch hour.

Felicity looked in around two o'clock. "How's it going?"

"It's going. It's definitely going. It's just not going any*where*." I blew out a big breath of air and rolled my eyes toward the ceiling for emphasis.

"It takes a lot of groundwork sometimes to make progress. Let me know if there's something I can do."

I appreciated her more and more.

At the end of the sixty names, I had cleared everyone except six: Nick Petrinko, Martin Garcia, Demetri

Kabalevsky, Laura Delaney, Andrew Carlton, and Gretchen Lewis. Two Russian-sounding names. Just because caviar is traditionally associated with Russia was not enough, but Petrinko had a judgment against him for $18,654.67. More than a blue-collar employee could handle easily. Kabalevsky had a fraud case filed against him. It was ancient news and dismissed more than a decade ago, but still, it showed a propensity for—or at least there had been an accusation of—dishonesty. Garcia was a mystery. There was a Martin Garcia with a federal criminal case in his background, but it would take more to find out if it was the same Martin Garcia who worked for Chairo. Laura Delaney was currently fighting through a nasty divorce with three minor children in the middle of the tug-o-war. The lawyer she had on retainer was a shark with a high billable rate, meaning she was fielding some serious legal bills and had financial motivation. Andrew Carlton had a criminal conviction involving drugs when he was just twenty-one. He was now in his mid-thirties, but drugs are hard to shake. Gretchen Lewis had a raft of small claims filed against her, some of them not yet resolved. One mentioned some petty embezzlement. Ben probably didn't know any of this about his people. It was the kind of stuff people kept hidden from their employers unless they had an actual conviction on their record they were forced to reveal on an employment application.

Mid-afternoon and I was through the employee list and

half braindead. I needed some fresh perspective. I remembered Felicity's advice to get to know other partners who might give me work. I also wanted to check in with the other new associates.

I wandered down to Carly's office first, peeping in her door. She clacked away at her computer keyboard but looked up when she saw me. I waved as I stood in the doorway. "I heard a rumor that Grayson Oliver Tripper III was back at the office."

Carly took on a pained look, her eyebrows knitted as she motioned me in. "After a manner of speaking. He's got an office here, but he runs the firm's Denver office. He's not here all that much. I guess most of our interaction will be by phone or email."

"What do you think of him?"

"Not sure. I heard rumors that he fires most associates who work with him within the first three months, so that's not very comfortable. But he talked to me about a multi-million-dollar litigation case he's working on. He's letting me draft discovery questions. I even suggested a motion. He said to move forward with drafting it."

"Sounds like he's impressed with you if he's taking your recommendation on filing a motion with the court."

"That's what I hope. I'm just really feeling the pressure right now. What about you?"

"Same show, different channel. Carbone has given me full autonomy on this caviar case, but I don't feel like I know what I'm doing. So far, I'm looking under rocks and not finding anything interesting. Well, unless you count the owner of the caviar company. He's definitely interesting." *Shoot. Overshare.*

Carly perked up, her eyebrows slightly raised and a tight, smug smile on her face. "*That* kind of interesting, huh? Do tell."

"Nothing to tell. A client. He's just not stuffy, that's all. I'll let you get back to work."

I slipped out the door before she could ask any more questions.

Making my way down the hall, I passed Vernon Wagner's office. Real estate partner. I hesitated. At law school, the advice had been that it wasn't *if* you got sued for malpractice relating to real estate law, but *when*. On the other hand, that area of law seemed interesting. I decided to take my chances. I poked my head in the door. He seemed deep in thought, with a thick deposition transcript in his hands, but he caught the movement and looked up.

"Hello, Mr. Wagner. I'm Skyler Ashford. I'm working with Mr. Carbone, but if he doesn't have my time filled up, I wanted you to know I'm interested in real estate law." I gave him a warm smile.

Wagner didn't smile back. It looked like he was sizing me up, purposefully keeping his face expressionless. "I'll keep that in mind. But you need to make sure to check with Tom first. I don't want any misunderstandings."

My heart went to my stomach. Had I overstepped an invisible line?

"Sure thing. I only meant if Carbone… I mean *if* Mr. Carbone is willing to share my time."

I wasn't sure if that sounded worse. I made an awkward retreat, backing out fast.

Did Felicity just set me up? This place is making me paranoid.

I debated my options, then decided I didn't want to experiment to determine whether the partners talked about the new associates—more like gossiped—as often and much as I suspected. I decided I'd better have a confessional with Carbone before the next partners' meeting in case he heard I talked to Wagner and was given a different impression of the encounter than what actually happened. I skulked down to his office. Joan shot me a look like she was waiting for more entertainment. I decided it was best to coat her with honey even if I'd rather sting her.

"Hey, Joan, how are you today?" I threw on my sunniest smile.

"Fine. You need something?"

"Just talking to a few folks on my break. I was hoping Mr. Carbone had a minute for me. Is he in?"

She gave me a look that conveyed she liked being in charge. Wanted to be asked. "I'll check."

She used the intercom option on her phone. "Mr. Carbone, do you have a minute for Ms. Ashford? She's standing out here in the hall."

I could hear Carbone bellow from his office. "What's she doing out there? Send her in."

Joan shot me a look like I was an idiot. I smiled back

like I didn't understand before walking into Carbone's office.

He looked up, cheeks slightly sucked in. "How can I help you, Ms. Ashford? Do you have some progress to report on the Chairo case?"

"Uh... not yet. I've been investigating the competitors and employees, but nothing solid. Do you have anything else you want me working on?"

"If you don't have anything to do, then sure, but I want you to concentrate on the Chairo case."

"About that. I was wondering...uh... if you're not here or there's nothing else you want me to do, I presume I need to keep up my billables and can work with other partners as long as you're made aware of it."

A look of confusion flashed over his face, quickly replaced with a scowl. "I would presume that they would talk to me first."

"That's my understanding also. I just wanted you to know that I was interested in real estate law and introduced myself to Mr. Wagner. I thought I should tell you that."

I think he started to say something, but then there was only a *humph*, and his lips pursed. "Is that all, Ms. Ashford?"

"Yes, sir."

"If Wagner or any other partner has work and you have nothing to do, take it. Billables are a priority. But right now, you need to concentrate on the caviar case. That's your priority, and I expect that other assignments will not slow it down. Figure it out."

He looked back down. I was dismissed. And glad to go. I couldn't tell how that went. I scuttled out of the office, trying not to give Joan the satisfaction of letting my face show how I felt. I figured he'd talk to Wagner the first chance he got, but at least it wouldn't look like I went behind his back.

Four o'clock. Although I was unsure what my next day would hold, I decided it would be good to check in with Ben. I asked Felicity to set up a conference call for tomorrow morning. I decided to make a master notes file to put together all my current leads, including any connections I could find. So far, that wasn't much. The employees who hadn't been cleared from my local court check, the list of possible sabotage attempts at Chairo, and the list of competitors with their details. I figured that bore a closer look. Those were all people on the production side of caviar. *What about consumers? Restaurants?*

After making a list of questions for Ben, I decided to call it a day. Then I had a second thought. It was already 5:18 p.m. How late would the timesheet bandit hang out? Presumably, until after I usually left. I filled out the paper and put it on Felicity's desk before gathering my things. I made a small commotion about leaving. I even went out to the back parking lot and moved my car to the far side of the front parking area before quietly returning to the office. Peeking around every corner, I snuck back to my office, leaving the lights out. I partially closed the door so I could see Felicity's desk, but it was hard to see inside my office. I quietly sat in a dark corner to wait.

After half an hour, I was going nuts with no

entertainment. I couldn't use my phone because it would create light. After an hour, I realized I needed to pee but couldn't leave. It approached seven o'clock. I decided I wouldn't wait more than another half hour. I had my eyes firmly watching Felicity's desk when the door was suddenly thrown open and the lights blazed on. My bladder nearly betrayed me, but nothing matched the look of utter surprise on the face of an extremely thin, black-haired, Hispanic janitor who burst into my office. He shrieked, "What are you doing here?" in high soprano.

"It's my office." My voice was highly defensive.

He de-escalated slightly. "What are you doing in the dark?" Now, he shot me a suspicious, quizzical look like I might be a nut case.

"None of your business." I waltzed past him as he was still opening and closing his mouth as if he wanted to give me a further retort.

As I retreated, I heard the vacuum and some mariachi music start up in my office. *Hmm… happy janitor.*

CHAPTER 6
CONSUMERS

The timesheet caper was still going on the next morning. Maybe the culprit got in early in the morning? In any case, Felicity wasn't there yet, so I could eliminate her. When she showed up, I went out to her desk. "Someone's been altering my time sheets."

"How could that be? I've been entering them into the computer system. That's secure."

"Yes, but I'm here before you in the morning. I've found altered timesheets. I've had to fill them out again."

She scowled. "How in the world could you remember the details? That could lead to inaccuracies and needs to be reported to the partners."

"I've been recording my time on an Excel spreadsheet I created. To begin with, it was to help me know where I was at with my billables, but it's ended up being a backup to ensure the paper version wasn't altered."

Her look turned to deep concern. "Why would anyone do something like that?"

"They've been shaving a point-one off the time entries. Perhaps they thought it was too little to be noticed, but it would add up to enough missing time to undermine me with the partners."

Felicity's mouth opened slightly as her eyebrows knit tight. "That's criminal. Fraudulent. We need to find out who because they need to be fired." She looked like she might fly at the culprit like a mother hen. I loved her for it.

"I staked out your desk from my office in the dark last night." Felicity stopped flapping and her mouth fell the rest of the way open. She abruptly closed it before asking, "And?"

"Nothing. I left after the janitor scared me."

She gave a soft laugh like she could envision the encounter. "Oh, that's Julio. I call him the dancing janitor because he's always got his earphones on listening to mariachi music if he's cleaning after hours. He dances around—sometimes even sings if no one is here—or if he thinks no one is here. Caught him once. He didn't hear me because of the earphones. Nearly jumped out of his skin."

The mental picture made me smile. "Same guy, except for the headphones."

"He's been here for years. I'll ask if he's seen anyone lingering around my desk."

"I think it may not be at night. Maybe they get in early. Before either of us."

"We'll get to the bottom of it. Why don't we just leave a dummy timesheet out, but you email your spreadsheet updates, and that's what I'll enter."

"Deal."

I called Ben. After a couple of rings, he answered. "Chairo Caviar, Ben speaking."

"It's Skyler. I thought maybe we could put our heads together and talk about what I've got so far. Is this a good time?"

"Absolutely. Fire away."

"Okay, five companies seem to be your main competitors: Czar Alexander, Caviars of California, Black Gold Caviar, LLC, Rusal Caviar, Inc., and Romanov Black Pearl Caviar, LLC. Maybe we can take them one at a time? Can you tell me what you know about those companies?

"Sure."

"Okay, what about Caviars of California? Looks like a woman runs that one."

"Marla. She's a force of nature. Hands-on, and a good businesswoman. We're always in a price war with them. I'm not sure how she keeps her prices so low. It may be business efficiencies."

"Okay...or she's buying on the black market?"

"That would surprise me. Marla is a staunch environmentalist. One of the biggest contributors to the River Conservancy."

"Or that's part of the front?"

"Aren't you a paranoid one."

"That's what lawyers do. Okay. Black Gold?"

"Never heard of that one."

"That might be because they were operating under a

fictitious business name of Tashir Caviar, at least back in 2008. They changed names again a few years later."

"Oh, okay, I know who you're talking about now. Yeah, they're still operating, but I've heard rumors that they're having financial troubles."

"They're not the only one. It looks like Czar Alexander was FTB forfeited back in 2002 with a forwarding address in Montana, but just because a company isn't in good standing doesn't always mean it's not operating."

"They went under a few years back. I had an ugly run-in with the founder, Sergei Chesnokov. He seemed to think that we undercut him, stole employees, and caused the company to declare bankruptcy. The truth is that he just wasn't interested in paying his employees fairly or keeping his facilities up to date. We ended up with several of his employees coming to work for us, but they had already left before coming to me."

"Which ones?"

"I'm not sure if I'd recall all of them, but Nick Petrinko, Raul Mendes, and Allyssa Forbes were three of them."

"Nick Petrinko. I have that name on a list of employees with questions about their backgrounds. But first, let's talk about that last company on my list. Do you know anything about Rusal Caviar, Inc. or Jacques Baudelaire?"

"Seems like there are quite a few Russians in the industry. Jacques is the exception. He's a Frenchman with impressive connections in the restaurant industry. They produce a nice quality product many chefs speak of highly. Other than that, I don't know much about him or the company."

"So, he'd have the connections to move illegal caviar in the restaurant market. Circling back to the employees, I tagged Nick Petrinko, Martin Garcia, Demetri Kabalevsky, Laura Delaney, and Andrew Carlton. Petrinko has a sizeable judgment against him, Kabalevsky had a fraud judgment a long time ago, Delaney is going through a nasty divorce, and Carlton had a criminal conviction involving drugs."

"Wow, I had no idea. What about Garcia?"

"Mystery man. There's a Martin Garcia with a federal criminal conviction, but there are a lot of Martin Garcias. I'm still working on finding out whether it's the same guy."

"So, we have a list of people to keep an eye on at the company. That's good. You putting the P.I. on it?"

"I will be. I figured I'd update you first. If she needs a cover story, I presume you can give her a fake job."

"This is starting to sound like something out of a crime T.V. show, but yeah. Wonder how she feels about fish?"

I recalled Victoria with her impeccable clothes, makeup, and stilettos. My imagination conjured a humorous picture of her wrangling a sturgeon. "I don't know, but her name is Victoria Delaney. She'll be giving you a call."

"Anything else?"

"Not for now."

"Got it. Bye, Skyler." We hung up the phone. I dialed Victoria to fill her in.

After lunch, Peter Mand wandered into my office. "How's the caviar case going?"

"Finally got a couple of leads, but nothing solid yet. How are your corporate minutes going?"

"We got those done. Hey, your case sounds way more interesting. What kind of leads?" He sat down in one of my office chairs as if making himself at home.

I laughed. "So far, a bunch of nothing really." I suddenly felt a little uncomfortable. "If you finished the corporate work, what are you working on now?"

"Melikian has me reviewing a bunch of product sales contracts, and he asked me to draft a partnership agreement. Bunch of tax provisions."

"Have you gotten work from any other partners?"

"Diane Walden is working with Melikian on some deals with real estate components, so I've gotten to know her a little bit."

"What's she like to work with?"

"She's pretty cool, but she's a typical trusts and estates attorney—you only make real money when your clients die. She's paying her dues drafting the trust agreements and wills. She won't be the age where they're starting to die off for another decade or so. Sounds morbid, but that's the way of it."

"I hated all that stuff in law school. Fee tails. Blackacre. Rule Against Perpetuity."

"Don't remind me. The other thing about trusts and estates is that you can't fix something if you screw up because the client's already passed away by the time you realize there's a problem."

Suddenly, a deep sadness appeared in his eyes, and his face grew slack. "It's especially hard to draft wills when my sister may be dying." He looked down at the carpet.

I drew in a sharp breath. "Oh, Peter, I had no idea. What's wrong?"

"Leukemia. They're trying some experimental treatment, but I'm not sure how much longer my family can afford it." He looked up and blinked. "Sorry. Didn't mean to talk about it."

He stood with a morose look, smoothing the same cheap suit I'd seen him in every day this week. I felt sorry for him. He seemed bored with his work and emotionally burdened. I didn't want a job that made me feel like I was just grinding along, stuck in the same office day after day. But now he loitered in my office. I didn't see any way I could help. I needed to get my billables for the day. I lied. "I've got a conference call in a few minutes."

He stood up a little straighter. "Maybe you can tell me about your case if there's something interesting. Take my mind off all the elderly clients and tax provisions." He shot me a crooked smile before walking out the door.

Peter hadn't been out the door for more than a few minutes when Felicity buzzed me. "Bob Colburn from Fish and Game on Line 2."

"Thanks, Felicity." I picked up the phone. "Skyler Ashford. You have some news for me, Mr. Colburn?"

"Bob, please. Maybe. We hit pay dirt out on the river last night. Four oversized sturgeons, one nearly seven feet long, were lashed alive to the riverbank with a light cable through their gills. Poachers do this to keep the fish alive until they find black market buyers, but I've never seen this many at a time. Honestly, it was a bit of luck that they were discovered. There are cliffs along the riverbank in the area as well as overhanging bushes. There's nothing around to give off any light. The poachers picked their spot well. The officers only saw a cable that looked out of place. When they pulled on it, a fish was attached."

"So, did you catch the poachers?"

"That's where it gets interesting. We got authority for a stakeout. Fish and Game officers waited until the poachers came back. Normally, we would have arrested them immediately, but this has the smell of a bigger operation, so we let them take the fish. We have night vision photographs of them as well as the license plate of the pickup truck that was used. We're hoping it wasn't stolen. The police are running the plates now."

"That's great news, Bob. First solid information we've gotten. I've got a few employee names who have some potentially suspicious background. I'll email my notes to you. Maybe something will link up with what you find."

"We appreciate any help you can give us. One more thing. There are rumors of black-market caviar sales to several restaurants in the San Francisco area. I've got a call in to local authorities there to find out more and see if we can exchange information. There may not be any ties, but it sounds like an unusual volume for local poachers to market."

"I'll pass that along to our private investigator. Appreciate the update, Bob."

"No problem." With that, we hung up. I was left wondering how wide a net needed to be cast...no pun intended. *Restaurants. Could that implicate Jacques*

Baudelaire?

My stomach began to rumble. The clock confirmed it approached noon. I was about to go to the break room to retrieve my brown bag turkey and cheese on whole wheat when Carly appeared at my door looking like she held back tears, her voice shaky.

"Skyler, I need out of here. I need someone to talk to. You willing to grab some lunch with me?" She bit her lip and sniffed, on the verge of losing it. Not something you wanted to do at the office where there was an audience. It was at that moment we became comrades.

"Sure. Let's get out of here." I quickly grabbed my purse and started walking rapidly toward the back entrance, Carly following. "I'll drive. You look upset."

We made it to my car before the tears came. That ruled out any decent restaurants where other people from the firm might lurk. I didn't ask her opinion. I headed for a little hole-in-the-wall taco place I'd spotted on my route to work. Not the usual choice for lawyers, and a little out of the way. As I drove, Carly breathed deep and dabbed her nose, trying to regain some control.

When we were seated, we ordered a couple of lunch special taco plates. I glanced to be sure napkins were available in case of a snotty cry before I asked. "What happened?"

She sucked air in hard, her voice coming out ragged and breathy. "That psycho Tripper… He… He… He's *nuts*,

Skyler."

My brows gently creased. "I thought things were going so well. Didn't he ask you to draft a motion you recommended?"

She transcended into tears. They morphed into volcanic anger, her eyes flaring, and her voice escalating. She was looking a little psychotic herself. "Yeah. He asked me to draft it, and then when I sent it to him for review before filing it with the court, I get this call asking me what the hell I thought I was doing."

"What?" I could feel my face distort with confusion.

"I'm telling you, he's a *psycho*. Acted like he didn't remember the prior conversation. Cussed me out for wasting time on the motion. And now all that billable time for research and drafting is going to get written off. And he thinks *I'm* the crazy one."

"Whoa. No wonder no one lasts working for him." I flinched, hearing myself. "I mean, not you. You're brilliant. I'm sure if you talk to another partner and explain…"

She hissed, "You know I can't do that."

I dipped my head. I knew it. The partners stuck together. They were bought into the firm together. They had to live with each other for the long run. But they didn't have to keep putting up with us. "What are you going to do?"

"I don't know. I guess I'm just going to have to figure out how to hack his personality."

"Maybe his secretary can help? She probably knows how he works. Felicity has given me a few tips."

She laughed, slightly maniacally. "Are you kidding? Right after my call with him, I could hear him on speakerphone with her. I've never heard such a stream of F-words without a breath between and used in every form of the English language. His secretary was bawling at her desk when I left. Problem is, he's a brilliant litigator, no matter how horrid of a human being he is."

I couldn't even reply. I just mouthed an "oh" and was grateful so see the waitress approach with our food.

After munching our taco plates and avoiding any more talk about the firm—a silent understanding that Carly needed to regain her calm—we headed back toward the office. Suddenly, Carly yelled, "Stop, please. Pull over there." She pointed toward a tiny flower shop.

I didn't ask. I just did as I was told. As she exited the car, I looked at my watch. "Carly, we've got to get back. It's been nearly an hour."

She nodded. "I'll be fast." She came back out just minutes later with a large bouquet of sunflowers. I shot her a quizzical look as she got in the car. "For Emma. His secretary. She deserves combat pay for putting up with that piece-of-work, contemptible oaf. It's the least I can do."

We drove back the rest of the way in silence.

I needed to update Carbone on the case. This time I didn't ask Joan's permission. I just peeked in the doorframe. When I saw he was there, I knocked lightly on the door. He barely looked up.

"Just a minute, Ashford. In the middle of a thought."

Fair enough. I lingered outside the door, catching Joan's sharp-eyed scrutiny. After five minutes, I'd begun to wonder if I should just come back later, when he bellowed. "Ashford. You still there?"

Why could this particular man make me feel both incompetent and like an unruly teenager going to the principal's office? I steeled myself for the encounter and walked in. "Yes, Mr. Carbone. I thought you would want an update on the caviar case."

He raised an eyebrow, grumbling, "About time. Where are we at?" After giving him a summary download, he sat back in his chair, playing with intertwining fingers. I thought I saw slight satisfaction on his face, then it faded as he leaned forward. "Who can we sue? We're not supposed to be the cops. We need to find a way to make a recovery for the client for the lost sales."

I thought of at least three sentences I'd like to say before I thought the better of it and responded audibly. "It seems to me that the investigation process will determine if there's someone we can sue. I'd certainly like for this to be a legal case instead of the unconventional assignment it's been so far." I figured I'd just stare him down.

He seemed impervious. He cleared his throat. "Well, as long as the client is willing to pay for this type of investigation. But it would be in the firm's best interest if we could take it to the next step to earn our keep."

"I certainly hope so, Mr. Carbone." I rose, figuring I should make my exit at this point. On the way out the door, I added, "I'll continue to keep you informed."

He ignored me. I nodded curtly to Joan, who watched for my expression as I exited.

Back at my desk, I dialed Victoria. No answer. I hung up without leaving a message. After a few minutes, Felicity buzzed me. "Ms. Delaney on Line 5."

When I answered, she whispered, "I saw the call come through with the law firm's caller ID, but I'm undercover here at Chairo. What do you need?"

"I just wanted to update you. Fish and Game has a lead."

"That's great, but if you could send an email with those updates, it would be easier for me. I don't want to blow my cover here. Ben tells me an unusually high percentage of females have reabsorbed their eggs. I don't think it's a coincidence. I think someone is purposefully spooking the fish."

I bristled at her use of Ben's first name, picturing those long legs of hers in a pair of waders, looking a fair sight better than when I'd first considered it. "Got it. I'll write it up and send it to you. Looks like you might need to make a trip to San Francisco to check on some sales of underpriced caviar to restaurants."

"There's only one of me. I need to follow up here, but I'll get on it as soon as possible."

It couldn't be soon enough for me. "Speaking of reports, I'll need them from you on a real-time basis." I felt catty. It probably came across that way. I didn't feel like a take-back.

"Of course, Ms. Ashford." Totally professional,

making me feel less so myself.

"Thank you, Ms. Delaney. I'll let you get back to your investigation."

After we hung up, I was mad. I wasn't sure at who. Maybe myself. I didn't like that so many people were getting to me lately. In every possible way. I needed to be a billing machine, not a confidante, a jealous female, a paranoid associate, and everything else jumbling around my head since I started this job.

There wasn't anything else I could do on the caviar case for the day, but it was only mid-afternoon. I wandered back down the hall to see Vernon Wagner. His door was open. When he saw me linger, he waved me in. "Something I can do for you, Ms. Ashford?"

"I talked to Mr. Carbone. It's okay for me to work for other partners as long as I'm making progress on the caviar case for him. I could use some additional billables. I want to keep my plate full and earn my keep with the firm."

He adjusted his seat in his chair, looking at me contemplatively. "Well, I do have a case that's been requiring a lot of hours. Cross-expertise even. A real estate development case I'm doing for a guy I've known since high school—Carter Wells. He's got some investors willing to purchase the dirt if he will pull in his expertise to obtain financing to build. Bond money, tax credits…a layered financing approach. They've got a problem with some species of garter snake the environmentalists have their panties in a wad about. We need a read on what it would cost to buy some alternative habitat or otherwise get them to stand down without killing the economics of the deal. Clay Voorhees is our attorney who specializes in that kind of environmental thing. There's also some tax analysis that Gerald Cobbs is handling relating to the financing. Why don't you talk to them about how you can help? Tell them I said it was okay."

"Got it, Mr. Wagner. I appreciate the work."

I exited his office feeling lighter. Excited for something different to sink my teeth into.

I went to track down Voorhees. I knew his office was at the far end of the hall, but I hadn't seen inside. I found the door closed. No one occupied the secretarial desk on the other side of the hall. I knocked lightly and heard a soft "Enter." When I opened the door, I was distracted as I looked around his office. It smelled of Patchouli. Plants overflowed everywhere, some in pots on a credenza, a large Ficus on the floor near his desk. In the gaps in his collection of books, tribal statuary perched on the bookshelves. I felt like I'd walked into the private space of some odd, exotic explorer.

Voorhees himself fascinated me. Standard lawyer suit, but slightly long, graying, curly hair and an unkept mustache and beard. Although he was sitting, he looked to be on the shorter side. The hairy tops of his hands were almost simian. He looked at me impatiently. I shook myself out of my thoughts.

"Skyler Ashford. New associate. Mr. Wagner sent me to see if I could help on the Carter Wells deal."

"Did he now? So, what do you know about environmental issues in real estate deals?" He looked at me pointedly.

"Honestly, not much, but I'm anxious to learn." I was hoping I sounded confident even though I squirmed inside.

"You're not a summer clerk, so any work you do has to be billed properly. The Rules of Professional Conduct require that a lawyer not charge a client for taking on work where the lawyer needs to learn the area of law. That means you'd be writing off the time you spend figuring things out, only billing for the time you actually provide value to the case, not learning about environmental law practice."

I cringed, but then I figured this was part of paying my dues. "I understand."

He reached for a thick file on his desk, offering it to me. "This is the information on the property. Litigation has been filed trying to prevent the development. A motion is coming up in a month. We need to file an opposition. Show me what you can do. I'll need it well in advance of our response date for my review."

I took the file. "Thank you." I wasn't sure if I meant it.

Settling back at my desk, I opened the file and started reading. The San Francisco garter snake is commonly regarded as one of the most beautiful snakes. The species had blue, red, and black stripes running down the length of its body and has been listed as endangered since 1967. Its habitat was thought to be limited to the San Francisco Peninsula and extended into San Mateo and the Santa Cruz Mountains. Apparently, our client's proposed building site was a known refuge for the colorful serpents.

Knowing the surrounding area would eventually be a hot housing market, Carter Well's investors, Odeion Real Estate Development, had been buying up land in the area for the last decade, including a large dairy farm. They convinced the dairy farmer, experiencing an economic downturn, to enter into an agreement where Odeion would own the land but lease it back to the dairy farm for the following decade. That timing appealed to the aging dairy farmer whose sons had shown little interest in making it an inter-generational business. The lease had expired, and the property was well-suited for building apartments for the burgeoning Silicon Valley housing market. Problem was, the garter snakes had loved the dairy farm and lived in harmony with its operation. The property also included ponds with red-legged frogs, the snakes' favorite food.

Researching the developer's options, one possibility was to buy up some habitat that could be explicitly designated for the preservation of the species while destroying another potential habitat site for our client's deal. This meant finding an alternative location with shallow, vegetated ponds near a hillside. The ponds also needed to have a California red-legged frog population for the snakes to snack on. Problem was finding an exchange property that wasn't priced through the roof. It was like paying twice to build in the expensive San Francisco Bay Area. That was only if the San Mateo City Council approved such an exchange.

Wells now faced a lawsuit from the Wild Waters Conservation Association, an environmental group claiming that the San Mateo City Council violated the federal Endangered Species Act by approving the construction. The Association named both the City of San Mateo and Odeion in its lawsuit, which had successfully delayed the developer from breaking ground for six months now.

As I set the file back down, I glanced at the clock. Already past five. It had taken hours just to grasp what was happening from the various letters and court documents passed along by Wagner. On the other hand, I found the work interesting, and getting up to speed on the contents of the client's file qualified as billable. Getting a grasp on the federal laws protecting endangered species and whether the environmentalists had any grounds for blocking the development would not be. At least not entirely. I was cross-eyed and vowed to come in extra early in the morning to get around the hours I would be writing off. If this kind of thing kept happening, I was going to run out of "earlier" morning hours to sacrifice to the firm, but that was the best solution I had for now.

CHAPTER 7
SABOTEURS

"Get up earlier!" was becoming my mantra. I arrived at the office at six a.m. since I figured I'd be writing off a chunk of time. For once, I found most of the offices dark. I rounded the corner toward my office to see Peter Mand replacing a paper on Felicity's desk. Before he could spot me, I ducked into a dark secretary's cubicle a few offices from my own. Peeking around the dim corner, I saw Peter glance nervously toward my office. Before he could turn his head my way, I hunkered down. After a few minutes, he passed by me. When I'd given him enough time to disappear down the hall, I crept out and walked up to Felicity's desk. The dummy timesheet— altered.

I couldn't believe it was Peter. Why would he sabotage me? I'd never done anything to him. Well, except for the fact that rumors flew that the firm never kept all of its first-year associates. But there was no clear evidence of that firing behavior, just paranoia and rumors that served to keep us scrambling on the hamster wheel. Even if he made me look bad, he had his own work to measure up to. It was more about being great at beating the billables game than knocking someone else down…wasn't it?

I tried to put it out of my mind and focus on my work. I still had to keep up progress on the caviar case, and now the opposition on the real estate case was due in a month. I'd better have a draft out within a couple of weeks just in case I'd missed something important. I diligently read up on the federal Endangered Species Act until eight o'clock when Felicity arrived. As soon as I saw her, I buzzed her intercom line. "Felicity, can you come to my office and close the door behind you? I think the timesheet culprit has been caught."

She hurried in, her eyes bright and curious. "What? Who?"

"I arrived early and saw Peter Mand putting a paper on your desk. He didn't see me. I hid in a dark spot, then checked the timesheet when he left. It was not the same as the one I put out last night."

Her expression grew troubled…sad. "He seemed like such a nice young man. Whatever reason would he have to do such a thing? He'll probably get fired."

"Don't say anything to anyone yet. I want to talk to him. He told me yesterday that he's been paying for his sister's medical treatments. He's emotionally distressed, but I'd hate to see him lose his job…or even his career. It's an act of moral turpitude. It's possible he could lose his legal license depending on how things get handled with the partners."

Felicity drew a breath in. "I'll leave it to you for now, Skyler, but we must protect the firm. Dishonest in one thing; he can't be trusted with other things. There's just too much confidential information involved with what we do. It's one thing for him to ruin his career, but could he jeopardize the firm? We can't let that happen."

"Just give me a day. I want to know what's behind his actions."

I figured there wasn't any reason to waste time. I marched down to Peter's office, strategy in hand--get him relaxed, then spring the direct question without warning like a deposition. I knocked on his semi-open door. He looked up from his keyboard. "Hey, Skyler."

"Mind if I come in?"

His eyes shifted slightly. "No, what's up?"

"I just wanted to follow up on our conversation the other day. Your sister. Are you helping pay for her medical treatments?"

His voice was halting. "I... I shouldn't have shared. It's no one else's problem. Uh... I... Yeah, I try to send the family money when I can."

"That's a lot of pressure. Is that why you've changed my timesheets to make me look bad?"

He scooted slightly back in his chair, face registering alarm with his eyes wide, his mouth slightly opening and closing like a fish. "Uh...what are you accusing me of?"

My eyes narrowed. "You can't lie your way out of this, Peter. I saw you this morning. I don't use paper timesheets. Now I have evidence of the tampering."

He deflated like a balloon, slumping in his chair, head down, unable to look me in the eye. "I'm sorry, Skyler. I really like you. It's just you got assigned to that darn caviar case."

It was my turn to be taken off guard, looking surprised. "What does that have to do with it? How is that connected to trying to get me fired to protect your job?"

He was silent. I glared, unblinking. I wasn't going away. Silence was my weapon of choice. He finally broke. "I can't tell. If I do, I'm afraid they'll hurt me."

I closed his office door. "Who? Someone involved with the caviar poaching? You know I'm going to the partners with this. It may be your legal career on the line, so who and what are you most worried about? I think you'd better come all the way clean."

First the blood drained from his face, then he started to look all puffy, his eyes misting like he was going to cry. "Gabe. It was Gabe. He told me he couldn't be connected but he wanted the caviar investigation to go away. I thought if I got you in trouble, it would slow things down. He paid me. My sister needed the money." Peter put his face in his hands. "He also said if I identified him, I could get hurt."

"Gabe?" I sat down with a plop on one of the guest chairs in Peter's office, my hands limp. "Gabe, as in Gabe from copying?"

"Yeah. I don't know how it's connected, but now I've told you everything. I may lose everything. My sister..." He trailed off.

"Look, Peter, this is serious. You've been caught, but it would be better if *you* tell Carbone. If I do, it looks even worse. I'm giving you until noon." I stood and walked out, still in shock.

My church-going Granny had always insisted that ugly words only make you sound less professional and in control. Today, I could hear her voice in my head, and my cuss filter was working full force on the way to my desk. I frantically motioned Felicity into my office, closed the door behind her, and filled her in. Her eyes were full of horror at the thought that there could be a saboteur working against a case in the office. My next call was to Victoria Delaney. When I gave her the download, there was silence on the line for a full minute.

"I already suspected."

My voice raised unintentionally. "What do you mean suspected? Suspected what?"

"Gabe."

"What the heck, Victoria?" Anger seeped into my tone.

"While you've been watching them, I've been watching you. The law firm that is. Investigating backgrounds. I like to know whom I'm working with. He was a new employee since I worked with Tom previously. As a precaution, Felicity filled me in on the timesheet shenanigans. I started running the new employees, you included."

"And what did you find?"

"You know Gabe's last name?"

Come to think of it, I didn't. "No."

"Petrinko."

"Same as Nick Petrinko, one of the employees I didn't

clear at Chairo Caviar."

"Precisely. I just don't know how they're connected so far. If they go underground, it will only make things harder. Any way to keep things chill with Gabe for a while?"

"That's complicated. He bribed another associate to try to sabotage me and undermine the firm's work on the case. I told him he needed to come clean with Carbone by noon."

"Shoot. That does compromise things...unless you think you can control the associate. Which one?"

"Peter Mand."

"I take it he knows that you're onto something?"

"Yeah, but he's scared. He could lose his law license. Gabe also threatened to hurt him."

"Tell him the firm can protect him from Gabe. Keep him scared about his career—cooperative and quiet. I'm calling Tom to update him."

"Victoria, I need to be part of that call or meeting. I'm a first-year associate. My job's not that secure."

"I get it. You're the hero of this story. We girls stick together. Don't worry. I'll get back to you soon. Bye."

Click. She hung up. And, no, I wasn't feeling all warm and fuzzy. Would Victoria give me credit?

When Carbone buzzed me, I was trying to get my head back in the opposition for Voorhees. Carbone's voice was stern and staccato. "My office. Now."

When I arrived, Victoria was already there. She must have dropped everything to come by, but you wouldn't have known it. No waders. Flowy black pants, a red satin shirt, and candy-apple heels. She and Carbone were talking, smiling, when I walked in. Carbone's smile disappeared the moment he saw me. Victoria remained relaxed, long legs crossed, her top stiletto moving up and down, dissipating energy.

I was standing until Carbone motioned to the second guest chair. "Sit, Ashford. Victoria has been filling me in on the situation with Gabe."

I looked over at Victoria, her arms relaxed against the arms of the chair. She gave me a nod, but what had she already told Carbone? I looked over at him. His mouth tensed. "Well, Ashford?"

"I presume Ms. Delaney has already explained that Peter Mand has been attempting to alter my timesheets, trying to get me fired not just because he was being competitive, but because he was being bribed to interfere with the caviar case. I guess he's got a sick sister, and he's trying to pay for some expensive medical treatments. She has leukemia and..."

Carbone barked, "I don't care about Mr. Mand's personal situation, Ashford. How will we keep him under control so we can investigate this guy in the copy room?"

"Gabe Petrinko."

"Whatever. How are you going to support Vicky's investigation?"

I looked at her for help. She said, "Tom, your associate here has given us the only break we've had in this case. I understand that Peter Mand is afraid both of losing his law license and his ability to pay for his sister's medical treatments. He's also concerned that these poachers could get ugly. If we bring him in on the situation, his best move will be to cooperate with us. I want to stay out of sight just in case Mr. Mand decides to tip the poachers. I don't want to blow my cover."

Carbone scowled. "All right, Vicky. I trust your judgment. You get out of here. We'll let you know how it goes."

Victoria rose to leave. Before reaching the door, she turned, nodding toward me. "Tom, this one's a keeper. Don't give her too much of your nonsense." Before he could respond, she stepped out.

I looked back at Carbone. He had one eyebrow raised. I wondered if he suppressed a slight smile—just a hint. There was a moment before he sighed and sat back in his chair. "She likes you. That says a lot. Let's call in Mand." He buzzed his secretary and roared, "Get me Peter Mand. Now."

I blanched. "He was going to come to you himself before noon. Victoria jumped the gun."

"More like didn't trust it to go down that way. We're getting a handle on this *now*."

The wait until Peter walked in was excruciating. Carbone just sat there, quiet. I followed suit, not knowing where to look. Finally, Peter appeared in the doorway, looking like he approached his execution but still unsure of the outcome.

Carbone barked, "Get in here. Shut the door behind you."

Peter obeyed, then shot me a look of betrayal, his hands clenched hard at his side. Seeing Carbone's expression, he glanced at me again, quietly hissing, "You told me you'd give me until noon."

Carbone leaned forward, hands on his desk like he was about to come straight over it. When he spoke, it was through gritted teeth. "She did nothing. Someone else was onto you. Onto Gabe. And now you've got to decide your future. Now, sit."

Peter stumbled toward the guest chair. He less sat than crumpled. "My sister…"

"I know all about your sister, and I don't care, but if you care, you'll cooperate. You're done here, but your law license is still in the balance. If you want to keep helping your family, you're going to help us."

Peter croaked, "What do you expect me to do?"

"Keep quiet, for starters. Report anything you can find out from Gabe to me. Keep up appearances. Don't interfere with our investigation. Know that we'll know if you violate our terms. Cooperate, and we won't report this to the State Bar for disciplinary action."

He sniveled, nodding. "I don't have a choice. I would never have in the first place if…"

Carbone didn't let him finish. "I don't have time for your whys. Now, get out of my office."

Peter nearly bolted. When he was gone, Carbone turned to me. "You have something to do? We've got one thin lead on the caviar case. If you think you need an atta-girl, you're thinking it too early in the game."

I gave him a slight nod before making a hasty exit.

He wouldn't have reported it to the State Bar anyway.

Too much potential for liability blow-back on the firm. But Peter doesn't seem to be willing to take the chance. That's good.

Passing Felicity's desk on my way back to my office, I paused. "I want you to know that I'm working on an assignment with Mr. Voorhees. A case for his client Carson Wells."

"Yes, good to update me on your cases. If you're working on any with deadlines, they need to be linked with your personal calendar." She tapped a few keys on the computer. "I see there's an opposition coming up in about a month."

"That's what I'm working on. I figured I should get a draft to Voorhees within a couple of weeks, but it's been tough. Carbone still wants me to keep the caviar case as my priority, and Voorhees warned me that I can't bill time getting up to speed on the law generally for the opposition, just case-specific research."

She shot me a knowing look, unconsciously rubbing her temple. "Remember when I told you to charge a forms fee?"

"Yeah?"

"Well, have you checked the firm's other cases and forms files to see if there's anything similar we've handled in the past?"

The blank look on my face mirrored the blank space in my head.

Felicity scratched her neck as her eyes went upward, not quite to a full eyeroll. "You can search for keywords. The computer will return any document this firm has ever done with the phrase. That would include any prior motions, oppositions, trial briefs...any kind of document you can imagine."

My mouth formed an "oh." "So, I could search for 'Endangered Species Act' and hope that Voorhees has drafted something else dealing with it that might help."

"Exactly. That database is a plagiarizer's paradise." She caught herself and turned in her chair toward me, eyebrows raised. "Not that I mean..."

I gave her a conspiratorial smile. "You mean that lawyers are the greatest plagiarizers in the world, and you'd be telling the truth. That's a great tip. I can't believe I didn't think of it myself. I'm so glad you saved me from even more non-billable hours."

She gave me a little smile and turned back toward her desk. As she grabbed her computer mouse, she looked back up momentarily. "Another thing. Voorhees has a temper." Her desk phone rang. She answered, "Felicity Banks. Ms. Ashford's and Mr. Compton's secretary." I was left wondering what she meant about the hippie-like environmental lawyer.

I'd barely sat down back at my desk when she buzzed me. "Mr. Colburn on Line 2 for you."

I picked up the line. "This is Skyler."

"Bob Colburn. Fish and Game. I have some strange news for you. But first, did you know the Federal Bureau of Investigation has an animal forensics lab?"

"No."

"Okay, let me give you the background first then. After the Endangered Species Act passed in 1973, Fish and Game wanted the FBI to help with solving related crimes, but they didn't have much experience with animals, plus they prioritized work on cases involving humans. Over the years, however, the animal forensics lab has expanded. They now handle more than five hundred cases annually, examining more than fifteen thousand pieces of evidence annually on average.

"Agents purchased caviar from as many companies in California as they could find on the market. We also took samples from sturgeon in various locations along the river. Our undercover agents were able to identify a restaurant in San Francisco making purchases from the illegal ring there. They seized some of the contraband caviar. It came in a tin labeled Torgovaya Kaviar Kompaniya. We had the animal forensics lab run comparisons."

"How does that work?"

"The adult sturgeon lives in the ocean but they return to their freshwater birthplace to spawn. This means we can match any prior records from caviar poaching with DNA from the sampled roe and get an idea of where the fish are being poached."

"That's great."

"But that's not what's weird. Some caviar in the contraband tin didn't come from the river."

"What do you mean?"

"Remember when I said we also tested the caviar sold by California companies? Those companies raise fish from their own stock. They end up with an identifiable DNA profile."

"And?"

"Some of the roe being illegally processed came from Chairo."

Silence. My brain scrambled. *They couldn't be involved, could they? Why would Ben hire us if they were involved? If not, how was their breeding stock's DNA getting into the illegal caviar?*

"Skyler, you still there?"

I forced my brain back online. "Yeah, Bob. I don't know how that's possible. Is Fish and Game investigating Chairo? How does this affect my investigation for Ben?"

"We're following all leads. I probably should tell you to keep this confidential, but I've known Ben for years. I can't believe he's any part of this. Just keep this information close. If I thought there was a possibility Ben was involved, I wouldn't have even told you."

"Thanks, Bob. I'll handle it carefully, but I'll notify Ben. We have a personal investigator on-site at Chairo. Maybe she can figure it out."

"I hope so. Good-bye."

As we hung up, I felt drained. My arms felt like lead as I picked the phone back up, first buzzing Carbone, then dialing Victoria to update the team. My last call was to Ben. He answered on the third ring. "Ben Akers, Chairo Caviar."

"Ben, it's Skyler. Has Fish and Game talked to you yet?"

His voice went somber. "Yes. I've known Bob for

years. We've worked together to help the wild sturgeon population. He filled me in. Chairo's fish are being used in this illegal operation. There are several options, none of them good."

"And they are?"

"Someone stole frys—newly hatched fish. That would be relatively easy to pull off, but there are two reasons it's unlikely. First, the DNA would have been diluted if Chairo's fish had been bred with fish from another source. Second, if they used our stock to create a new population, it would have taken years. I guess it's possible this thing's been going on that long and just gained momentum, but that seems unlikely. The more likely option is that someone has stolen full-grown females."

"Those things are huge. Not exactly the kind of thing you hide in your pocket."

"Exactly. It would have to be an inside job. We might not notice given the thousands of fish in the tanks, but they would have to be careful not to take too many, plus a five or six-foot-long sturgeon isn't exactly easy to sneak out of here."

"I can't see that happening in the daylight."

"Me either. It would have to be someone who works at night. That narrows things down. On that list of people you hadn't cleared, the only one with access who has worked evenings is Nick Petrinko."

"We can't let him know you're onto him. I've alerted Victoria. You should pass on our supposition to Bob at Fish and Game. Between them, I'm sure they'll arrange a stakeout. Get to the bottom of who is behind this."

"It's not that hard to catch sturgeon in the wild. It's

easy. It's just illegal if you don't have tags and take more than three in a year. Stealing doesn't make sense. There's something more to this. It feels personal."

"I agree."

After saying goodbye, I decided to do some internet sleuthing about this guy, Nick Petrinko. Also, our copier guy, Gabe Petrinko. Same last name. It was beginning to sound like it wasn't a coincidence.

I had about an hour before lunch. I figured that was almost as much time as it would take to find everything I could about the two Petrinkos on the internet, then I'd switch to working on the opposition for Voorhees after lunch. First Gabe. I entered his name in the local court's online case information search parameter. Nothing. Then again, Gabe was usually a nickname. His name was probably Gabriel. I changed the search parameter, and there were three hits. It was an unusual enough name. I felt pretty good that they related to "our" Gabe.

First hit was a petty theft. Misdemeanor, but showed propensity in his character to break the law. Second hit was possession of unlicensed firearms discovered during a traffic stop. A little more concerning given his threats to Peter. He'd gotten off with a fine and some community service. Last hit was an assault. He'd served six months for that one, but it was a couple of years ago. Surprisingly, the law firm hadn't picked up on it. He'd probably lied on his job application. It wasn't as if they were hiring a lawyer, so it likely slipped through the cracks, but still, it was sloppy for a firm that took so much pride in security.

I looked closer at the docket for the latest criminal case against Gabe, listing the parties, attorneys, events, and filings. Something caught my eye. There were *two* defendants in the case, the second one named Nicolai Chesnokov. Where had I heard that name before? My brain went into search mode but came up empty. I reviewed my file notes. Five pages in, I found it. Not exactly the same name, but close. Sergei Chesnokov, the founder of Czar Alexander Caviar, the company that had gone bankrupt. The guy who blamed Ben for all of his business problems. Money and greed were always motives in sturgeon poaching, but this added a personal element. I felt like we were getting closer to figuring this whole thing out.

I rang Ben. It went to voicemail. "This is Skyler. I may have a break in the case, but I'm not sure. I need to run some information past you."

He was probably at lunch, which is where I should be. I rang Victoria. She answered on the first ring.

"Victoria, I'm tracking some new information on the case. Are you out at the caviar farm, or could you meet me for lunch?"

"You're in luck. I just got out of a meeting with a client not far from you. Meet at Le Parm for Italian in half an hour?"

"See you then." We hung up. I patted myself on the back. Not only could I bill my time eating lunch, but Victoria would probably pay for it, then the firm would reimburse her for a business lunch. About time I got smart. I could use an hour out of the office. At an exceptionally nice restaurant at that.

I walked into the restaurant and looked for Victoria. I was running late, so she'd probably already arrived. After a few seconds, I spotted her wave from the far side of the room and joined her at a cozy table. She was looking gorgeous as usual. Skinny black pants with a matching jacket and black patent heels today. A jewel teal silk peeked from the jacket, matching the understated jewels dangling from her ears. I wasn't overweight, but she made me feel fat anyway. I didn't care. I looked through the menu, settling on lobster ravioli in vodka sauce and an iced tea.

After the waitress took our orders, Victoria leaned forward and asked, "Okay, what's the lead?" I explained. She was silent, thinking for a few minutes. The waitress brought our beverages. Victoria took a sip of her diet cola. "So, what's the connection between the two Petrinkos and the two Chesnokovs?"

"That's the question, all right. I was hoping you could help with that."

"Petrinko is a common Russian name, but Chesnokov is a little more unusual. You say Ben had a run-in with Sergei Chesnokov?"

"Yeah. Apparently, the guy blamed Ben for all of his business woes and the financial insolvency of his company. The corporation was FTB forfeited a couple of years ago. I'm not sure if they had any assets after the bankruptcy. I can pursue that angle further and let you know what I come up with. Do you have any news?"

"Since we learned about Gabe and his possible relationship with Nick Petrinko, I've been closely tailing Nick. He's met with a few fishermen who seem suspect, but I haven't caught anyone with a fish…at least not yet. I talked to Bob Colburn yesterday. They're doing a stakeout of Chairo at night, so I'm staying out of their way. Since Fish and Game has its eyes on Chairo, that frees me up to go undercover to try to buy some illegal caviar in San Francisco. I'll be driving into the city and staying there a few days."

"I'm curious. How will you make connections with the illegal distributor?"

"I've always been a good networker. I helped an upscale restaurateur in San Francisco about five years ago. He suspected his partner was embezzling, but he had to be careful about making accusations. I infiltrated and got the information he needed. Tom ended up handling the legal case against the now ex-partner. I've already made a call. The restaurant will make it look like I'm a new sous chef. I'll start nosing around about buying caviar at a discount."

"Can you cook?"

She laughed. "You'd be surprised. I manage pretty well in a kitchen, but I won't be trying to cook for his customers. That would be a stretch. I'll ask other chefs at other restaurants if they know how to cut corners on the budget."

"Is the embezzlement case how you met Mr. Carbone?"

"Tom? No. We go back further than that. I handled something personal for him. That would be inappropriate to talk about."

I burned with curiosity.

I came back to the office full and slightly sleepy—the after-lunch doldrums, just as I needed to focus on research. I wandered down to the coffee room to find some liquid motivation. Gerald Cobbs stood at the coffee machine. I'd seen him in passing and heard stories. Former Green Beret. Trained as a tank commander. Still volunteered some weekends with the Reserves as a training officer. In his late thirties and groomed with military precision, he looked the part—like a wall of muscle. He was now an L.L.M.—tax specialist attorney. He was also the guy working with Wagner and Voorhees on the real estate development deal. He couldn't have been more the opposite of the hippie environmental law attorney.

I figured I should make introductions. "Mr. Cobbs. Good afternoon. I'm Skyler Ashford. I'm working on the Carson Wells case involving the San Francisco Garter Snakes. I believe you're doing the real estate tax analysis?"

The pod brewer made its last annoying, sputtering noises, signaling the end of the brewing cycle. He removed the spent receptacle, threw it into the trash, took his coffee cup, and turned. "Glad to meet you, Ms. Ashford." He looked me firmly in the eye.

"Skyler, please. Can I ask what part of the development deal you're working on?"

"I'm going over the proformas right now, and we're putting together a binder to submit to obtain tax credit financing for the project. A low-income component to the apartment development will qualify it for that round of financing. We're already in the chute on the bond financing.

This one is very multi-layered. Appreciable time has gone into making the financial side pencil out. It would be a shame if the whole thing gets killed over some snake."

"Yes, sir."

He gave me a curt but polite sharp nod. "See you around, Skyler. Good luck with that opposition. We need to win that motion."

After he left the breakroom, I brewed my coffee pod before heading back to my solitary office. It felt empty this afternoon. I needed to do something with that bare bookcase to make the space my own.

I had barely logged into PACER, the website for the U.S. Bankruptcy Court, and finished my coffee when Felicity buzzed. "Ben Akers on Line 4."

I picked up the receiver. "Ben, thank you for returning my call."

"What's the lead?" His voice sounded anxious.

I filled him in on the Petrinkos and the Chesnokovs. I heard him blow out a lungful of air in a huff over the phone. "I thought Sergei had put that out of his head years ago. Moved out of state even. You sure there's a connection?"

"We know Gabe has a reason to want your investigation to go away. His prior criminal accomplice has the same unusual Russian name as the guy who blamed you for his business going under. That seems more than coincidental. At least enough that we need to dig deeper. Victoria and Bob are putting their heads together to keep an eye on Nick Petrinko on the night shift to see if they can catch the fish thief red-handed. And Victoria's headed to San Francisco to follow up on the restaurants and whether Jacques Baudelaire could be involved."

"Yeah, Bob talked to me about a new guy coming in undercover. They installed night vision cameras in some hard-to-spot locations. I'm a basic farm boy at heart. All this FBI-type stuff feels surreal."

"Hang in there. We're making progress."

"Uh… Skyler…I've been meaning to talk to you…outside the office. I mean…"

"Yes?"

His voice softened. "This is awkward. I wanted you to know that I'd like to ask you out, but I don't think that would be appropriate while this case is going on. Maybe that's unfair to tell you, but I guess I thought you should know."

I hesitated, not because I didn't want to go out with him—I definitely did—but because it *was* awkward with the case. He got that right. His voice brought me out of the thought.

"Skyler? Dang, this is why I shouldn't have said it over the phone."

"Sorry, Ben. I mean, I'm not sorry. I like you too, but you're right about the case conflict. What if I screw it up, and you end up hating me? What if Carbone disapproves of dating a client? There are so many things in the middle of getting to know you better on a personal level."

"We can push the pause button. But I at least wanted you to know what I was feeling."

"Pause button. Agreed."

As we said our goodbyes and disconnected, I felt deep

confusion about how I was supposed to feel. I decided I needed to push the pause button on my emotions too, as tough as that was going to be.

I logged back into the Federal PACER website, searching the bankruptcy court records relating to Czar Alexander Caviar, Inc. They'd owned the real estate where their business was located. The bankruptcy trustee allowed a foreclosure to move forward. The property had been sold at the courthouse steps to a company, Pacific Coast Investments, LLC, a California limited liability company. The rest of Czar Alexander's assets had been gutted to pay creditors pennies on the dollar.

On a whim, I decided to look up Pacific Coast Investments, LLC. Was it a third-party, arm's length buyer? The Secretary of State's website showed it was filed through Zoom Legal—a company often used to create entities anonymously. I pulled up the filing history. Those were often uninformative, but when I pulled the initial Statement of Information, a document required to be updated annually showing the members of a limited liability company, the sole member was...Nick Petrinko? As in, the guy who worked at Chairo?

I quickly printed out the related documents into PDF format and placed them in my computer file before buzzing Carbone. After I explained my findings, I heard a snort of contempt. "If the Petrinko and Chesnokov families are in this together, it sounds like Czar Alexander never really went out of business. This wouldn't be the first time I saw a straw man used in a purchase. We need to follow the real estate sale further."

"Find out how the property is being used today?"

"Correct."

"This sounds like something else that Victoria could help us with. Maybe Ben knows something, too."

"Get on it." He disconnected abruptly.

I loved the progress on the caviar case, although it was obliterating my progress on the opposition for Voorhees. I saw a long night in my future.

I figured it made sense to call Ben before updating Victoria in the event he had some additional information. When he picked up, I filled him in and asked, "Do you know anything about the old site for Czar Alexander Caviar?"

"Yeah. Another caviar company opened up there after Czar Alexander's bankruptcy. World's Finest Caviar. Not the most creative name, but hey, whatever."

"I'll check into them."

He asked, "Do you think Sergei Chesnokov is behind this?"

"It's starting to feel like it, but we need to piece together solid evidence."

"I'm glad you're on it. Are you calling Vicky, or should I?"

"Hmm… If I do it, you get billed."

He laughed. "Okay, then I'm doing it. I shudder to

think how fast the firm is working through that ridiculous retainer Tom Carbone asked me to pay."

When I hung up with Ben, I buzzed Felicity. "Can't we pull a real estate litigation guarantee on a property?"

"Well, yeah, but a guarantee costs significantly more money than a simple property profile. If you just need the basics, that would show every document recorded on the property. I could get that for you for free with our broker connections."

I gave her the address for the old Czar Alexander plant.

It was now almost three o'clock in the afternoon. I could finally start combing the firm's document database for anything helpful to my snake case. A search for the "Endangered Species Act" yielded some interesting hits. I copied them to a new file on my computer's desktop file, "Skyler's Snake Research." I also searched for "environmental opposition" and found a slew of documents. Most dealt with hazardous materials and petroleum leaks, not critters, but there was one that had a good basic outline of what I needed to present. What was becoming apparent was that winning the motion was an uphill battle. Winning the entire case in court would be uncertain and costly. They needed to find a negotiated solution if it were possible.

Several hours later, I came up for air only to find Felicity's cubicle dark. I glanced at my clock, surprised. After six. As soon as my eyes caught the time, my stomach decided to comment. I wondered if the doors would be locked for food delivery and what my options were. I wandered down the hall toward the break room to check out who else was still working.

Voorhees' office light was still on. So was Cobbs'. I'd heard that the financial end of the development deal was on the front burner with some pressing deadlines. It looked like Carly was still working too. Tripper continued to be a handful. She was trying to manage him and find a way to discreetly jump partners without causing a political disruption. I didn't envy her.

I stopped off for a cup of fully leaded before peeking in Voorhees' office, just past the break room. Voorhees sipped something from what appeared to be a gourd with a stainless-steel straw. Spa music featuring Native American flutes played in the background. He saw me and motioned for me to come in. "I see you're putting in the hours too. How are you progressing on the opposition, Skyler?"

"Not as quickly as I hoped. That's why I'm here late. Making up time on it."

"Cobbs and I are probably pulling an all-nighter. Wagner is coming back after some birthday party his wife wouldn't let him out of." He took a sip from the gourd with a look of relaxed satisfaction.

"Is there any hope of the environmental case reaching a negotiated settlement? Seems like this could otherwise keep the project from moving forward for years."

"That's what Wagner was pressuring me about earlier. They need dates certain for their financing. I can't provide them. We may have found a piece of land with the proper terrain and water but no red-legged frogs. That won't satisfy the environmentalist group that filed the lawsuit."

"Can I ask what's in the gourd?"

"Ah...yerba mate tea. It's from Argentina. A favorite of the last pope. Mate is like a natural energy drink. It's traditionally drunk out of a gourd with a bombilla—a straw with a filter on the bottom to separate the mate leaves. Much better for you than the caffeine in that coffee." He nodded to my mug with disdain.

"Thank you for the information. I'll let you know when I have the first draft of that opposition."

When I returned to my office, I thought about ordering some Yerba Mate tea. The gourd and bombilla were pretty cool looking. I could use some energy. Unfortunately—or thankfully—the first thing that popped up on my computer when I typed in "yerba mate" was a NY Post article opining, "Drinking this tea is as dangerous as smoking 100 cigarettes." Apparently, some studies contend there is a link between a carcinogen in the tea and esophageal cancer. Many other articles touted its health benefits, but I decided to stay away. Sometimes things that looked healthy on the outside possessed hidden dangers.

I got back on track with my legal research. I had almost finished a decent explanation of the facts from our client's perspective and an outline of arguments that needed better case citations when I heard a commotion. Angry voices. They seemed to be coming from the far end of the hall. My natural curiosity got to me. I started walking toward the sound. As I entered the hallway from my office, I recognized the voices as Wagner and Voorhees. They stood just outside of Cobbs' office. I stopped near the hall of partner portraits, unsure if I should get closer. A stream of curse words resounded more clearly than whatever they argued about, excepting a few phrases that hinted it was unsurprisingly something to do with the Carson Wells development case.

Voorhees' face turned redder and redder. Without warning, he pulled back and threw a punch aimed right at Wagner's face. With good aim and sufficient force, it could've done some damage, but for Cobbs. The tank commander bounded from his office door, caught Voorhees' right hook mid-air, and crunched his meaty hand around Voorhees' clenched fist. He led Voorhees toward his office door by the fist like a kid being dragged to the principal's office by the ear. I heard a booming, "In here," as Voorhees disappeared into Cobbs' office, not voluntarily. I wouldn't have believed it if I hadn't seen it with my own eyes. Wagner was left looking pale and stunned, recovering in the hallway.

He turned and saw me. A look of profound embarrassment crept over his face, going from pale to pink. He turned abruptly, gathering himself, and barked, "What are you still doing here?"

I felt like a puppy with its tail curled between its legs. I looked down as I replied, "Working on the Carson development case, sir. The motion about the snakes."

His face eased slightly. I could see his breathing slowing. "It's getting late, Skyler. We should all go home and take it up another day."

"Yes. That sounds like a good idea."

CHAPTER 8
SERPENTS AND FROGS

When I got in the following day, Felicity already had the Title Report I'd requested waiting on my desk. The property previously owned by Czar Alexander Caviar, LLC had been purchased by Pacific Coast Investments, LLC, but I already knew that. There was no mortgage recorded. It appeared that they had purchased the property from the foreclosure all-cash. The only thing recorded on the property was a Memorandum of Lease indicating that Pacific Coast Investments, LLC had leased the property to World's Finest Caviar, Inc. The Memorandum of Lease was just a summary to advise third parties a lease agreement existed. It didn't provide the terms of the lease. Was it a legitimate agreement with a third-party caviar company? I doubted it. It felt like just another layer in an elaborate scheme to put distance between Chesnokov and whatever he was up to now. Something to make it feel legitimate from the outside.

At this point, I was pretty sure I was just dealing with a bunch of shell companies, but I went to the Secretary of State's website and did a business search on World's Finest Caviar, Inc. The result was about what I expected. Formed by Legal Zoom with no indication of who the real parties were behind the deal. The Annual Statement listed a bunch of non-Russian names that I didn't recognize, but that document wouldn't list shareholders. I still had no idea who was really behind the company. It might not even matter. In the world of business entities, it was easy for things to be all smoke and mirrors.

Things were awkward with Voorhees, Wagner, and Cobbs after last night's altercation, especially since there was a witness—a lowly associate. I already turned in my first draft of the opposition to Voorhees by email and waited for feedback. I bumped into Wagner getting coffee. With the break room otherwise empty, we had some privacy. I avoided talking about last night's personal interactions. "I heard you were searching for a site that might be acceptable as a substitute for the garter snakes and could be traded as an environmental concession. Any success?"

He grimaced. "A couple with sufficient water. The right kind of pools and terrain. It's just those blasted red-legged frogs."

"What do you mean?" I found a coffee cup, stuck it under the brewer, and started a pod dispensing liquid inspiration.

"The sites with water don't have the frogs those miserable snakes like to eat. Picky eaters or something. The site won't be approved as an exchange unless we buy real estate with snakes and provide their snacks."

"Why don't you let that opposing environmentalist group relocate the frogs?"

He looked at me flabbergasted—completely dumbfounded. His mouth moved several times with nothing coming out, then, a look of profound contemplation, brows knit. "Would the frogs stay? Populate?"

My coffee pod made the revolting death sputters that signaled it was done.

"I guess you could ask the environmentalists. We're lawyers, not biologists, right?"

He continued to look at me with a perplexed expression. Since he didn't say anything further, I took my coffee cup, gave him a nod, and made my exit.

When I got back to my desk, there was a voicemail waiting. "Skyler, it's Victoria. I've been hanging out with my chef friend in San Francisco, doing some digging. There seems to be an influx of unusually low-priced caviar on the market through a contact they know only as Dominic. I was able to make a buy and meet the guy. Seems Russian…and very tight-lipped. The caviar is labeled Torgovaya Kaviar Kompaniya—the same as the stuff Fish and Game seized that matched the DNA from Chairo. I've alerted Fish and Game on how to get in touch with the seller. They'll follow him to see if they can find more associates."

I tried to ring Victoria back. It went straight to voicemail. I also tried to call Bob. Voicemail as well. I figured he might be involved in all of the surveillance.

Things seemed like they were on the brink of a revelation, but I couldn't get in touch with anyone with more information. I took a deep breath, telling myself to practice patience, but I felt ants on my brain. What I could do was update Carbone. I buzzed. No answer. I finally gave in to an act of desperation and buzzed Joan. She explained that he was in a deposition all day.

Having given up on any immediate progress on the caviar case, I wandered down to Voorhees' office. The door hung open. I knocked gently. He looked up and motioned me in.

"Skyler, I just got done reviewing the opposition. Excellent draft." He shot me an approving smile.

I smiled back, standing tall and confident. "I was hoping you might let me argue the motion. I made several supervised court appearances when I participated at the clinic in law school. I think I'm ready."

His smile faded. "That's out of the question. You need to cut your teeth on something with less at stake. There will be other hearings."

Now my smile faded too. I blinked and caught myself chewing my lower lip. "Perhaps I could at least come along and watch arguments?"

What started as a look of uncertainty from Voorhees began to border on annoyance. "We usually don't send two attorneys to a hearing. If you went, it would *not* be billable."

"Oh. That's reasonable. We wouldn't want to double-bill a client. Even if it's non-billable, I would like permission to come and watch the arguments. After being involved with the research and drafting, I feel invested."

"*Hmph*" was all I got back. I didn't move. After a few moments of silence, he said, "Let me think about it."

"Thank you." I made my exit, unsure why I signed myself up for even more unbillable time. But it was good to care about a client. Or at least care about case outcomes. Wasn't it?

My first week was past. Tomorrow would be an easy day—a firm meeting and a Mandatory Continuing Legal Education session, both billable. All I would have to do is sit back and relax. But the rest of this day loomed, a daunting blank slate.

Carbone was out of the office. He'd said I could work with other partners if he knew or if my billables were threatened. Curious about Daniel Tellis, the litigation partner who didn't have an associate assigned, I walked out of my office but hesitated. Felicity looked up, more with her eyes than her face. I tilted my head and gave her a little shrug. "Carbone's in deposition, and Voorhees seems happy with the opposition. I thought I'd introduce myself to Tellis. If I don't come back in an hour, send a rescue squad."

She gave a little chuckle.

I asked, "Any advice?"

"No. He's a straight shooter."

That's good. I walked down to Tellis' office with a

little more confidence. His door was cracked open. I knocked and received a friendly, "Come on in."

When I entered, he stopped what he was doing, looking up with a closed-mouth smile. "Skyler, isn't it? Wagner was telling me about you. You're working on that caviar case with Carbone?"

"Yes. But that's my problem today. I'm on hold waiting for information from almost everyone on the caviar case, I finished a draft for Mr. Voorhees, and Mr. Carbone is out all day at a deposition. He didn't tell me he was going to be gone. I don't have any other work lined up. You know how it is. Billables. I was hoping you might have something you'd like some help with."

He leaned slightly back, allowing his executive chair to rock back gently. "Ah, I see. Yeah, I was a first-year associate once. A long time ago, but I remember the billables dance. Of course, as a partner, there are different pressures." He paused for a moment. "But let's see, I do have some things I would like to get off my desk."

He leaned forward, thumbed through a stack of files on his desk, and pulled out a folder, not very thick. "Client came in the other day with a simple case involving breach of contract. Need a demand letter. The goal is to write a letter that will force an agreement quickly. The client is willing to accept a payment plan for what he's owed in return for a stipulated judgment where we hold onto it and don't file with the court unless payments aren't made. If there is a default, the agreed-upon judgment would be filed with the court without delay. We could proceed directly to collection without a trial." He handed over that file and took out another. "This one is similar, except our client is the defendant. Mr. Kramer. He agrees he owes the money, but he can't pay it until his business is paid by its distributors. We need to get the opposing attorney to give us more time. Initial negotiations were unsuccessful. A lawsuit has already been filed. If the attorney will not agree to an extension of time to respond to the lawsuit, I need you to draft a demurrer—a motion that identifies deficiencies in the complaint—so they will be forced to amend it to correct the problems and stretch out our time to respond." He handed me the file.

"What if I can't find any grounds for the motion?"

He shrugged. "There are almost always deficiencies. You just have to find them and be creative. We'll file the motion on this one even if they aren't substantial issues— ones that we might otherwise ignore because the motion costs money. In this case, it's worth the money to buy time."

I nodded. He added, "If you have any questions, let me know."

"I appreciate that." I took the files and returned to my office, happy to have something with some substance to keep me busy the rest of the day.

I worked happily on Tellis' files until six p.m., feeling a sense of satisfaction that my billables were staying on track. I was even a little ahead of expectations. I emailed the draft demand letters to Tellis. I was about to leave, my computer turned off, and my purse in hand, when Wagner stuck his head in my doorway. "Hey, Skyler, I thought you'd want to know the Carter Wells development case has settled out of court. Now, we're just left with the financial work."

"Oh… Thank you for letting me know." Then I remembered that meant there would be no hearing. My shoulder dropped, and my purse dropped off it. "I guess that means I won't get to hear the opposition argued."

Wagner was hanging off the side of my doorframe. "Good thing, too. Those things are messy."

"Yeah, guess so." I pulled my shoulder bag back up. Wagner gave me a good-natured wave. "See you tomorrow."

CHAPTER 9
SOME SNAKES HAVE FANGS

I arrived the following morning in a light mood. My entire morning schedule was taken up with the firm meeting and continuing education seminar. The subject matter was "Updates on Sarbanes-Oxley Requirements." All about corporate reporting requirements, it sounded like a real yawner, but all I had to do was stay awake, and it counted both for billables and the required continuing education hours I had to report to the State Bar Association.

I walked into the large conference room. Most of the partners were already there. I gave a Carly and Peter a discreet wave. Carly nodded and shot me a slight smile, but Peter scowled and looked away. A large spread of breakfast goodies—donuts, muffins, and fresh fruit—graced the large counter at one end of the room. I took my place in a short line and loaded a small plate with a blueberry muffin and a few chunks of cantaloupe. Looking around, I spotted an empty spot next to Diane Walden. I put my plate down before going back and making myself a coffee. As I took my seat and took a bite of my blueberry muffin, Diane said, "Skyler, I remember you from the associates' welcome lunch. How are you liking life at the firm?"

I chewed faster so I could swallow and reply. "A few adjustments learning the territory, but the work is interesting."

She took a relaxed sip of her coffee. "If there's something about the firm's policies you don't understand, my office door is always open to you."

I set down my muffin, turning my body toward her. "You have no idea how much I appreciate that. I'd love to do lunch sometime. Maybe you could give me some pointers on how to be a rainmaker—bring new clients in."

"I'll look at my calendar."

I could tell by the tone that she was placating, and it probably wasn't going to happen. It wasn't that she wouldn't want to, but taking on a mentoring role was a big commitment. But maybe I was wrong. I hoped so.

As I took the last bite of my muffin, Daniel Tellis stood from his seat at the head of the enormously long conference table. "Good morning, everyone. After the firm meeting, we'll have our continuing education seminar. For the benefit of our new associates, these meetings are usually once a month. It's the end of the billable month for everyone. For our new hires, we understand you've only had a short month of billables, but we want to check in with you as a partnership group."

My stomach started doing little flip-flops. I had no idea they had a meeting about billable's progress.

Tellis picked up a document from the desk and consulted it. He went over the billable hours for each associate, making comments. He saved the first years for last. "Carly, I see you've slightly exceeded your billables expectation. Good work. Peter, I see you're a few hours short. It's just the first weeks, but it can be difficult if you get too far behind. Can I ask if there have been any challenges to meeting the expectation?"

Peter had the wide-eyed look of someone on the hot seat. "I, uh…my sister's been sick. My mom needed me to sit with her several late nights at the hospital. I guess I've been tired and a little distracted."

Tellis pursed his lips and nodded his head, his expression sympathetic but his voice firm. "I can understand, but we all have personal lives and personal pressures, Peter. It does not change the billable hours expectation. If there's a reason you won't be able to keep up your billing hours, you need to talk to Ted Melikian."

Peter's head hung low, his eyes focused on the chocolate sprinkled donut in front of him. "I'll get it figured out." He shot me a dirty look, knowing he was going to be let go no matter what happened with his billables.

Tellis moved on…to me. "Skyler, you're way off. I see you at the office late sometimes, so that's surprising. Do you have any explanation?"

I drew in a sharp breath, surprised. Suddenly, I couldn't get another breath as it caught in my throat. I croaked, "I don't understand. I should be on track."

A look blending slight irritation with a heavy helping of confusion passed over Tellis' face. He cleared his throat. "Well, you need to take a look at your timesheets and talk to Tom about how you're going to deal with this." His eyebrow slowly raised as he stared at me momentarily before moving on.

I couldn't tell you a thing about the Sarbanes-Oxley

Act when we were done. I spent the entire hour-long seminar quelching my instinct to bolt to check the time-keeping software. I was also avoiding Carly's looks that telegraphed she wanted the download on what just happened as well as a slight smirk every time I caught a glance of Peter. When it was finally over, I avoided making eye contact with anyone and hastily escaped from the conference room without a word.

I quick stepped to my office, shut the door, then buzzed Felicity, asking her to join me. Hyperventilating and panicky, Felicity took one look at me and asked, "What's wrong?"

I sputtered, "Firm meeting. Didn't know they would discuss our billables with everyone. Tellis says I'm way behind. How can that be?" My hands flat on the top of my desk, I felt my entire body tense.

Felicity's face crinkled. "I don't know. I've been entering the timesheets you send me by email into the time tracking and billing software. It looked like you were right on track."

"I know!" Now I was getting angry. "Is there any way you could have made an entry error?" I told myself to lower my voice. Felicity was on my team. I pulled up my Excel file, searching for answers I knew wouldn't be there.

Felicity tensed. "Just a minute." She quickly exited my office. She returned a few minutes later with a printout. She handed it to me and sat down in my guest chair in a defeated slump. "Look at it. That's a report of your billables. Look at the work on the opposition."

I turned to the page reflecting research and writing work on the development case and compared the entries to the numbers on my computer screen. "Okay. So, the hours here match what's on my Excel file."

"But look at the column to the left."

My brows knit in puzzlement. I consulted the paper. More time increments were indicated, but they only seemed to be next to the entries on the Carter Wells case. I looked up at Felicity. "What are those numbers?"

"Write-offs."

It took a minute to compute. "I didn't write off any of my time."

"One of the partners must have."

I drew a slow, deep breath in as I raked my hand through my hair. I looked again. It was almost half the time I spent on the case. I stared at Felicity for a moment, trying to get my bearings. "Who? Why?"

"Any partner can write off an associate's time. They might do it because they think you took too long and it's an unfair amount of time to bill the client. They could do it because you logged more time than they did at a meeting. They have total discretion. It's usually the partner assigned to the case."

"Voorhees." It came out as an ugly hiss. I felt the blood draining from my face, my body growing cold.

Felicity sat up, leaning forward. "Likely. At least you know. Now you need to find out why. Carefully. Without making enemies."

I rubbed my hand through my hair several more times,

then down my face. I was sure I was now a mess. I didn't much care. Felicity shot me a sympathetic look. "I've got to get back to my desk. Mr. Compton was expecting a callback from opposing counsel on an important matter, and I've got several subpoenas to prepare for him."

I nodded. In a small, defeated voice, I whispered, "Thanks, Felicity. At least someone is on my team."

She gave me a crooked smile as she opened the door. "Always. Do you want the door open or closed?"

"Closed, please. I need a minute to get my head straight before I face Voorhees."

I gathered my thoughts, then went to the ladies' room to ensure I was presentable before confronting Voorhees. When I approached his door, it was open, acoustic guitar spa music spilling lightly into the hallway. I knocked. "Mr. Voorhees?"

"Skyler, what can I do for you? Did you hear the case about the garter snakes settled? Wagner came up with a solution no one else thought of—relocating the frogs."

What the heck? That was my idea. My brain hiccupped. Do I say it? Do I take credit? If Wagner took credit, would Voorhees even believe me? Not the time to accuse a partner. Too many bogeys coming at me all at once.

"I'm not here about the case. I'm here about my billables. A huge chunk was written off relating to the Carson Wells case. I was wondering if you did it and, if so, why."

He looked at me strangely, suddenly still as a statue. "It wasn't me." After a moment, he added, "You might ask Wagner. Wells was his friend. I suspect he might have done him a favor in the billing department." He looked back at the paper on his desk, staring hard.

I gasped. "At my expense?"

Voorhees picked up his gourd full of Yerba Mate and shrugged. "Happens. I know I didn't write off any of your hours, Skyler. You'd need to talk to him directly to find out if he did." Vorhees was keeping his face neutral, but I thought I felt a tone of disapproval under the required partnership façade.

"Thanks for the information." I gave Voorhees a nod as I exited his doorway. Maybe I understood why he needed the jungle of plants and relaxing music in his office.

My cuss filter processed a heavy-duty workout as I stomped down the hall toward Wagner's office. At that point, I wasn't thinking about being polite. I just wanted answers. I burst into Wagner's office without an announcement. "Did you write off my hours on the Carson Wells case?"

He didn't even blink. "Yes."

"Why? Why would you do that to me?" I could hear myself starting to border on "hysterical female" but couldn't contain it.

"It was my discretion to lower the total of the bill. I had no idea you were so slim on your billables. You seemed like you were doing fine."

I let out a huff. "I *was* before you threw me under the bus with the other partners. You should explain to them. You should put the hours back. If you want to give your friend a discount, do it out of something else." *Like your hours.*

His voice was completely cold and matter of fact. "I can't revise the time. The bills have already gone out for the month. And I wouldn't anyway."

Did I sense some regret? If so, he wouldn't show it. And I had probably burned up any goodwill by flying at him with the accusation.

As he stared me down, I didn't know what to do. He was a partner. If I kept this up, I could get myself fired. On the other hand, it felt like I wasn't standing up for myself. At least my attempts weren't getting me anywhere. He finally won the stare-down. As I broke off, he said, "You'll be fine, Skyler."

Fine? After all that, "fine" was the best he could do? I took my cue to exit. After all, there were only so many sources of billable hours, and he was one of them, except now I knew to watch him. Garter snakes opposition...humph...now I knew who the real snake was. And this serpent had fangs that could hurt me.

I was so mad after leaving Wagner's office I couldn't see straight. When Ben called and asked if I could come out to the caviar farm to discuss the case, I couldn't wait to escape the office. I spent the hour drive considering my options and possible responses to Wagner's insults.

By the time I arrived, my head had cooled considerably. I was looking forward to seeing Ben again. He rounded the corner as I walked up to the office building.

Today, jeans, a blue plaid shirt, and the black rubber boots best suited for the fishponds. A broad smile appeared when he caught sight of me. I got a little fluttery before I squelched it. He waved. "Skyler. Come on in the office."

He escorted me into the small administrative lobby then back into the minuscule office that held his desk and a guest chair. "I heard from Victoria about the tins of caviar being sold in San Francisco. Those restaurants were previously some of Chairo's best customers. Now, this has gone beyond wildlife trafficking. It feels like customer piracy. Anything we can do about it legally?"

I thought for a moment. "We know Nick has title to the former Czar Alexander facility. That should be worth a fairly sizeable amount. Plus, I suspect he's pocketed money from the poaching. If that's true, there's enough money to warrant pursuing a recovery. Typically, an individual company wouldn't have a claim against a poacher, but there are some elements here that are personal. Directed specifically at your company. We might be able to bootstrap the personal attack into a civil case, but first, we'd need to connect Nick directly to the sales of black-market caviar. Maybe also the theft of Chairo's sturgeon. Perhaps we can make claims of Interference with Contract or Interference with Business Advantage. We'd have to obtain all the evidence to determine what civil claims might exist. It's too much money not to try.

He stared at me with a look I couldn't interpret, then blurted, "Your brain is kinda sexy." From another man, that would have been inappropriate, even sexual harassment. But from Ben, and in the tone he said it, there was only a genuine compliment and sense of appreciation. I think he had one of those moments when you say something, and then a second later, you hear it, because a deep blush began to creep up all the way from his neck to his face. His mouth opened, and his eyes widened. "I didn't mean…"

"…and I didn't take it that way."

He let out the rest of the breath he was holding.

I asked, "Have you heard from Victoria today?"

"Nothing after telling me about the undercover caviar purchase from Dominic and sending the sample to Bob."

"That was yesterday morning."

"Yeah, I've been meaning to check in with her."

I stood up. "I'll take care of that when I get back to the office and let you know if she's found anything else."

He rose and walked me to the door. "Hopefully, this thing gets wrapped soon, so we can talk about dinner out."

I gave a low chuckle. "That's if you don't sue. Civil cases can take years in court."

"Maybe I need to find another law firm to do that." He gave me a sad puppy dog look.

I feigned shock and disapproval. "And cheat me of all those billable hours?"

With a final jesting smile, he closed the office door as I waved and turned to go to my car. I walked to my vehicle, got out my keys, and that's the last thing I remember.

When I came to, I found myself in what appeared to be the dark trunk of a hatchback. A strange odor overwhelmed the coffin-like space. And what was that slapping up against my back? Something…breathing and alive? Human size?

We drove for a long while. I didn't know how long I'd been out, so there was no way of relating time to distance. I tried to reach around to feel for my purse and realized my hands were zip-tied. As my brain struggled to work out what had happened, I realized the back of my head hurt. With the continued movement of my unintended companion trying to get free, I wondered who else had been kidnapped along with me.

After what I guessed was half an hour, we pulled in somewhere. The car parked. I heard the driver get out. A few minutes later, the hatch opened. Bright light flooded in, temporarily blinding me. I blinked. Focused. Nick. Pointing a gun. "Don't mess with me, Skyler. I could leave you in the trunk. If I let you out, are you going to cooperate?

I nodded. What else could I do? Gun still pointed, he took out a knife, cutting the zip ties so I could maneuver out of the vehicle as he stepped back. He waved the gun toward a door, eyes furtively glancing side to side. I started to walk toward the door. A sign on the building read, "World's Finest Caviar, Inc." I glanced back at the car and saw my companion—a colossal, seven-foot-long sturgeon, barely alive and gasping.

As I went through the dark doorway, I considered whether this was my first and last opportunity to try to shove Nick and run for it. But there was too great a distance across an empty asphalt parking lot. The odds were, I'd be shot if he had the guts. A stunt like that only worked if you were a character in a book or a movie. Not for an associate attorney facing someone who was beginning to look like a Russian mobster.

The facility appeared to be completely gutted and empty—a dark, vast, echoey space. It had likely been used to house tanks and equipment similar to what I'd seen at Chairo. Clearly, World's Finest Caviar, Inc. was a front, and yet I heard voices, and a light illuminated a room beyond. Nick motioned for me to walk toward it. Signaled me to halt. With the gun still on me, he knocked at the door. A middle-aged woman wearing a face mask answered with a hint of a Russian accent. "Why are you knocking, Nick? The door was…"

She stopped mid-sentence as she saw me. Saw the gun. Her eyes went somber. Nick commanded, "Hold the door open." She complied with a sharp look aimed at Nick.

As I entered the lit room and glanced around, I noted two men in addition to the woman. One I recognized—Gabe. It must be after-hours at the law firm. Gabe's face took on a hard quality, unlike anything I could have imagined from our interactions at the office. He grabbed a nearby heavy chair and shoved it in my direction. "Sit."

When I sat, he grabbed a length of nylon rope lying nearby and wrapped my midsection and legs, tying me to the chair. As a further precaution, he kneeled and lashed the chair legs to one of the heavy, metal tables in the room. When he stood back up, he looked at Nick, anger flashing in his eyes. "Why did you bring her here? Lead her to us?"

Nick set the gun down on another table. "She's that attorney you sent me the picture of on my phone, right? The one we're supposed to keep from finding out too much? Things have been getting hot, right? I figured your uncle would want to interrogate her. Find out exactly how close they're getting. Whether we have to move the operation."

"Did you make the connection with the fishermen?"

"Yeah. I can't take any more fish from Chairo. That chick, the P.I. you sent me a picture of...she's been hanging out, pretending to be an employee. I don't trust that she's the only one watching. I'm not taking that risk anymore, but Amarpal got us a big female. Maybe seven feet. I'll bring it in." He looked at the other man. "Alexei, give me a hand."

So that's the other guy's name.

Gabe hissed, "Don't use names."

Nick threw his hands up with a sneer. "She already knows yours and mine, doesn't she? Why does it matter?"

Gabe stared at me, mouth slightly open, licking his top teeth with his tongue, deep in thought. After a few minutes, Nick and Alexei returned with the fish, still weakly thrashing in their arms. They heaved it onto the table where the face-masked woman stood. She'd now donned a surgical gown and neoprene gloves. She grabbed a device with a metal rod, held it to the fish's head, and pushed a button. Electricity streamed through the rods, stunning the fish. She expertly sliced the immobilized sturgeon open its entire length and removed a colossal ovary stuffed with roe. Despite her face mask, her eyes showed her smile. "This is at least a thirty-thousand-dollar fish."

Gabe looked over at Nick. "After you dump the carcass as far away as possible so it doesn't connect back to us, we'll pack up and head out."

Nick nodded his head toward me. "What about her? What are you going to do with her?"

"As you said, my uncle will want to talk to her. As soon as we get this caviar processed and ready to take to San Francisco, we'll load her too."

It's going to get trickier for someone to find me if they take me further away. I said, "It doesn't matter what you do with me. Everything I know is on the law firm's computer under password protection. Hurting me will only add years to your crimes."

Gabe let out a low rumble and sneered at me. "You mean like my computer password? You really think any of those files are still there?"

Maybe not the files on the main server, but you probably didn't know about my desktop files, and you don't know what Carbone, Victoria, and Ben know. Are they in danger?

There was little I could do. I watched as they salt-processed the tremendous harvest of roe into caviar, put it into tins, and packed them in dry ice. After midnight, Gabe remarked, "I'd better get out of here. I have work in the morning." He leered at me. "I'll tell them you're out sick so they won't worry."

CHAPTER 10
RUSSIAN MOBSTERS

The men took the dry-ice packed boxes of caviar tins, load-by-load, out of the building. When they were returned, Nick picked up the gun. He looked at me and gestured to the other woman. "Cut her feet loose. Zip tie her hands."

The still-masked woman did as she was told. She snapped at Nick, sarcasm dripping from her voice, "Can you handle her from here?" He didn't bother answering. We were back to gun-pointing. When we exited the building, I took a breath of fresh, unfishy air and looked up at the starry night sky. It crossed my mind that it could be the last time I would see it. There was a large semi-truck now parked close to the building, now loaded with the tins of poached caviar. A huge, muscular driver was already in position. Nick motioned for me to get in the back of the truck. I struggled with the height, eventually rolling in. The doors shut behind me. I heard the sound of locks being shut. It was dark. And very cold.

The truck started up with a loud rumble and lurched forward. I wondered if I could gauge time and listen for sounds along the route like I'd seen in a recent movie. I soon realized that was Hollywood, not real life. I also realized that my body was traumatized by the bash to my head, the zip ties cutting into my hands, the humiliation, the stress, and the fear. Despite everything, as the truck settled into a rhythmic roll and the miles passed, I dozed off. A blessed, temporary escape.

I woke to the sound of an automobile horn and heavy traffic. *We must be near The City, as the locals called San Francisco.* After another twenty minutes or so, the truck lurched to a stop with the sound of an air brake. The engine turned off. Men's muffled voices. After another five minutes or so, clanging indicated the doors being opened. Nick and his gun greeted me. The driver stood by, ready to unload the cargo. I rolled, sore, out of the back of the truck, almost losing my balance. The huge driver caught me and stood me back up.

I took in my surroundings. A large, seemingly abandoned warehouse building, presumably on the outskirts of San Francisco. The truck was parked alongside a raised cement loading dock. A slight hint of nearby salt water hung in the air, along with the smells of diesel, asphalt, and stale trash. Nick motioned for me to walk toward the loading dock ramp. When we reached the top, he knocked on a heavy steel door. A very Russian-looking man answered. Nick said, "Vanya, we have a visitor. Tell Sergei we brought the woman lawyer for interrogation."

Vanya responded with a deep frown, his jaw tensing.

"Why are you bringing her here? This is the one place no one knew about." His strong Russian accent made him difficult to understand.

Nick squinted back at him. "Sergei should decide whether she has useful information. Are you just going to have me stand out here in plain sight with a gun pointed at her?"

Vanya grunted and removed his bulk from the doorway. Nick shoved me through the entry, then followed. The warehouse was a large, open space, apparently used for a little of everything. Cots in one corner. Empty shipping boxes and supplies near a large table in another area. A long table with a hotplate and microwave on top. Next to it, a large-size dorm refrigerator and a small table with metal folding chairs. A half dozen or more people milled about, all with some degree of distinction that made me think they were of Russian descent.

Vanya disappeared to a distant corner. Nick motioned for me to sit in one of the folding chairs. He looked deep into my eyes. I could smell his stale sweat. "You see, we have a large operation here. Many people. Most are carrying guns or knives. The area is remote. Don't make things messy for me." He walked off to talk to another man.

My hands remained bound. I looked toward a woman nearby and asked, "Do you think you could help me get a drink of water? I'm so thirsty I feel ill."

She evaluated me for at least a minute, then walked across the room and talked to Nick. He glanced back, brows knit. I saw her arms gesture, then his arms raised to the air. Afterward, he turned back to the men. She walked to the table with the microwave and withdrew something from underneath. A plastic bottle of water. Returning to my side, she whispered, "You will not make trouble for me if I do you this kindness?" I shook my head. She unscrewed the cap and brought the bottle to my lips, helping me drink. As I gulped, her eyebrow raised, registering surprise. When I had finished about half the bottle, I was still thirsty, but the men who had been talking with Nick walked in our direction. She screwed the cap back on the water bottle, threw the bottle in a trash can, and exited to the far side of the room, where others helped organize the boxes being unloaded from the truck.

As the men approached, it seemed that one was the leader. His face bore deep wrinkles. Gray-blue tattoos on his forearms peeked from the rolled-up sleeves of the white button-down shirt he wore with dark trousers. Well-muscled but completely bald, the top of his head peppered with old-age spots. His cloudy blue eyes, framed by silver-gray eyebrows, were sharp and perceptive, his mouth thin and perpetually pursed. He spoke in a deep, calm voice with a Russian accent. "My name is Sergei, Ms. Ashford. I have heard much about you and your sleuthing skills. It has caused me a great deal of headaches."

Purposing to keep my voice equally calm, I met his blue eyes. "As you have caused Ben Akers 'a great deal of' headaches."

"This may be true, but Mr. Ben took everything from me. All of what this nation calls a dream. He stole my employees...my business. He thinks he knows caviar. But the birthplace of gourmet caviar is Russia. California exploded with people making caviar. This...this...farm boy comes in and brings technology and tells everyone the caviar is better." Sergei's voice rose ever so slightly, then became dismissive. "He stole from me, so I stole from him. So what?" As he shrugged, his eyes closed and his eyebrows raised. When they quickly opened again, the look in his eyes was not hurt but tinged with revenge.

I asked, "Is this your answer to business competition?"

His tone changed. Boastful. "The Russian mob has been involved in caviar since I was a child, Ms. Ashford. Life was hard in the old Soviet Union, and the sturgeon fishing was good. People here in America were happy to have our Russian Beluga caviar. The restaurants loved us. Then the fishing was not as good, and some crazy Russian defected and decided to help Americans make caviar. Except he was not so crazy. The sturgeon fishing is good here. So is the roe for the caviar. The business? We tried your American dream, but it was broken. Now, we do the business as we know it. Now, we do what is necessary to survive. I have found old friends to join me."

"And what about me? What do I need to do to survive?" My eyes searched his eyes.

He motioned with a raised chin to Nick. "Bring the other." He looked back at me. "We have no use for you. Nick was unaware we already knew everything we needed."

Nick returned, strong-arming a woman. Victoria.

"The two of you have caused me much inconvenience, but I am not a cruel man. I am a businessman. This business has existed long before me. Long before you. It will not stop. We will just take it elsewhere. Disappear. We have many associates worldwide."

Victoria shot me a glance confirming my conviction to stay silent.

There was a lot of activity over the rest of the day. We

were watched but ignored. At the end of it all, they had packed up not just the caviar but any trace they were even in the building. That is, except for us. We were both lashed to chairs that had been, in turn, lashed to a heavy steel pipe coming out of the wall. As a last measure, we were gagged.

Sergei was the last out of the building. Just before he left, he said, "We'll see how good your clues were now. I am not a killer. They will either find you soon, and all is well, or they will find you later, when it is not so well for you. I just need you silent while I finish making the necessary move of my goods...my business."

As he left the building, he looked back, one eyebrow lifted, his lips pursed as they almost always were, then he turned out the light. The small click of the switch seemed loud as we were left in the dark with the echoes of the large, unoccupied space around us. The metallic slide and click of a chain and a lock being put on the door outside resounded in the otherwise looming silence.

My ears strained in the darkness. I could hear Victoria breathing, lashed to another chair nearby. Occasionally I heard her jerking violently at her restraints, then silence. For two days, the only hint of time I had was the change in the dimness within, from gray when sunlight snuck through cracks of windows above or when it was pitch dark. You go a little crazy in a situation like that. You also figure out a lot about yourself and your priorities. There's a lot of time to think about little things.

On what I think was the dawn of the third day, I heard voices outside, then the sounds of a metal cutter crunching through the lock to the door. Sunlight came in, along with Bob Colburn and three armed colleagues from Fish and Game. Through eyes screwed nearly shut, I saw him blink at the darkness as I blinked at the sunlight. When our eyes adjusted, Bob rushed forward, his eyes wide with concern, searching us for any sign of injury. The other men, one dark-skinned and one Asian, both in Fish and Game uniform, both stood at full attention, guns pulled, eyes searching the darkness to ensure we were alone.

Bob pulled off our gags, then swiftly pulled out a knife from his vest and cut our zip ties, first Victoria's and then mine. My mouth was so dry from the gag I could hardly talk. When I tried, nothing intelligible came out. Bob looked at the dark-skinned officer. "Evan. Quick. Grab some water bottles from the vehicle."

Victoria leapt to her feet, angry, her voice reduced to a hoarse whisper. "Did they get away, Bob?"

He looked at her incredulously. "Let's deal with how you are first."

The Asian officer disappeared into the darkness with a flashlight. He returned and lowered his weapon. "All clear, Bob. Looks like they took every shred of evidence they were ever here."

"Thanks, Haru."

Haru looked at us. "You must be Skyler and Victoria. So glad we found you. You've had us all very worried."

Evan came back with the water bottles. Thankfully, he brought two each. I couldn't take it in quickly enough. When I had guzzled one full bottle and was one-third through the next, I finally came up for air and found my voice. "Bob, the leader is Sergei Chesnokov, but I think you already knew that. It was Nick Petrinko, who was working at Chairo, stealing ripe female sturgeon. He's likely the one who was sabotaging the equipment. He was also coordinating poachers on the river. Gabe, the copy guy at the law firm, is Gabe Petrinko, Chesnokov's nephew. The families are related. Sergei said they were working with the Russian mob and relocating their caviar business. You need to move fast to catch them."

Bob grinned. "We'd worked through most of that, thanks to your prior reports to me."

Victoria cleared her throat. "I'm more interested in how you found us."

"That was Haru here, so I'll let him explain."

The Asian man grinned. "Victoria told Bob she'd purchased some black-market caviar from a guy named Dominic. We followed that lead and set up another bogus buy. While Dominic was selling caviar to our undercover officer, I put a tracking mechanism on his vehicle. We'd tried to tail him before, but he was pretty cagey. The tracking device finally got us this address."

Bob put his hand on Haru's shoulder. "It was good work. When we didn't hear from Victoria for a few days, our antennae went up, but we were still gathering evidence and not ready for a raid. We needed to catch them with the product in their possession. Then Gabe showed up for work saying he'd run into Skyler leaving the night before and she was not coming in because she was sick. We didn't get that information until yesterday when Ben called your office and couldn't reach you, Skyler. He got worried and tracked me down. That just didn't sound like you. When I called the law firm, I found out Gabe had not come back to work after that morning. With both you and Victoria out of contact, we went on high alert and decided to pull the trigger on the raid, hoping to find you."

Victoria sat, looking pale. "Glad you did. It's been a long few days."

Bob said, "Let's get you gals out of here. Evan and Haru can process the warehouse for any evidence. You two look like you could use a burger and fries as soon as possible."

I stood up, stiffly stretching. "And a shower. But I wouldn't say no to a burger and fries first."

After I'd convinced Bob that I didn't require a medical check and that the fast food was probably what I needed the most, he agreed to drive me home. I'd wolfed down a double-patty cheeseburger and a large fry by the time we got there. I waved him off with a promise to call the next day before heading straight for a long soak in my tub.

I'd just changed into pajamas, my hair still wet, when a knock sounded at my door. After what I'd just been through, it made me jump. I padded to the door and cautiously looked through the peephole. Ben.

Opening the door, I met a frantic look on his face, as if he hadn't slept in days. "Skyler. Thank goodness you're okay. I came as soon as I got the call from Bob."

"How did you get my address?"

"You weren't answering your phone. I got the address from Felicity."

My phone! It's now in the hands of the Russian mob. If they unlock it, they can get my address. My personal identity information.

Ben asked, "Can I come in? Just for a minute."

I realized I'd been holding the door only partway open. I stepped back. "Of course. I heard you helped alert Bob that something was wrong."

His eyes flashed, then narrowed. "When we began to suspect there was something foul going on, I was ready to take Nick down. Good thing I couldn't find him."

"Yeah, good thing because he carries a gun. Not at all the guy you thought he was. He was much more prepared to off me than even the boss of the operation."

"I knew they took you against your will...but guns." Ben's eyes went wide with the realization. "I never have imagined there were actual mobsters involved with the black-market caviar sales."

I sat down on the couch, exhausted, looking up at Ben who still stood at nervous alert. "We got close enough that they're moving their business operations. Hopefully, it means you'll get your customers back because they aren't buying from the poachers. On the other hand, Sergei said they were relocating but staying in business. Could that mean another country? Or could they do business more remotely?" I patted the couch cushion next to me.

Ben sat on the edge of the couch cushion, still tense. "Well, if they relocate it has to be somewhere with sturgeon. The roe has to be processed promptly. There aren't that many places here in the United States that provide what they need. I'd hate to think they'll get away just to set up shop elsewhere. Chairo breeds its own stock and replenishes the river. These criminals are fishing the sturgeon to extinction."

"This may be the end of the road to our investigation."

Ben smiled gently at me. "Or the beginning of another road. Maybe we can finally make that dinner date. But you must be exhausted tonight. I'll let you get some rest. We can talk more in the morning now I know you're all right."

After Ben left, I questioned myself. *Was* I all right? How much should I worry about Sergei coming after me? Was the investigation over?

CHAPTER 11
BACK TO THE SALT MINE

When I walked into the office the following morning, Cammie gave me one of those stares like when a person doesn't want you to feel like they're staring, but they just can't help themselves. I figured the office gossip mill had been going full tilt about my kidnapping. I waved and smiled casually. "Morning, Cammie." She gave me a self-conscious smile back. "Good morning, Skyler." She ducked her head as I passed.

As I walked through the Hall of Partner Portraits, my heels echoed, announcing my arrival. I felt eyes on me from the secretarial stations. The moment I got to my office, Felicity jumped up from her desk and followed me in, closing the door behind her. "Skyler, I'm so glad to see you. I had a bad feeling when I heard you were out sick. Then to learn you were kidnapped! That's insane. Are you truly feeling well enough to be here today?"

"I'm fine, Felicity, but thank you for asking. I feel safer here than I do at home. The Russian mafia has my mobile phone. I don't know if they care enough to crack the code to get any information, but that makes me a little uncomfortable."

She gasped. "Have you reported that to Bob? To the police?"

"Not yet. If you could get Bob on the line for me and maybe help me get a new phone, those are the first things on my mind today."

She scrutinized me like a mother hen. "Of course. Right on it. You let me know if you need anything else."

"Just do me a favor and don't talk about it around the office. I already feel like a circus freak on display."

She nodded and left.

A few minutes later, she had Fish and Game on the line. "Bob, I realized last night that Sergei has my mobile phone. That means he has personal identity information, including my home address. How worried should I be?"

Bob said, "We're still working the case, hard. I don't know why they would come after you, but I have the F.B.I. involved at this point, as well as local authorities. I'll see if they can send regular patrol cars in the evening around your office and apartment."

"Thanks, Bob. Do you have any new leads?"

"Not really, but if they continue to do business in the area, they'll be fishing the river. We've increased patrols."

"You know, they were leasing that San Francisco facility, but the World's Finest Caviar facility is in Nick Petrinko's name. It's worth at least five million if not more depending on the improvements. I can't see them just walking away from that kind of asset."

I could hear Bob's brain cogs turning even over the phone. "That's a good thought, Skyler. If you have any theories on that, I'd like an update."

"Sure."

We hung up. I continued to think about what loose ends Sergei could have left. There didn't seem to be much.

Before I could do anything else, Carbone walked into my office without knocking and with a scowl on his face. He plopped down in my guest chair. "How the heck did we end up with a Russian mafia mole in our office? Who dropped the ball vetting Gabe?"

As if I'm supposed to know?

I scowled back. "I'm not sure what your office policy is about background checking copy room help. I just know he was hired about the same time I was. Nick Petrinko worked at Chairo. He must have overheard Ben talking about hiring the law firm and alerted Sergei Chesnokov. They would have needed to work fast to know whether we were a threat."

"If word gets out that a mobster had access to our client files..." He drew a breath in and held it, face drawn. When he finally let it out, he stared out the window behind me. "He erased all of the files we had on Chairo. Ransacked the paper file too. This borders on malpractice. Maybe even crosses the line. We're exposed."

"I know I was supposed to keep everything in the client files, but I have my notes on my computer desktop. Those were not erased."

Carbone turned toward me, eyes intent. "How much information?"

"Enough. And I know the trail back to the rest. That's what worries me. They know where I work and where I live. They could have killed me when they had me, but I still feel vulnerable now."

"You put the file back together and get me a report as soon as possible. I'll assign someone to walk you out at night. I'll suggest that the firm pay for you to stay at a hotel for up to a couple of months. Until we have a better idea how this ends."

He never asked me how I was doing. I had the impression he was keeping the file safe, not me, but I had to be polite...professional. "Thank you, Mr. Carbone."

He stood. "You let me know if you need anything else to get this turned around." Carbone exited my office without another glance.

I opened the file with my notes. As I read them, I tried to envision what I would do if I was a mafia boss. For one, I would have an exit plan, and he had a jump on us.

I buzzed Felicity. "Get me an updated Title Guarantee on the old World's Finest Caviar site as soon as possible. Have the title company put a rush on it."

"You know that's going to take a couple of days. It's normally a couple of weeks."

"Just tell them I need it as soon as humanly possible."

When I hung up with Felicity, I thought about calling Victoria, but then I realized her phone was probably in Sergei's possession also. The last thing I needed was Sergei knowing I was still looking for him. I called Fish and Game instead. "Bob, we can't call Victoria's phone. Sergei has it. But I need to get in contact with her. Any idea?"

He chuckled. "I would give you her office address, but it happens she's sitting right here with me. I'll put us on speakerphone."

I heard a small click on the line, then Bob said, "Vicky, it's Skyler. You have a new burner phone number you can give her?"

"Sure. It's 555-1608."

I replied, "Thanks, Victoria. I'm in the process of getting a new phone today. I'll text you the number when I get it."

She asked, "So, why were you trying to reach me?"

"I've been trying to think what Sergei's options are for an exit plan. Or maybe a continuation plan. Bob's watching the river for poaching activity. Would it be worthwhile for you to see if there's any activity with your chef contacts in San Francisco?"

Bob exclaimed, "Isn't that how she got kidnapped?"

"I'm not suggesting she make any purchases. At least not unless your men are involved. But maybe the chefs would be more willing to talk to Victoria rather than an officer from Fish and Game about how they're cutting costs."

Victoria's voice. "You're still determined, aren't you? Chances are they're out of the country by now. If not, he'd be lying low."

"Unless he still has some thirty thousand dollars of valuable and perishable caviar to unload quickly first."

Silence. Then, "It wouldn't hurt to make a few calls."

"Thanks, Victoria."
We hung up.

My mind focused on closing down Sergei. It felt like the only way to make sure I didn't need to find a new place to live. I made a few calls and put locks on my credit. Took all the precautions you have to when someone sinister has your personal information. When I was done, I realized that I was still responsible for billables to keep my job. My mind went numb. It all felt like too much.

I remembered I'd left off with the letters for Tellis, so I figured that would be the best place to start. I made my way down the hall to his office. My heart wasn't in it. Stares and whispers from the secretarial staff continued along my way. Over it, I stuck my head in the attorney's open office door and found him engrossed in his computer. "Mr. Tellis, am I interrupting?"

He looked up, then gave me a double take. "Skyler. I heard about the kidnapping. You're back already?"

Unfortunately. "Of course. Couldn't stay away." I put on my best team-player smile. "Last thing I did was those letters for you. Any follow-up? I have some time available."

"As a matter of fact, we got a response on the Kramer letter. They're playing hardball. We need to file that demurrer. You want it?"

"Sure. I'd like to do the court appearance also."

"That makes sense if you draft it. I'll have my secretary, Amy, bring the file to you."

I thanked him and exited.

While I waited for Amy to retrieve the file, I continued down the hall to check in with Carbone. He was on the phone with a client, but when he saw me in the doorway, he motioned me into his office, gesturing for me to sit and be quiet. I planted myself in a guest chair, waiting, listening in.

"Yes, Ms. Singh, we'll need to obtain the reports from all of your farm neighbors regarding pesticide applications and soil amendments before we can determine if we have a chemical drift case against the property owner or the aerial crop-dusting company for the damages to your vineyard. We also need the reports from the processor regarding your grape deliveries. Can you get those to me by next week?" Silence…then, "Yes, just call my secretary to set up a meeting after we receive the documents. Thank you, Ms. Singh. We'll talk soon."

He hung up the phone and turned his attention to me. "Skyler, what can I do for you? Do you have another thought on how to track Sergei?"

"No, sir. I'm waiting on the title report on the World's Finest Caviar property, but that will take another day or two. In the meantime, I'm trying to keep busy. Do you have another case for me?"

He looked at me contemplatively, sitting back in his chair, fingers intertwined. "I've got two. The first is a transactional matter—pretty basic business sale. Our client is Marco Demaris. He owns a large fuel distribution business, Demaris Energy Enterprises, Inc. He's ready to retire. He's in the process of negotiating a sale of the business to a competitor, Dorian Fuels, Inc. You need to consider the tax ramifications in structuring the deal. Reach out to the corporate C.P.A. as necessary. It could either be a sale of the stock or assets. If it's structured as a stock transfer, remember to protect against the ongoing liabilities of the corporation. You up to it?"

"Absolutely. You said you had another case?"

"Our client Landon Greene owns a hotel. It's been targeted by an attorney well-known for suing as many hotels as possible under the Americans with Disabilities Act—the A.D.A. They move from one geographical target to another. They're in our area now. He's alleging that Greene's hotel is in violation of the A.D.A. because the stripes for handicapped unloading are two inches too narrow and a door required a few ounces too much effort to pull open." He gave me a sneer of disgust, lip slightly curled.

Pathetic. He's all for the client paying the bill. No sympathy for the handicapped hotel guest. My stomach turned as I realized that I was being asked to take the side of the hotel. "Why doesn't the hotel just fix the problems? It doesn't sound like they're difficult to remedy."

Carbone's face tensed. "That's what makes me angry. Our client is a good man. He's perfectly willing to make the changes necessary to be in full compliance with the A.D.A. requirements. All they had to do was make him aware of a deficiency. It's just that federal law places a minimum on attorney fees that a plaintiff gets if they bring a lawsuit under the A.D.A. Our client is essentially being blackmailed for the minimum attorney fees."

I swallowed, searching for the right words. "Uh... Isn't that fair?"

He blinked and then stared at me, perfectly still. "Maybe, if it weren't for the scumbag behind this guy. The opposing attorney...his only work from what I can see is turning the A.D.A.'s good intentions into his personal goldmine. He finds a couple of handicapped people who are desperate, greedy, or morally damaged enough to help him. He trains them. Supplies equipment, like the device to measure the push strength required to open a door. They drive around just to find any minor violation and then squeeze the hotel for the minimum attorney fees as a settlement. Sometimes they check into the hotel, but sometimes they take pictures of the parking lot from their car and drive on. They don't even require anything to be fixed. They even agree—for a price that is—they won't sue that location again. They either move on to another area, or the attorney finds a different handicapped person willing to fuel his underhanded profit center and do it all over again anyway."

As I took in his explanation, I felt both empathetic for the handicapped community and intensely angry on behalf of the hotel owner. I said, "That's wrong," but my voice lacked conviction. *That's not how federal protections should work. Something is broken when a well-intentioned law can be used in a way that feels...almost criminal?*

Carbone gazed out the window, took in an audible breath, then blew it out hard. "We need to write a letter negotiating the best deal we can for the client. If you can find a way to get them to agree to anything less than the statutory minimum as a settlement, it's a win. Our client won't see it that way, but it is. And then we need to draft the settlement agreement and explain to the hotel owner, Landon Greene, why he needs to sign it even though he feels like this whole this is some grifter's scam."

I sat, hands folded in my lap, looking down. "Will he make the changes? For the benefit of the handicapped people who aren't unscrupulous?"

Carbone sighed and looked back at me, his voice uncharacteristically quiet. "He's a good man. Landon has already contacted an A.D.A. expert to check over the *entire* facility to make sure it's fully compliant. The way that…that attorney uses this plan for his personal wealth-building, probably paying the actual handicapped man a pittance of the recovery…it's revolting. It doesn't make it easier for Landon to do what he thinks is right." He turned back toward the window, deep in thought.

"Isn't there a way to still encourage respect and inclusivity of the handicapped community without allowing this kind of thing to happen?"

"Not without a senator championing a new approach to the law."

"Why doesn't our client write his senator?"

He looked at me incredulously. "You know how many bigger things are on senators' plates? Besides, you'd have to come up with a better approach that accomplishes the A.D.A.'s intentions without leaving room for the pirates."

I saw what he meant. My arms went limp with helplessness. Carbone picked up his phone and buzzed Joan. "Can you get the Greene and Demaris files for Ms. Ashford, please?" He looked back at me. "The law can be harsh."

I nodded, stood, and exited, still feeling dark and a little like I had something nasty on me.

When I walked past the break room, Carly spotted me and walked quickly to catch up. "I heard you were kidnapped by Russian mobsters. Is it true?"

I kept walking and answered in a low voice. "It's true, but I'm trying to keep things low-key today."

She continued to follow me back to my office. When I walked in, she followed and shut the door. "Seriously? I can't imagine. What were they like?" She plopped down in my guest chair with an expectant look.

I could feel a pounding at the top of my skull. "Like Russian mobsters. Look, I'm trying to keep my mind off of that experience." My voice came out a bit harsh.

She ducked her head. "I'm sorry. I didn't mean to make you relive the trauma. Are you okay?" She leaned forward, looking closely at me.

"Yeah. And I'll be better if they catch the guy. How's it going with Tripper?"

She sat back and started humming the first bars of the gunfight music from "The Good, The Bad, and The Ugly." "It's a standoff whether I'll get fired or quit first. There's no way to keep him happy. I keep hoping the other partners will let me work with someone else, but…." Her voice trailed off. She shrugged, her face tense.

"I'm sorry. You don't deserve to be treated like that."

Her shoulders relaxed slightly as she stood. "I'd better let you get back to work." She walked to the door and grasped the doorknob then looked back at me. "If you need to talk, we've always got our taco joint." She paused. "You know I'm not going to let them fire me. I've already put out my resume to other firms." Before I could respond, she left.

I did some quick checking on the A.D.A. just to see if I could find a miracle Carbone had missed. Unfortunately, he was right. Best to just write the smallest check possible, then it was up to the hotel owner's conscience…or a fear the plaintiff would come back…when and whether to make changes. *I mean, if they had written a demand letter and the owner didn't make changes, I could understand, but this was just extortion under the color of the law.* I shook off the thought. It didn't help to get emotionally involved in a situation where the necessary legal action was clear.

After writing a polite settlement offer letter on the A.D.A. case, gritting my teeth all the way, I turned my attention to the demurrer. The complaint seemed straightforward. I couldn't find much wrong with it, but all I needed was a single irregularity under the pleading rules to file a motion and drag things out until the client had the money to settle. After an hour of reading through the rules of pleading and the necessary allegations required for each claim, I was ready to put something together. It was more legal art than substance, but it would pass scrutiny in court. A cup of coffee and another hour later, I had a draft ready. That left the business purchase, but it was close to four o'clock, and I wasn't sure where I was sleeping tonight.

I walked back down to Carbone's office. I could have just buzzed him on the intercom, but my legs could use the stretch, and it allowed me to see whether he was busy before I made my request. As I passed the coffee room, I saw him inside and diverted. "Mr. Carbone, you mentioned some security and the firm paying for a hotel room for a short time while we decide if the Russians are a threat. I noticed you have a security guard now posted at the entrance to the office."

He looked up from the brewer, almost startled. "Oh…yes. I had Joan book a hotel for you. Check with her." He rubbed the back of his neck and took a deep sip of coffee, black. "Anything else?"

I hesitated, unconsciously biting the inside of my lip, and looking down. "Uh…you mentioned someone walking me out, but I have to get some things from my apartment. I was hoping someone could go with me?"

He looked at the clock on the breakroom wall. "Uh, yeah." Offering a small smile that didn't seem to reach his eyes, he said, "I'll have one of the guys go with you when you're ready to leave. Just ring Joan, and we'll send someone down to your office. Anything else?" He made a slight noise at the back of his throat.

"No…and thank you."

He nodded curtly and left.

After an hour of work on the purchase contract, I figured I'd better let my escort get his job over with. I buzzed

Joan. "This is Skyler. Can you email me the hotel reservation, please, and send down whoever is playing bodyguard tonight? I presume that's the security guard."

"Check your email for the phone reservation. And the guard has already left for the night." She sounded indignant and hung up without any polite goodbyes.

I neatened my desk. Peter walked into my office. I looked up. "How are you doing, Peter?"

He shifted his stance. "Carbone assigned me to take you home and make sure you don't get kidnapped again." His voice sounded irritated. *Did Peter still blame me for telling Carbone about his involvement with the timesheet caper? Surely Carbone can't be serious. If Peter was taking bribes from Gabe, how can I trust him?* I froze. He saw the look on my face. "I took some fast money to help my family. It's not like I was working for the mafia, Skyler. We might not be friends, but you can trust me for this."

I reluctantly gathered up my purse and phone and stood. As we walked down the hall, I felt a deep sense of discomfort, walking slower than my normal pace, eyeing Peter's back as he walked in front of me. As we passed the Hall of Partner Portraits, I heard a familiar voice from the lobby beyond. "Skyler."

Ben. I started breathing fast, realizing I had been partially holding my breath. "Peter, wait. I see Ben Akers. I'll just be a minute." I walked through the echoey passageway and realized I was slightly trembling. "Ben, what are you doing here?"

"Figured it was close enough to quitting time that I'd come by and check on you. First day back and all."

I took a shallow breath, blinking. "Uh...Carbone

booked me a hotel for security and assigned Peter to take me to my place to pick up some things." I gave Ben a nervous smile.

He scowled back. "No, he's not. I'll take you."

I looked back to where Peter waited at the other end of the portrait hallway. Slowly turning back to Ben, I uneasily searched his eyes. He drew himself up, shoulders back. "You tell him that I'm taking you."

Feeling my breath let out, I smiled at Ben. "Just a minute." I hurried back to where Peter stiffly stood, tapping his foot.

"Peter, you're off the hook. Ben is walking me out."

He frowned. "You sure? Carbone put me on the assignment." He looked to where Ben shot him a steely stare.

Tapping his arm gently, I said, "Yeah, I'm sure." He swiftly turned and proceeded down the hallway toward his office without another word.

I walked back to Ben, smiling with relief. "You driving?"

"You bet. We'll come back later if you'd like to pick up your car."

Ben walked me out to the front client parking lot. "I hope you don't mind." He pointed to a restored old pickup truck. Rounded hood. Fully chromed. Wooden back. On the doors, "Chairo Caviar."

I beamed. It was so Ben. Classy but not stuffy, and with a sense of fun. "I love it."

I stepped onto the running board and loaded in, then we were off. Cranking the window down with the old-fashioned manual handle, a light breeze blew through my hair. Ben turned up some funky jazz on the radio. We sailed along in our little world until he pulled up at my apartment complex. I immediately grew somber, furtively glancing in every direction as I got out of the truck. My mind played out scenarios in the event someone was lying in wait inside. I tried to keep my voice light. "Ben, you know they got my mobile phone. They could have my address."

"Are you worried? That's why I'm here. But if they wanted to hurt you, they would have already done it. Let's get your things and get you out of here."

"Yeah, you're probably right." I kept looking everywhere, watching for any signs of movement in the shadows. When we got inside the apartment, I was on alert for anything out of place. After a quick walk around, I felt reasonably sure no one had violated my sanctum.

When I pulled a large suitcase from the entry closet and rolled it toward the bedroom, Ben asked, "Is there anything I can do to help?"

I breathed out. "Uh…no. I just need to pack some things. I'll try not to take too long."

He called out from the living room, "Take your time."

I called back, "Sodas and stuff in the fridge. Help yourself."

When I emerged, Ben was asleep on the couch. I

chuckled to myself at his light snore. *Some protector.* I gently nudged him, and he woke with a start. "Sorry, Skyler. Been a rough few days."

"Tell me about it?"

"Well, this girl I have feelings for got kidnapped, and I didn't sleep much until she was found." He gave me a lopsided grin. "You ready to get out of here? Where are we going?"

"Carbone has me booked at a hotel for a few weeks. I've got some ideas on tracking Sergei. I don't know if anything will pan out, but I'd feel a lot better if I could sic the authorities on him."

"Me too, although I don't like you being involved. I'll drive you back to your car. You want me to follow you to the hotel or walk you in tomorrow?"

"Nah. I think it will be okay."

We drove back, I got my car, and we said our goodbyes. He asked, "Do you have a new phone number?"

I laughed. "You didn't have the old one. But yeah, I'll text you."

He tucked his head, studying the ground. "I'm sorry I got you involved with this whole thing."

"I'm not. You didn't. Besides, how else would I have met you?"

He nodded and I noticed that he stayed, watchful, in the parking lot until I had driven off.

CHAPTER 12
MIDDLEMEN

Waking up at the hotel was surreal. It took me a minute to remember my surroundings. I felt uncomfortable. I decided to get showered and dressed right away and get out of the hotel. Anxious to have something to do to keep my mind off Sergei, I got to the office even earlier than usual, letting myself in with my security code. A few other attorneys were already at work, which made me feel more relaxed.

I got in a couple of solid hours reviewing the information concerning the business purchase Carbone had assigned to me, then called the client's accountant to get her viewpoint on the deal structure. After deciding to recommend a stock purchase, I scoured the firm's documents database for similar transactions, reviewing several and saving them to my desktop where I could copy and paste provisions easily. By noon, I had a decent draft of the necessary documents ready for Carbone to review before they would be forwarded to the client.

Carly strolled in around noon. "Want to grab some lunch at our taco joint?"

I felt small and helpless as I replied, "No, I'm not comfortable going out just yet."

Head tilted to the side, she asked, "Anything I can do?"

"Bring me something back?"

She gave me a saucy wink. "Sure thing."

Voorhees passed my office, leisurely walking, gourd and bombilla in hand. When he saw I was in, he veered through the doorway. "Skyler, I've been meaning to talk to you. Were you the one who came up with the frog relocation plan? There were a couple of things Wagner said that didn't add up. It didn't sound like his idea."

I winced. "Well, did he tell you it was his idea?"

Voorhees gave a low chuckle. "Excellent deposition technique, counselor. Answering a question with a question. But I want an answer." He looked at me with an unwavering stare.

"I believe I mentioned relocation of the frogs to Wagner when we ran into each other in the break room, but I'm sure I don't want to cause any problems." I looked back at him, eyebrows raised and pinched over pleading eyes in what I hoped was a signal not to get me fired.

He took a sip of his Mate "tea" and tilted his head slightly. "Don't worry, counselor. I won't cause any waves for you. But I'll know. And I have another case I'd like you to work on with me if you're interested."

"Great timing." I breathed out. "Care to come in and take a seat?"

He moved to my guest chair. "Deal is a fight for a sales territory. Tasty Treats, LLC has developed a huge market in the grab-and-go snacks industry." He took another draw on the bombilla.

"Oh, yeah, I know them. They have those cute little fruit pies."

He grinned. "I take it you're a fan. So, Mandy's Market Supplies, Inc. has claimed they have an exclusive right to sell Tasty Treats products to supermarkets and mini marts in the State of California. Our client, Snack King, LLC, has had a great relationship with Tasty Treats and has been acting as a distributor for them for the last six months. Mandy's sued Tasty Treats and our client, claiming a violation of their alleged exclusive sales territory. Their claims are based on a contract signed between Mandy's and Tasty Treats more than five years ago. If you look at the contract, it offered an exclusive territory, renewing every three years, but only if Mandy's met a minimum sales volume. More importantly, Tasty Treats interprets paragraph five of the agreement as promising Tasty Treats would not make direct sales to supermarkets and mini-marts, but not that they would refrain from selling to competing distributors."

"What's the status of the lawsuit?"

"Mandy's filed a motion for a preliminary injunction asking the court to order our client to stop selling Tasty Treat products until the court makes a final decision on the claim."

My brow wrinkled. "That could take years if Mandy's can drag things out. By that time, Mandy's will take over all of Snack Kings' customers."

"Exactly. But if the court isn't convinced that Mandy's has a strong case and meets all of the requirements for such a harsh order, the more recent status quo will be maintained, so our client can keep doing business as usual until the court can sort out who's right."

"How much is at stake?"

"About twenty-five million in sales this last year. And growing. Mandy's couldn't even keep up with the customer demand that our client can. They aren't big enough to handle it."

My heart did a little skip as I took the file. It was a lot of responsibility. A client's business, or at least a huge chunk of it, hung in the balance. "When do you need this done?"

"Hearing is in a week-and-a-half. I need at least a day to review the draft and make any last-minute changes, but I'd like it turned around in three days. Are you up to it? The kidnapping and all?"

"I appreciate you asking, but keeping busy keeps my mind off of the thugs."

He nodded, stood, and left my office.

Carly dropped by with my tacos. I went to the break room to eat since I didn't want my office to smell like a spicy restaurant. By the time I returned, the Snack King file sat on my desk.

I started reading through the documents. Mandy's was not just claiming that Snack King was interfering with its contracts, but also that Tasty Treats was selling to Snack King at a lower price than it sold the same products to Mandy's. But looking at the notes from our client interview,

Snack King bought in huge quantities. Massive truckloads. They got a quantity discount that Mandy's could also have if they sold a larger quantity of products. Also, Mandy's had provided no evidence with their motion that they met the minimum sales volumes.

It appeared that Mandy's was named after the founder, but the current president was her grandson, Vincent Gordon. His attorneys had written a letter to our client giving two options to settle: agree to pricing terms on old accounts and not to take new accounts, or buy Mandy's for six million dollars. *Is this just an attempt by Vincent Gordon to force his own golden ticket for his retirement?*

I spent the rest of the afternoon doing some internet research on the background of Mandy's and also our client, Snack King. The President of Snack King was Scott Bosendorf. Based on the picture of him on the website, he was in his mid-forties and very physically fit. *Must not eat the snack food he sells.*

I evaluated the contract carefully. The paragraph about exclusive territory was ambiguous. I could see how Mandy's was trying to interpret it to mean they were the only company allowed to sell in California, but it could also easily be read that Tasty Treats was only prohibited from making direct sales in California but could utilize distributors. Usually, an ambiguous provision would be interpreted against whoever drafted it, so the person causing the confusion had the disadvantage. I didn't know which company had drafted the contract, but it didn't matter since there was also a "No Interpretation Against Drafter" clause that nullified the usual rule of interpretation. *Is there anything else that might provide a clue as to what the parties' intentions were when they first negotiated the understanding?*

Voorhees had already asked the client to dump every shred of communication they had with Tasty Treats. That section of the file would be worth reading, but it was really more important to understand the prior relationship between Tasty Treats and Mandy's. Mandy's had made no argument revealing evidence of their interpretation. The law would favor keeping things as they stood until the court could hear evidence at trial—arguing that it was the "status quo." What could be offered as evidence now was limited.

Promptly at five o'clock, Cammie buzzed me from the front desk. I picked up the phone. "Ben is here for you. He says he's supposed to walk you out." She had a question in her tone but wasn't asking out of professional courtesy. "Should I send him back?"

Permission to enter the inner sanctum? "Yes."

A minute or so later, he appeared at my office door, entered, and sat. "If you need to work late, I'm happy to find a magazine from the lobby, but I'm not letting Peter near you now we know he was in cahoots with the Russians."

My billables flashed through my mind, then a picture of Ben sitting in my office trying to look interested in last month's "Financial Times." The snack foods case would have to wait. "Just give me a minute to log out of my computer." When it was secure, I grabbed my purse and stood.

As we walked toward the door, Ben suggested, "Since I'm acting as your bodyguard, it seems like we could get some dinner together, and it wouldn't be an unsanctioned date."

"Hmmm…" I weighed the potential outcomes. "As long as we're not calling it a date…yet."

His eyes were shining as he shot me a look like a toddler who just got handed a lollipop. "Jardin de Cuisine it is, then. Unless you don't like the best French food in town."

I basked in the moment, savoring it like a cat in a sunlit window. "Whatever you say. You're the bodyguard."

We got a little table toward the back. We ordered appetizers and lingered over dessert. It felt like we were old friends. The best kind of start for something more if it was meant to happen.

CHAPTER 13
LOAN TO VALUE RATIO

As I slunk into the office a little late the next morning, the Hall of Portraits seemed especially judgmental, as if they could sense I'd enjoyed an evening not thinking of them once. Felicity already sat at her desk. She did a double take that made me wonder if she could see the glow I was feeling. But there was no time to be giddy. I needed to get the opposition to the preliminary injunction motion back to Voorhees with plenty of time if he needed to make edits. Worse yet, I needed time for the client to review his proposed declaration since the court would only accept his testimony about the facts, not a lawyer's recitations in the arguments.

I was deep into it when Felicity walked in with a manilla envelope. "The title report on World's Finest Caviar's site. This is the fastest rush turnaround I've ever seen them do, but I told them it was of the utmost importance."

She lingered, curious. Her eyes wandered to the document as I removed it from the envelope and placed it on my desk. I thumbed through the pages quickly. It was just as

I had suspected. I looked up at Felicity's watching eyes. She asked, "Anything interesting?"

"They took out a loan secured by the property. It was within days of when they knew we were getting close. They couldn't sell the property that quickly, but they must have pre-qualified the corporation for the loan about the time Gabe joined the firm. They could close quickly if things got hot."

"But wouldn't a loan only be for a portion of the property's value?"

"You're right, but the right lender...it's a little more than four million dollars. About an eighty percent loan-to-value ratio since they pledged property they owned free and clear. They must have been willing to sacrifice nearly a million in order to get the rest liquified quickly."

"Why didn't they sell the property earlier?"

"I'm not sure. It was purchased all-cash at the foreclosure sale under Nick Petrinko's name while the company was going through bankruptcy. They couldn't use a loan that would potentially disclose names revealing the true owners, so they used Nick. Maybe soon afterward the real estate title was too hot to make another transaction that might trigger the bankruptcy trustee's attention. If that happened and the bankruptcy court realized there was fraud involved, they would have lost the property permanently. The bankruptcy case didn't close until recently, even though the business stopped operations a long while ago. Maybe they promised Nick something? There are a lot of possibilities. We may never know. All we can do now is follow any paper trail breadcrumbs we can uncover."

"Who is the lender? Can you get any information from

them?"

"Some bank I've never heard of—Greenhouse Bank, Ltd. Banks normally won't give out customer information without a subpoena. We'd need to file a lawsuit to get that and the response would take time, plus we don't have sufficient information yet to file a complaint with the Superior Court."

Felicity grew still, her voice quiet. "Sounds like it could be another dead end. Or at least a roadblock to slow us down while the criminals are getting away."

I pushed the paper away and looked up, trying to sound more confident than I felt. "I'm sure we'll find something more. Thank you for helping get us this piece of the puzzle quickly." I turned back to my computer.

Felicity shook her head. "You're a determined one."

I wasn't sure where to go with it, but I did know Sergei had to get the money released from the loan. He hadn't told the bank he wanted it for a pleasure trip. There had to be more to the transaction. I couldn't issue a civil subpoena to get the court's records without filing a lawsuit, but maybe Fish and Game could under criminal law, so I rang Bob and explained. "I know that a loan was taken out secured by the facilities purportedly used by World's Finest Caviar. We know the name of the bank, but nothing else about the loan. It has to be fraudulent. Does Fish and Game have any power to get further information?"

"Under California Fish and Game Code Section 12028,

we formed an Environmental Crimes Task Force that coordinates with local authorities, including the District Attorney's office. Let me see what I can do, Skyler. I'll get back to you within the day." He sounded like he was in a rush. He hung up.

I needed to work on the Tasty Treats case this morning, but I wanted to burn Sergei more. I decided to look into the bank. Was it legit or some shady institution?

When I looked it up on the internet, its deposits were FDIC backed and all the things you'd expect to see. Just an unfamiliar name. Probably because they didn't have banking locations in California. Should I alert the bank to the potential fraud? I looked for the contact information page. Montana? Where had I seen that before?

I never would have put it together without my file. Thank goodness I'd left my notes on my desktop instead of the firm's main server where they were supposed to be. When Czar Alexander Caviar, LLC had filed its last Statement of Information with the California Secretary of State prior to its bankruptcy, the primary mailing address listed was in Montana. Could one of Sergei's people have slipped up? Given us a lead to where Sergei had gone? Out of the country or...Montana? It was just a P.O. Box, but it was something. I called Bob back and filled him in.

I was about to open that Tasty Treats file when Felicity buzzed me. "Victoria on Line 3."

I picked up. "Skyler Ashford. Victoria?"

"I made those calls to the restauranteurs in the Bay Area. It seems that their source of discount caviar has dried up. Dominic has disappeared from the scene. At least for now, they're lying low, or else they've ceased operations."

"Thanks for checking. At least we know where they aren't. That actually makes me feel better. The firm has me booked at a hotel for a couple of weeks for security reasons while we see if we can learn more. I didn't like the idea of the Russian mafia having my home address. What about you? How are you doing?"

"A little jumpy, which is not like me. But I'm fine. I sleep with a pistol. This isn't the first case that's taken a weird turn for me. I've had a gun pointed at me before. Just never tied up and left to die from dehydration if someone didn't find me first."

I filled her in on the loan, the bank, and the Montana address.

Victoria sighed. "I think I've done about all I can on this case, but it sounds like Bob might have some resources. I'll send my bill. If you need me on another case, you know where to find me."

"It would be a true pleasure."

As much as I hated the drama of this case, I'd miss Victoria.

I needed a stretch, and Carbone would expect an update. I walked down to his office to fill him in on the latest. As I got up to leave his office after the download, I hesitated, but couldn't help myself from asking, "Why did you assign Peter to walk me out? Isn't he the one who was working with Gabe? Working with the black marketers that kidnapped me?" I stood, looking down at him sitting at his desk.

He leaned back and crossed his arms. "We knew what his motivation was. Gabe no longer works here, so that motivation was gone. Peter still has a professional oath to uphold."

Carbone's judgmental gaze made me flinch. I felt myself shrinking inside. I couldn't continue to look back at him. "I see. Well, I don't need him to do anything anymore."

He gave me a dismissive nod. "He doesn't work here anymore."

"Since when?" I took a half step back.

"Since yesterday afternoon. We gave him an hour to pack up his things and leave. His work was not to our standards, and we no longer needed him relating to the caviar case." He picked up his computer mouse and looked attentively at the monitor.

I was still for a moment, taking it in, then I turned to leave.

As I reached the doorway, he added, "We always lose one of our new hires for the year. You're safe as long as you keep up the good work for the firm."

On the way back down the hall, I spotted Carly in the break room and swung in for a cup of liquid motivation, extra leaded.

Her eyes looked distant as she waited for her coffee. I gave her a small smile. "So, what's Tripper got you working on now?"

She mumbled, "An agricultural insurance case."

"Sounds like a snore. What's it about?"

"Seems that since California's recent weather changes, the agricultural insurance companies have been scrutinizing loss claims they would have simply paid in the past. They're looking for any indicia of fraud. Frankly, it feels like they're fishing for it." She shook her head as she took her cup from the brewer and stepped back.

I inserted a new pod and waited for my coffee to brew. "And this case? You sound frustrated."

She spoke rapidly, a strain in her voice. "I am. The farmer experienced a huge loss. More than a quarter million. But neighboring farms didn't seem to have the same degree of loss that our client did. It's got the insurance attorneys entrenched in their position. We're trying to demonstrate that our client's property is closer to the river, lower down, and subject to a slightly different microclimate than the neighbors."

"So how are you going to do that?"

"Tripper has me trying to find historical weather data. There used to be a lot of CIMIS—California Irrigation

Management Information System—weather stations around, but they've closed a lot of them over the past few years. Plus, that only gets us information from the closest reporting station, not directly on our client's property." She scratched her forehead. "The insurance company is digging deep on this one, claiming good farming practices are in question. That means we have to demonstrate the client farmed correctly—irrigation, water quality, soil amendments, pesticides, herbicides—you name it."

"How can you get all of that information after the crop year is finished?"

Her lips pursed and her jaw tensed before answering. "That's the problem. You can't. That is, unless the farmer has taken soil, water, and leaf samples during the growing season." She broke eye contact and let out a deep sigh. "Good grief, it seems like the farmer can't just be a farmer. He has to be a farmer, a good businessperson, a scientist, and more, including someone who keeps records of everything about his crop just in case he needs it to prove an insurance claim."

I felt a little sick feeling in my stomach. "Tripper expects you to figure it out without the samples from last year?" *I wonder how Tripper will react if Carly can't produce forensic scientific evidence. He's been unpredictable in the past. Is her job on the line?*

"It's likely going to come down to testimony from the crop consultants who were working with the farmer as well as his field manager and chemical company representative. They witnessed conditions in the field while the crop was growing. The client also took a few photographs."

"That's not as conclusive as hard science, but the

insurance company couldn't possibly have the kinds of samples that the farmer doesn't, could they?"

"They have general information about soils in the area and water. It's up to us to prove good farming." She gave me a nervous smile.

"How could general information possibly trump the personal testimony?" I felt inner scrutiny for asking her more questions. It had just popped out.

"The farmer used both well water and bought irrigation district water when the crops needed more water during the drought. The drought has caused salt build-up in many farms' soil. If the dirt shows that kind of salinity issue and the farmer can't prove he pumped sufficient water from the irrigation district that wasn't affected, it could hurt his case."

I touched Carly's tense arm briefly. "You've got this. You're the smartest attorney I've met here. Just don't let Tripper get to you."

"He pulls one more f-bomb attack, and I'm done with him." Her voice seethed with controlled anger. She gave me a forced smile. "I've got to get back to it. We'll do taco lunch soon." She left the break room, leaving me feeling uneasy. I grabbed my completed coffee and threw away the spent pod before returning to my office.

When I sat back down in my office chair, I stared at the empty bookcase on the opposite wall. I had done nothing to make the office my own. Nothing to express my personality. There was nothing that belonged to me except my newly reframed diplomas, displaying my professional accomplishments. I pondered the strange fact that I couldn't muster a desire to change it. It suited the empty feeling that I had inside.

Felicity buzzed me. "Bob on Line 2."

I picked up the line to hear Bob's excited voice. "Skyler, we have Nick Petrinko in custody on charges."

"How?" It was my turn to sound surprised and excited.

"We had a list of suspected poachers' license numbers—vehicles to be closely watched. Fish and Game officers were trailing some suspected poachers. They were led to a meet-up with Nick Petrinko far away from the river, where he thought he would be in less direct danger of discovery. They caught them with five female sturgeon and charged them all with wildlife trafficking. Additionally, Petrinko was charged with possession of an unlicensed firearm."

I felt myself go cold. "That means they're still operating in the area. Sergei is still in business. I'm still not safe in my own apartment."

"I'm not sure about that. We have Petrinko in custody. There's sufficient evidence to get a warrant to search the World's Finest Caviar plant."

"When are you going to do that?"

"Tonight. I thought you'd want to know. There's still a chance we can catch up with Sergei. Cut the head off the snake, as they say."

"Yeah, Bob, I really appreciate the call. I hope you find something tonight. Let me know."

There was silence on the line.

I asked, "Bob, am I missing something?"

"They're going to have to cut Nick loose within twenty-four hours unless you press kidnapping charges. You know it's hard to get the court to give a poacher more than a slap on the wrist, and illegal possession of a firearm is only a misdemeanor with a fine and up to six months in jail. It's not like they could keep him on those charges. But if you hold him accountable for your abduction, you'll have to face him in court."

"But...but...he..."

"And he's already hired the best criminal attorney in town." Bob sounded dejected.

"Victoria could do it." I cringed inside as I heard myself.

"She already agreed to do so, but you would add a second count. Add more jail time. You need to know that the District Attorney will be contacting you. I thought you should be prepared."

"Yeah. I get it. It just makes me shudder to think I'll have to testify against him in court. I've already had a couple of nightmares where I see him pointing a gun at me."

As we hung up. I felt a sense of dread, knowing Nick had never left town and Sergei could still be in the area.

When Ben arrived to escort me out of the office, I told him about my phone call with Bob. He sat sullenly in my office chair. "Nick's still doing business on the river?"

"I'm sorry. I'd hoped there was no more threat to your company."

His eyes narrowed. "That's the least of my worries. I don't like the idea that he's still in the area because of you."

I lowered my eyes, "I feel bad about you driving all the way over here every day to make sure I'm okay."

Ben asked, "Are you on a lease or a month-to-month at your apartment?"

"Month-to-month." My voice grew quiet. "Are you implying I should pack up and move?"

He grew tense. "Don't you think so?"

"Are we going to have our first fight about it?"

He looked away. "If it's for your own good."

I grabbed my bag and stood, frowning. "Well, at least I can let you get on with your babysitting duty tonight as quickly as possible."

His eyes softened. "It's no duty. I'd just like to see you without you looking over your shoulders for assassins."

We walked out of the building in silence.

CHAPTER 14
CAVIAR COWBOYS

The moment she spotted me in the main hallway, Felicity rose from her desk to meet me before I could enter my office. "Bob from Fish and Game called. He said it was important. He asked for your voicemail."

I thanked Felicity, hurriedly dumped my purse, and punched in the numbers to connect me to my office voicemail account. "You have two new messages and one old message which must be saved...." I sighed. *Beep.* "Hey, Skyler, this is Morgan Delaney from…" I hit the code to skip the message. *Beep.* "Skyler. It's Bob Colburn. That search last night paid off. We caught two more people red-handed, processing sturgeon roe. There were boxes already packed in dry ice with overnight shipping labels to an address in London. We also seized a computer. I thought you'd want to know."

Montana. I was right about the bank loan. But London? Maybe that's the new market?

I rang Bob back. "Do you think Sergei is selling black-market caviar in London?"

"We're not sure, but that's a strong possibility. Thanks

to the DNA samples we ran, if contraband caviar shows up there, it can be compared to determine if the origin was in this region."

"If he's gone out of the country, we'll never catch him."

"Keep the faith. This isn't over yet. There are international agencies pursuing wildlife trafficking. I've already started making connections. We're able to provide valuable information."

"What about the bank loan?"

"I figured you'd call and ask me about it. I wanted to tell you personally. The bank was told the loan was for machinery and operational upgrades for caviar processing. They required the money to be paid directly to vendors. The drawdowns went to a company called Aquaculture Adventures, Inc. We're looking into it now."

"I'd be willing to bet Sergei is behind Aquaculture Adventures, Inc. and used a false front to wash the money."

"You and me both. We just have to figure out how to show it, trace where it went from there, and hope there's a way to freeze the funds."

As soon as I hung up with Bob, I went online to see what type of information the Secretary of State for Montana had for registered businesses. It wasn't much different from California, except you couldn't view PDF copies of documents. Copies would have to be requested if I wanted to see details. Luckily, a search for Aquaculture Adventures showed that it had changed its agent for service of process from a P.O. Box to a Commercial Registered Agent. There wasn't a familiar name, but it was the same P.O. Box address that was previously used for Czar Alexander.

I felt like things were coming together again. We knew Sergei was operating out of Montana. The caviar might be shipping to London, but it seemed that Sergei would rather play cowboy than go back to the motherland.

I called Bob back, explaining the connection.

He said, "I'll contact Montana Fish and Wildlife and have them coordinate with local authorities. Hopefully, we can get a stakeout on that post office box."

"That's great, Bob. I feel like you've got a real chance of catching Sergei now. If the bank did a draw directly to Aquaculture Adventures, would there be any information on the check? Where it went?"

"I'll find out."

I didn't like the idea, but my next search was for available apartments. Ben was right. I was tired of staying at a hotel. I figured the firm wasn't going to pay for it much longer. I barely got the thought out when an inter-firm email notification popped up on my screen:

"To: Skyler Ashford

From: Thomas Carbone

Subject: Hotel Costs

Dear Ms. Ashford, the partners have convened and graciously agreed to extend   payment for hotel accommodations for one week from this date. Please be advised   that any further stay will be your financial responsibility.

Kindly,

Thomas Carbone"

Kindly indeed.

I got back to the list of available apartments, checked out three websites, including floorplans and pricing. Narrowing it down to two choices, I decided to visit during my lunch hour.

I buzzed Carly on the intercom system. "I'm thinking about moving after the whole mafia's got my mobile phone thing. I'm going to look at two apartments over the lunch hour. I'd like some company and a second opinion. You game?"

She paused for a dramatic moment. "Only if you buy lunch."

"Fast food it is, and you're driving."

"See you at noon."

The morning passed relatively quickly. Voorhees set up a meeting in Conference Room B with Scott Bosendorf, the President of Snack King, to gather information for a declaration supporting our opposition. It took up the rest of my time until lunch. When I got back to my office, Carly lingered in my guest chair, legs crossed, tapping away at her mobile phone. When I entered, she gave me a sidelong glance. "I've been waiting. It's five after twelve. No time to waste. Where were you?"

"Voorhees had me in a client meeting. Couldn't be helped."

She let out a huff. "Well, let's get going, and I'll tell you what I think of your potential palaces. Since you made me wait, I'm demanding a large fry and extra-large soda with my fast food."

"Sold. Let's go."

After acquiring the promised greasy burgers and accompaniments, which we ate in the car as I drove, we arrived at the first potential new apartment, pulling up to the manager's office. After a short explanation, she took us to a one-bedroom unit on the second floor, overlooking the back of the property.

Carly walked into the kitchen and called out, "Small." She continued to the living room. "But it has a fireplace. Nice."

I followed her into the bedroom and immediately went to the window, opening long curtains covering a sliding glass door. There was a balcony overlooking the pool.

Carly joined me, peering out. "You know you'll end up with noise when a bunch of college frat boys decide to take a midnight swim, right?"

"I like the idea of the second floor for security. My current apartment is on the first floor and my bedroom view is a parking lot, so it could be considered an upgrade."

She laughed. "You mean college frat boys instead of cars for a view?"

I smirked. "You never know."

I snapped a few pictures of the place before we left to check out the alternative choice. We followed the same procedure, comparing notes on the way back to the office. Carly said, "I liked the second one better. It's got easier freeway access and it's quieter. No fireplace, but the bathroom was less cramped. With all the restrictions in California, you really can't have a fire in the fireplace anyway. Just for show."

I sighed. "You're probably right. I just hate the idea of all the packing and unpacking. Someday, I'll get a house, then I'll feel like I'm a grown-up."

She took her eyes off the road briefly as she shot me a wide-eyed glance. "You're a law school graduate working for a law firm handling multi-million-dollar cases. Not just any law firm, but one that hires only top prospects. You don't feel like a grown-up?"

"I guess I just always had the white picket fence vision of my life. Husband. Career. Two point something kids. Oh, and a cat."

She giggled. "You could get the cat now. I think that apartment has a pet deposit option. You know… just in case you don't get the husband right away, you could be a cat lady."

"Speak for yourself."

We arrived back at the office still giggling. I called the manager of the apartment sans pool views to let her know I'd sign a month-to-month rental agreement, then called my current apartment manager to let her know I planned to move out in a week. I didn't care if I had to pay double rent for a couple of weeks because of the cancellation notice requirement. Next, I called a moving company and scheduled them for early next week. After it was all done, I breathed a sigh of relief.

As I passed through the Hall of Partner Portraits, Carbone was barreling down the hallway from the other end. "Skyler. Where have you been? I've been looking for you."

"Lunch?"

"Well, you've got less than half an hour to prepare for a client meeting. I'm double-booked. I need you to meet with Ms. Vartabedian in Conference Room A. Get the file from Joan."

Carly was right behind me. She shot me a knowing look, one eyebrow raised, as she silently headed to her office.

I followed her, heading to retrieve the file. When I got to Joan's desk, she looked up at me with a smile I didn't like for reasons I didn't yet know. I forced a smile back. "Mr. Carbone indicated I should take the meeting with Ms. Vartabedian and that you had the file ready for me."

She continued to smile in her creepy way. "Right here." She handed me a slim file.

Her mannerism made me wonder what else had been handed off to me as I made my way back to my office. I only had a few minutes to review the file, but when I opened it, all it contained was an intake sheet for a new case.

I buzzed Felicity. "Mr. Carbone asked me to take a meeting with a new client, Ms. Mary Vartabedian. Do you know anything about her?"

"I've heard the last name before. I think Mr. Carbone represents a Mr. Vartabedian concerning his restaurant franchises—possibly her husband or son? I don't know anything about Mary Vartabedian, but if I'm right about her association with an existing client, her relation is a frequent flyer. Can't seem to stay out of trouble with his business dealings. A bit of a hand-holder, but it makes the firm a lot of money."

"Thanks, Felicity." I hung up the phone.

So, a relation of a frequent flyer client. I need to keep the family happy with the firm's representation.

A few minutes later, Cammie buzzed me. "Ms. Vartabedian has arrived for her meeting. Joan informed me you're handling it. I've got her settled in Conference Room A."

I retrieved a yellow legal notepad and a gel pen and took them, along with the file, to Conference Room A. I opened the door to survey the client. An elderly woman with gray hair done in one of those football helmet styles of yesteryear. She was well-kept and tidy, wearing a modest dress. At the side of her chair sat an enormous purse that contrasted with her petite frame. In front of her on the conference table lay a folder full of papers. She looked up at me with expectant eyes that immediately clouded with disappointment. "Thank you, dear, but they already offered me coffee." She looked at her wristwatch.

I closed the door behind me. She looked up again as if

I hadn't heard her correctly. I put on my best smile. "I'm Skyler Ashford, the attorney assigned to your case."

"Oooo… I was supposed to meet with a man."

I managed not to roll my eyes.

"Yes. Mr. Carbone. But he's double-booked this morning. He's still the lead attorney. I'm his associate. He asked me to meet with you." I took the chair on the opposite side of the table and sat down, my notepad and pen ready.

She broke eye contact, lips pressed tight. "I see."

"Can you tell me why you've come in today?"

She snapped, "Of course I can. My son is a very important client at this firm, and he told me you would fix my problem. You see, I have birds. Well, I don't have birds, but I make a lovely place for the birds. Little chickadees, you see. They come to my garden where I put out the feeders. The neighbor's cat keeps disturbing them. It makes me very *angry*." She expelled the last word with a huff that cut off then looked at me expectantly.

"I… uh…the cat you say?" I rubbed my nose. "We can't really get a court order against the cat roaming the neighborhood." I felt the room receding as she peered at me like I was an idiot. I asked, "Is there anything else? Is the neighbor otherwise trespassing or causing disturbances?"

Her eyes gleamed. "Why, yes. She's got stacks of firewood and…well, junk…and she's been piling dirt up against the fence. I've got pictures." She withdrew a phone from her purse and proceeded to thumb through pictures as I waited.

Cats and dirt. No wonder Carbone didn't want to take the meeting. Double-booked my butt. He's probably out playing golf with some retired judge and left me to deal with the biddy. But if her son is a money-maker client for Carbone, I have to placate her. Hmm... How long can it take to find a picture?

She grinned, pointing the outdated phone toward me. I honestly couldn't see the picture very well the way the screen was catching the glare from the overhead lights, but it didn't matter. A pile of dirt and a fence. I asked, "Is that on your side?"

She giggled. "Oh no. When she wasn't home, I went around to her side and took the picture."

I groaned inside. The neighbor wasn't trespassing, but our client was. "Ms. Vartabedian, I appreciate the information, but you should not enter your neighbor's property without permission. That could cause a problem."

She blinked. "It's not me putting dirt on the fence. She's going to cause rot to the fence. The weight against it is going to cause it to lean or fall. Plus, it's my property!" She looked intensely at me, flushed and agitated.

This was not going well. I assured her, "I'm on your side. I just don't want you to give your neighbor any excuses." *Excuses for what? I needed to get this on track quickly.* "Is the fence leaning?"

"No."

"Does the fence have apparent rot or other damage?"

"No. But it's going to. Her big dog jumps against the fence when the cat comes into my yard."

"Yes, any fence will have age-related damage in time. You said it's your fence, but the law says that a fence on a common property line is the responsibility of both neighbors. You can't control what she does on her side of the fence, but if it causes actual damage to the fence, you can come back, and there's a statute that requires her to pay for half of the replacement cost. The entire cost if she caused the damage."

She looked at me like my remote control was missing a few buttons. "I told you, it's *my* fence. It's my fence because it's on my property."

I knew my voice held uncertainty. It felt like blood in shark-infested waters. "Why do you think it's your property?" *How should I have phrased that?* I bit my lower lip.

She moved her slightly gnarled hand possessively on top of the file of papers in front of her. She glared at me with a look of distrust, sighed heavily, slowly opened the file, and slid a paper halfway across the table. "They told me so."

I reached to retrieve the paper, half expecting to be met with a schoolmarm's ruler to the back of my hand. It was a reduced-size copy of a surveyor's map. I caught myself with my mouth slightly open as I strained my eyes to examine the small print closely.

"You had a survey of the property done?

"Well, you're looking at it, aren't you? Are you sure you don't need Mr. Carbone to come in here, dear?"

I could feel a pained expression overtaking my face. "No, no, not at all. It's just... I wish we had started here. This doesn't indicate where the fence is located. I believe you're telling me that the common fence is located on your side of the property line. Correct?"

"Yes, yes, you're finally hearing me."

I took a deep breath and tried to smile confidently. "I might not be able to get the cat to understand where the property line is, but this is important. We need to get the fence relocated to the proper place. It's especially important if you want to sell or if you leave the property to someone in a trust or will."

"I'm not planning on selling. I just want her to respect the fence."

"The fence itself is less important than the correct property line."

"Whatever you say, dear. Talk to Mr. Carbone and do something about her."

I felt like I'd been dismissed, and she still didn't understand. "Is there anything else in that file pertaining to the property?"

She reluctantly slid the folder toward me, locking eyes with me.

I took a cleansing breath and forced another smile. At this point, I just wanted her out of the office so I could look at something logical, like paperwork. "I'll walk you to the lobby. We'll drop these with Cammie at the front desk. She can make a copy for our file before you leave. That way, you can keep your originals. I'll get back to you after I've had a chat with the surveyor. We'll likely try writing a letter to your neighbor first to see if we can get cooperation to move the fence onto the correct property line." I stood up, both files in hand, and opened the door.

She gave me an unsure nod, stood, and followed me. Once I'd dropped her off with Cammie, I returned to my office to have a silent scream.

When I'd recovered sufficiently from Ms. Vartabedian, I logged back onto my computer. There was an email waiting from Bob. "Skyler, Montana authorities were able to get a copy of the information about payments to Aquaculture Adventures. I'm attaching it to this message. It looks like the bank required a wire transfer rather than a check. That means we know which bank the loan money was sent to. The lender is pretty upset about the probable fraud. Montana is working on a warrant to get the information about the receiving bank account and put a freeze on any funds."

There wasn't much I could do on my end except keep Carbone and Ben updated.

Felicity buzzed, "The District Attorney's Office on Line 1 for you."

I picked up the phone reluctantly. "Skyler Ashford."

"Good afternoon, Ms. Ashford. We've pressed charges against Nick Petrinko for the kidnapping of yourself and Victoria Delaney. Ms. Delaney has already agreed to testify. I need to know your position."

I cringed on the inside but kept my voice confident. "I was told you would be calling. Yes, I'll provide testimony. Is he likely to get out on bail?"

"That depends on whether the judge thinks he's a flight risk and what amount of bail is posted—whether he can pay that amount."

"Has Ms. Delaney already informed you of the connections Nick Petrinko has to the Russian mafia?"

"Yes, we're aware of the uniqueness of this case. We'll be asking for significant bail. I'll need you to come to my office to provide more information."

"Please call back and talk to my secretary, Felicity. She has my calendar. She can schedule a time."

"We appreciate your cooperation."

The call shook me. I worked on the letter for Ms. Vartabedian, but that only took about half an hour. I sent it to Mr. Carbone along with notes from my meeting. By that time, it was only about four-thirty, but I was done for the day. I felt like a squeezed-out tube of toothpaste both mentally and physically. I phoned Ben and told him I would be okay to drive to the hotel by myself. I wanted to leave right away because of a headache. I needed to pack up my apartment.

CHAPTER 15
SMOKE AND MIRRORS

Bob called in the morning. Montana officials were able to get information on the bank account opened for Aquaculture Adventures. Under the "Know Your Customer" Laws implemented in the Patriot Act, the bank was supposed to ask for enough information to understand who was opening the account. Unfortunately, the exact documents required are not mandated under the law. It appeared that the bank was sloppy, only requiring proof of incorporation, a Board of Directors resolution authorizing a corporate bank account, and a business license. All could be easily faked or legitimately obtained without an actual intent of doing business. It was easy enough to create a corporation that looked legitimate with all the formal paperwork—smoke and mirrors.

Once the money from the loan was transferred to the bank, Sergei's next trick was getting it out. It appeared there were a series of cashier's checks. They looked like they were made out to legitimate businesses and individuals. Sergei likely either created more false companies or bribed some businesses in trouble and promised them a small cut for their assistance. Criminals find criminals. The bottom line was that the only traces of evidence led to those individuals, and there was nothing left in Aquaculture Adventures' account.

Bob also let me know that the stakeout on the P.O. Box proved a bust. If the money was gone, it would be unlikely Sergei would return there. By now, with Nick unable to communicate and his California caviar source ceased operating, Sergei must know that the trail was hot again. He had laundered enough money to go anywhere in the world and retire if he wanted... It just didn't sound like his personality.

Carbone called me into his office. "I've got another case I want you to work on."

I looked at him warily.

"Our client, McTavish Fuels and Oils, is a supplier of petroleum products to gas stations. They were just served with a lawsuit by an ex-navy officer, a woman named Amy Whitmore who most recently worked for a regional airport. She contends that our client was in the chain of suppliers that exposed her to chemicals that caused her to develop mesothelioma."

"Mess o' what?"

"It's a type of cancer that invades the thin layers that cover internal organs. It's a sad thing, but our client never supplied chemicals to anywhere she could have been exposed."

"So, why can't we just send the opposing attorney

documents that show the client should be dismissed."

"There's a dance to this. This particular attorney practically makes his entire living on these types of cases. He solicits clients and then sues one Big Oil company. He knows they have deep pockets, but also that they have the money to drag things out in court. He needs a fund for the lawsuit. That's where the next layers come in. He sues some little guys who are likely to settle out early and give him...say, fifteen thousand dollars a pop to fatten his war chest. Then he goes after the medium-sized suppliers like our guy. By the time he's done, he's gotten enough in nuisance settlements for a fat payday, or he's got enough money to take a shot at the bigger defendants if he can prove the link between their products, her exposure, and her disease."

"But she's got a type of cancer that's been linked to this type of exposure."

"Don't be a bleeding heart too quickly, Ashford. Just because there's a link between an exposure to a product our client sells and the plaintiff's disease doesn't make our client responsible. This attorney solicits these clients like an ambulance chaser. He doesn't care if suppliers like our client supplied the products. He just knows insurance will pay to avoid the question. Plus, people accept exposure to petrochemicals every day of the week. He would have to show the client did something negligent. He's just out to bleed an insurance company."

I shook my head. I see. "It's another case like the A.D.A. deal where there's potentially a legitimate legal case, but an unethical attorney...or at least a highly questionable approach." I looked up at the ceiling. "What do you want me to do?"

He handed me the file. "Talk to insurance counsel. They may let us handle it, but more likely it will get farmed out to one of their inside attorneys. In the meantime, while we still have control, see if there's any way to get our guy out early. Insurance will probably hand the defendant fifteen grand just to avoid paying the attorney fees necessary to draft a summary judgment and get the client dismissed on legal grounds. Doesn't matter that our client didn't do anything wrong. This kind of thing makes me sick." His lip snarled.

I nodded, rose, and exited to go back to my office to review and think. After an hour, I could see there wasn't an early motion to avoid the lawsuit. We'd be drug through processes of discovery where we would send questions to get more information and receive likely several inches of written questions to answer. They were right. By the time we got to the point where we could file a summary judgment to get out of the case, it would cost more than they could probably settle for next week. The insurance companies were making a business decision on these types of cases. I couldn't blame them, but it was encouraging…enabling…lawsuits against innocent companies.

Then I had a thought.

What if Big Oil was as sick about this kind of case as Carbone? It must be costing them substantial attorney fees every year. I didn't mind them getting bled if they caused some woman's cancer, but if they were just part of some slick lawyer's formula that fed off companies that didn't do anything wrong? What if that lawyer got his legal funding cut off?

I could feel my heartbeat get faster. I practically ran to Carbone's office. When he saw my grin, he got a confused look. "Come in, Skyler. What's going on?"

"I have an idea about the McTavish case. What if we got Big Oil to indemnify us?"

He scratched his neck, staring at me for a moment like I'd lost it. "Why would they?"

"You said the little guys were getting used to build a war chest. What if they wouldn't cooperate?"

He let out a little snort. "C'mon, Skyler, you know better than that. Our insurance company is going to want to settle to avoid potential bigger liability later, even if we're right that McTavish wasn't in any supply chain."

I could hear my voice getting higher-pitched. "I'm talking about not needing the insurance company. What if Big Oil agreed that if all the little guys would lock arms and all refuse to settle because Big Oil would pay the bill if we got hit with a judgment? If they would do that, our clients wouldn't be at higher risk, and Big Oil would have the advantage of its deep pockets with a plaintiff that doesn't have settlement money to spend to fight them?"

His face turned serious as he rocked back in his executive desk chair. He took in a deep breath, then slowly released it, silently blinking. After another moment of stillness, he looked back at me. "That would take an agreement with most of the defendants and the agreement of Big Oil—PetroCom in this case. We'd have to promise them we weren't involved in the supply chain where the plaintiff was allegedly exposed."

I waited. He let his head fall to the back of his chair, mouth slightly open, eyes to the ceiling. When he looked back at me, he sighed. "Okay, I'm going to give you the contact information for the head of the legal department at

PetroCom. You can pitch it to them."

I succeeded in keeping most of my happy dance inside, but a smile snuck out.

Carbone waved me off. "Get out of here before I regret it."

I decided not to give him time for a take-back. As soon as I was back in my office, I direct-dialed Dietrich Hoffman, head legal counsel for PetroCom. "Good afternoon, Mr. Hoffman. I'm Skyler Ashford, an associate at Wagner, Tibbs, and Cobbs. Thomas Carbone gave me your number to discuss the Amy Whitmore Case. Our client, McTavish, was sued along with PetroCom."

A big and slightly gruff voice replied. "Tom, huh? Yes, I just heard about that case. What can we do for you?"

"I'd like to suggest we enter into a JDA—Joint Defense Agreement—so that we have privilege and confidentiality relating to our conversations and can coordinate our defense."

He cleared his throat. "We often do a JDA, but isn't this going to be sent to McTavish's insurance?"

I took a deep breath. "That's the unusual part. Mr. Carbone was explaining how the smaller companies usually settle in these cases, essentially funding the rest of the case against deeper pockets like your company."

His voice deepened, nearly a growl. "That's about right."

"What if we all agreed not to settle?"

"How would you get all the defendants to do that?" His tone said he was just humoring me.

"If PetroCom indemnified against any losses for defendants that can reasonably demonstrate they weren't in the supply chain and agreed to reimburse the attorney fees to get the smaller companies out on legal grounds."

There was silence on the line. For a moment, I thought I'd been disconnected. Then… "Intriguing thought, Ms. Ashford. I'll have to give it some consideration. Even if I decide it's a worthwhile strategy, something like that would have to go to our Board of Directors."

I hadn't thought of that. That was complex. "Of course."

His voice softened. "I'll get back to you before your client is required to respond. Goodbye, Ms. Ashford."

As we hung up, I was left with the feeling that I had just made a friend. Maybe my first step in building a reputation in the legal industry as an out-of-the-box thinker. I had a moment of elation where I felt like I could conquer my fledgling career.

I left the office early, knowing it was time I'd have to make up on the weekend or late at night, but the movers were scheduled to take my things to the new apartment tomorrow. I'd packed the little stuff in boxes, thankful it was a small apartment. I wanted to be there, watching. Not just the movers, but watching that we weren't being followed. Making sure my new location wasn't on Sergei's radar…or

Nick's if he ever got out of jail. This was a good time to move before he was cut loose.

The movers showed up before my last cup of coffee kicked in. A burly threesome, they muscled the entire contents of my apartment into the moving truck in less than an hour. As they started toward my new apartment, I was set to follow in my car. I lingered back a moment, watching to see if anyone tailed their truck, feeling like I was emulating a crime T.V. show. I glanced carefully in my mirrors as I set off, making sure no cars followed. As I drove, I became abnormally cognizant of the cars around me, making sure they turned off and went about their own business. As we arrived at the new place, I sat outside as the men unloaded the truck and drove off, making sure no one else entered the complex that didn't belong.

As they unloaded the sofa, one of the movers asked me, "Don'tcha wanna tell us where to put the stuff, ma'am?"

I hesitated before answering. "No, just put it where you think it should go. I'll rearrange it later."

He gave me a quizzical look for a long moment before moving back toward the truck and reconvening with the other two men. He shrugged at them. They both shot me a confused look before mumbling something and getting back to work. I stayed vigilant on guard duty.

When the furniture and boxes were finally unloaded and the movers off, I walked in, shut and locked the door, and breathed out a big breath. Not having supervised the furniture placement, I was pleasantly surprised that it wasn't too far off from what I would have instructed. Apparently at least one of the muscular, short-on-words movers had some interior design intuition.

I'd clearly labeled the boxes with their room locations. They were neatly stacked around the apartment, waiting for my attention. Those containing kitchen items were placed just outside the narrow kitchen space. I began opening boxes, searching for the one item I cared about in the moment—the coffee maker. After tearing open three boxes, I finally located it, along with filters, a grinder, a mug, and some whole-bean, dark roast beans. With a smile of satisfaction, I set a pot brewing. I usually took my coffee with cream, but black was going to do nicely today.

When I heard a knock at the door, I nearly squeaked. *No one has this address! Could they have followed me?* Another loud set of three knocks. I slowed my breathing and looked around for a baseball bat. *I don't own a baseball bat. What else is heavy you could use as a weapon? Wait, you're not going to open the door, are you?*

I slunk to the door and peered out the peephole. Ben. Letting out a held breath, I released the deadbolt and opened the door. He held a grocery bag. Looking into the new apartment, he said, "Are you going to let me in? Carly gave me the address. I brought some basic provisions."

I let out a hiss, practically pulling him through the door. "Were you followed? I've been so careful."

He blanched. "They don't know this address, and why would you think they would follow me?"

"You own Chairo—the company that started this whole thing." I saw the wound in his expression and immediately regretted the accusatory tone in my voice. "I mean...I didn't mean it that way. I'm just jumpy." He still held the grocery bag, looking stunned. I looked at it and then back to him. "You brought groceries?"

"Just some basics."

"Gonna bring it to the kitchen? I've got coffee made but no milk. You want some?"

"I've got milk, but no coffee." His face looked like it wanted to smile but wasn't sure after the welcome he'd received.

I took the bag from him. "Sounds like a perfect match...if you can find another coffee mug."

He looked at the boxes then knelt and began gently looking through the three open kitchen boxes, finally coming up with a misshapen ceramic mug that said "I Flunked Anger Management" on the side. He held it up, giving me a raised-eyebrow snicker. "Something I need to know?"

I pursed my lips and laughed. "My brother's idea of a funny graduation gift."

He stood and handed the cup to me. I filled it with coffee then took a half-gallon jug of milk from the grocery bag now on the counter, adding a splash of milk. "What else did you bring?"

He took a sip of coffee, nodding toward the bags on the counter. "You planning on putting it up?"

I began taking items from the bags and putting them in the refrigerator and cupboard. A loaf of bread, jar of peanut butter, eggs, pasta noodles, spaghetti sauce, some ground beef, and...blinis with a jar of caviar? I looked up in surprise to see him grinning. "A little housewarming present."

"Do you want some now?

He made a face. "Not with coffee. But I could stay and help you unpack if you'd like."

"After some coffee?"

He nodded and filled his cup before proceeding to my

small dining room table just off the kitchen. "I bet we could have this place in shape tonight if we put our minds to it. Besides, I might learn a thing or two about you rifling through all your belongings, like who's this brother?"

I took a slow sip of coffee. "Harry. Big brother. Bought me the mug. Then there's Matt. Little brother. Like really little brother. It was the shock of my life when my folks told me my senior year of high school that they were pregnant."

He almost sputtered some coffee. "No way! How'd you react?"

"No kid wants evidence their parents…uh…still like each other." My eyebrows raised before I ducked my head. "It was awkward when Mom showed up to my high school graduation in a maternity dress."

He leaned in. "So, what was it like having a baby come live with you?" He took another sip of coffee.

"*Mmm…* He was a pain in the butt…but so cute. At least until he scribbled on my college homework and threw tantrums in front of my friends."

"Now?"

"Mom and Dad still live in Del Mar, a beach town near San Diego. I visit for holidays. They have a hard time visiting me because of the little guy. He's in fifth grade now. We used to video chat, but I've been jammed for time since I started at the law firm, and he's more interested in video games than his boring, much older sister."

"What about Harry?"

"Engineer. Works building bridges overseas. He's always been an adventurer."

As we hit the bottom of our coffee mugs, he stood and looked for a nod of approval before beginning to take things out of the various boxes marked "kitchen" and asking where I wanted them stowed.

We pulled the kitchen together in about forty minutes. Another half hour and the miscellanea that went in the living room had been unpacked. He looked at me uncertainly. "Any more boxes we should unpack tonight?"

"Just the bedroom and bath. I think I should handle those. I'm not ready for you to find out that much about me."

"Then I'm going to get going. Laurel's been onto me about a strategic planning meeting." He rolled his eyes. "She'll be ready to ground me for life if I'm not prepared for it tomorrow morning."

"Hey, I like Laurel."

"Yeah, she's good for me. Keeps me grounded. I've got to keep her happy." As he spoke, he rose and started walking toward the door. I followed. He gave me a quick hug. "See you soon, Counselor."

CHAPTER 16
MOVERS & SHAKERS

Another work morning. Another day where I needed to scrounge assignments. After making the rounds with several partners, I had a few demand letters to write and some jury instructions to draft. Enough work for one day, but I could see how the "you kill it, you eat it" philosophy would work to my advantage. I didn't know how to stalk the prey. There are a lot of rules to soliciting legal clients. Under the Code of Professional Conduct, it's illegal for an attorney to solicit or contact a potential client directly if you know they have a legal problem. Even a simple postcard to new businesses had to be prominently marked "Attorney Advertising" on the envelope. Plus, it's not like selling other products. It's a downer to try to find people with big problems and then convince them you're the right person to solve them.

I'd heard somewhere that joining organizations like the Women's Chamber of Commerce was a good way to network and potentially meet clients. The problem was, those meet-and-greet lunches and other meetings weren't billable time. It would be just one more thing to try to fit into my day. Was that really how to find clients? I decided to put it on the back burner for now.

I was already in a blue funk when Carly walked in, looking unusually peaceful, and closed my office door behind her. "I've decided I'm leaving the firm."

I looked up with surprise. "Did you already find another position?"

"I had some interview opportunities, but then I thought more about it and decided to hang out a shingle on my own."

I gasped. "You're going into practice all by yourself? The overhead. Where will you find clients? Are you going to have any staff? How can you answer phones and be in court at the same time unless you do?" My brain fired questions like a machine gun right out of my mouth.

She raised a single eyebrow. "I'll figure it out. I'm not waiting around to get fired from this place." She looked around furtively.

"I have it from good authority that after Peter was let go, we're both pretty safe."

Her lip curled. "That's if you're not working for an insane attorney. There will be a lot of stress starting a new practice, but it's got to be better than the brain damage I'm sustaining here. At least I can choose the cases."

In her position, she had a point.

She looked pointedly at me. "What about you?"

"I...um...I've been getting along better with Carbone...I think."

She snorted. "Is it worth it?"

"I don't know anything else to compare it to since this is my first job out of law school."

Carly silently nodded. After a moment, she stood and

turned to leave. "You could find out."

She had a point. If it wasn't the work stressing me out, it was the lack of work. I continuously felt like a puppy waiting for the newspaper to hit me from behind. And I had no control over what cases I took, and little control over what partners I worked for. Was this, and all the insane hours that went with it, what I wanted for the next five years or so until I could make partner? If I stayed, what would that do to me? Who would I be by the time I made partner?

With my visit with Carly echoing through my head, I did a quick search to see if any law firms were hiring nearby. Not here in the Sacramento area, but there was one in San Jose, California that popped onto the screen: Clark, Cooper & Abrams, LLP, a "family-friendly" law firm...or so they said. They were located right on the banks of a small, quiet river. The pics online looked calm. The antithesis of what I'd been feeling here. On a whim, I filled out the online application for an associate's position and attached my resume.

Felicity buzzed me. "Mr. Hoffman from PetroCom on Line 5."

My heart did a skip as I picked up the line. "Skyler Ashford. Mr. Hoffman, how can I help you?"

"Good morning, Ms. Ashford. I wanted to personally let you know I thought your suggestion was intriguing. A touch of brilliance even."

I didn't *mean* to interrupt. "And?"

"But the Board of PetroCom is not ready to take the risks associated with indemnifications."

My ego deflated rapidly, first bouncing around the room like a balloon that had been blown up and then let go of without tying it off before landing flaccid on the ground. "Thank you for letting me know. I'm sorry we couldn't find a way to lessen the chances of insurance settlements fueling the lawsuit."

He chuckled. "Pun intended?"

I realized what I'd just said and felt a blush, glad it was a phone call so he couldn't see. "Guess I just pun-ted." I rolled my eyes at myself.

He laughed lightly again. "We don't see enough young lawyers brave enough to come up with inventive ideas. Keep in touch, Ms. Ashford."

"Thank you, Mr. Hoffman. I really appreciate the call. Goodbye."

As we hung up, I considered that he could have just called Carbone. I might not have gotten the board of a huge corporation to take a risk on my idea, but I counted it as a win anyway.

Felicity buzzed again, sounding slightly agitated. "Bob from Fish and Game on hold for you on Line 2."

"On hold?"

"He asked to wait until you were off the other line. Could be important."

I felt a little breathless as I picked up the line. "Bob?"

"The news is a mixed bag." His voice was somber. "We were able to freeze some of the funds, but now our legal counsel is dealing with all the small companies the rest of the money was sent to. Most hadn't transferred the funds out of their accounts yet. The World's Finest Caviar real property is under a *lis pendens*, notifying the world that there is a pending lawsuit so no one will transfer title. We've been successful in locking down most of Sergei's assets here in the U.S., but that means he has no reason to stay. Our contacts overseas are watching for him."

I replied, "Minimally, on the civil law side, we've got Nick on conversion based on the theft of female fish from Chairo, but his criminal trial could cause some delays. Then there is the matter of actually collecting."

Bob's voice lowered. "I know that's not what you wanted to hear, Skyler. But it is a huge win for the sturgeon population."

That afternoon, I got an email from the recruitment director of Clark, Cooper & Abrams, LLP wanting to schedule an interview. Problem was, they wanted me to travel on Easter weekend. Traffic would be brutal. The last time I'd made that drive on a holiday was to visit a friend at Thanksgiving, we didn't get over 25 m.p.h. for an hour-and-a-half. I'd watched my back bumper and several inattentive drivers narrowly escaped rear-ending me. It wasn't an experience I wanted to repeat. I felt it was a bit cheeky, but I asked if they'd be willing to fly me down, especially since

I wanted to visit family in the area while I was there for the interview. I was a little shocked to find a link to a plane ticket in my email a few hours later.

I called my cousin Jessie. After four rings, I almost hung up before I heard a familiar, "Hello?"

"Jessie, this is Skyler. I'm going to be traveling near you the Friday before Easter. You guys up for a visit?"

"Oh, Skyler! I haven't seen you in ages. That's perfect timing. We're hosting a big party for Easter on Saturday. Brian and I would love for you to come. You'll never recognize me. I'm about seven months along expecting twins."

My brain pinged an acknowledgment. "Wow. How did I miss that announcement?"

She giggled. We actually didn't announce until a few months ago. We were trying to keep it just between us for a little while, but with twins, that's not easy to do for very long. I'm getting ginormous."

I shook my head as I held the phone, absorbing the news. "That's great, Jessie. I'm so glad I'll get to see you soon."

I was a little shook up from the call. Jessie was my closest cousin out of more than a dozen. I remember Christmases at Grampa Frank's and Grammy T's houses. We little girls would take our dolls and make a fort under the branches of an enormous orange tree in the front yard that had been allowed to overgrow until its branches touched the ground, forming a good-sized hollow around the trunk. It had been our little place away from the rest of the world. It was hard processing that she would soon hold not one, but two little babies of her own. It made me realize how much life had passed since then.

I buzzed Carbone, telling him I planned to take a couple of vacation days just prior to Easter. No need to alert him to my real mission.

CHAPTER 17
UNSETTLED

Waking up the next morning, I felt disoriented—still adjusting to the space of my new apartment. I leisurely stretched, becoming reacquainted with my surroundings, my inner self finding its quiet place before I started my day. I contemplated the fact that I'd been at the law firm for a short time, but it felt like I'd lived a lifetime there. I'd learned so much about law firm life...at least life at this particular office. I'd met someone who made my heart flutter. I'd been kidnapped. I was now a material witness in a criminal case and had to move to evade the Russian mob. Now, was I considering moving away from the area? Most of it, I wouldn't miss...but Ben?

I kept thinking of him intermittently almost the entire drive to work. As if he could read my thoughts, almost as soon as I got to the office parking lot, my personal mobile phone rang. Ben's caller ID. I answered, "What's up Ben?"

He paused before he spoke. "I've been thinking... So much has happened since we first talked about going out on a date. It seems like it should be okay for us to have dinner together—officially. What do you think?"

I took in a quiet breath. "It's against firm policy to date a co-worker or a client unless that's been disclosed to the firm. As a client, the Rules of Professional Conduct would also apply to a relationship."

I could hear the smirk even over the phone. "Really, Counselor? I looked those up. It only applies to a sexual relationship. I'm only inviting you to share a meal, not my bed."

I could feel the heat of a blush like a volcano as my eyes went wide, then I ducked my head, glad he couldn't see my face. "Really? You looked it up? I don't remember it like that. I just remember it was a problem to date a client."

"I get it. Most of the websites that discussed the rule indicate it's wise not to date clients; however, they all seemed to imply there was likely more to dessert than some chocolate cake. Let me be clear. I'm not that guy. As old-fashioned as it might sound to some, I'm saving myself for marriage."

My voice came out like a whisper. "There aren't many men doing that these days, but I like that. I'd like to save myself for someone special, too."

"Then we don't have to worry about Professional Rules of Conduct 1.8.10, and I'm making reservations for tonight unless you want to interpose an objection to the question, Counselor."

I broke a closed mouth, half smile, still feeling vulnerable. "I don't think there could be an objection to such a well-researched question, *Counselor*."

"Any particular cravings? French? Italian? Chinese?"

"You seem to be such a good researcher, I think I'll leave that up to you." *Cravings, huh? I'm already getting what I'm craving—some alone time with Ben.* I couldn't stop smiling. *At this rate, my jaw's going to cramp.*

"See you at six then."

I echoed, "See you at six," before hanging up, my heart still feeling warm and full. I got out of the car, went into the office, traveled up the elevator, and walked past the Hall of Partner Portraits, ignoring all of their silent judgmentalism. They seemed to all be wondering why I was smiling in light of it. When I approached my office, Felicity gave me a warning look. My grin faded. I knit my brows in a silent question. She mouthed, "Carbone," pointing toward my door. My mouth formed an "Oh" as I slowed my approach.

Entering, I found Carbone sitting in one of my guest chairs, deep in concentration, phone in his hands, presumably texting. He looked up. "Ashford, I've been waiting. I thought you usually got in by seven-thirty. It's nearly eight."

I continued to my desk, quickly stashed my purse, and sat. "Yes, I'm usually in earlier. I moved. Adjusting to my new apartment and location."

"I want you to get a complaint on file against Nick Petrinko personally and the shell corporation that holds the real estate." He didn't look up from his phone.

"Isn't he in custody?"

"Doesn't matter. You can have him served even if he's in jail. The entity can be subserved."

"Is this what Ben asked us to do?"

At that, Carbone's head raised with a stern glare. "This is what will benefit Mr. Akers' case and possibly recover some of the money he's lost."

I decided to keep my mouth shut. "Anything else, sir?"

"No, that's it. Let's get this thing going in a courtroom where we can bill for being attorneys instead of playing amateur cops."

He stood, gave me a look I couldn't interpret, and walked out the door, leaving me feeling unsettled.

How do I feel about poking the hornet's nest so soon? I'm already testifying in a case that could send Nick Petrinko to prison for a very long time, but this is going after assets the mob thinks are theirs. Then again, I guess the feds are already doing that. The lawsuit is just one more source of trouble for them. It is my job. It's a meaty billable hours assignment for today. Besides, it's Carbone's signature on the complaint.

I spent most of the day drafting the complaint against Nick Petrinko and Pacific Coast Investments, LLC, the company holding title to the World's Finest Caviar site. I came up with a long list of claims against them, including Interference with Prospective Business Advantage and various frauds. For the intentional frauds, I alleged a right to recover punitive damages. By mid-afternoon, I had something solid I was pleased to email to Carbone for review.

I'd worked long past the lunch hour and was starving, but I didn't want to overeat before my date with Ben. I picked up my phone and punched in an order for a small chef's salad delivered from a local restaurant. The app estimated delivery within twenty minutes. I wandered down to the break room for a coffee while I waited. As I rounded the corner, I spotted Carly sitting at a table with two other associates. I waved a casual greeting before choosing a dark roast coffee pod and commencing the brewing process. When my coffee was ready, Carly waved me over.

One of the associates stood to leave, saying her goodbyes as I walked up to the table. The other associate was a man I guessed to be in his early forties with a short beard and mustache. As he smiled at Carly, his hazel eyes crinkled. Carly said, "Skyler, have you met Arnesto?"

He shot me a disarming smile. "I don't believe we've formally had the pleasure. Arnesto Miranda. I work with Mr. Tellis on litigation matters. I've been away from the office these last three weeks on a long trial out of town, but I've heard about your escapades with the caviar case, Ms. Ashford. You're quite the talk of the office. Are you recovered from the recent trauma?"

Should I be truthful? "I'm not sure I'll ever be completely over it, but I'm functioning."

His smile turned down to a low simmer as true empathy reflected in his deep caramel-colored eyes. I decided he might be one of the good guys. He said, "I hope the scars will fade, sooner than later." Glancing at the clock on the wall and then at Carly, he stood. "I'd best be back at my desk. I'm expecting a new client soon." He glanced back at me as he stood. "Truly a pleasure meeting you, Ms. Ashford. I'm sure I'll see you around now that I'm done with that marathon of a civil trial."

Now that it was just me and Carly in the break room, I leaned in and lowered my voice. "I have an interview with a firm in San Jose."

Carly's eyes registered surprise. "Which one?"

"Clark, Cooper & Abrams, LLP."

"When?"

"Just before Easter weekend. I told Carbone I was taking a couple of vacation days. He doesn't need to know everything…including that I'm dating Ben Akers."

As her eyes widened, she broke out in a wide, close-mouthed grin. "How long?"

"He told me weeks ago he was interested, but we're having dinner for the first time as a couple tonight." I put my finger to my lips, signaling her to keep things quiet.

"You're turning into a real rebel." She laughed under her breath.

"You should talk. You still making plans to leave?"

"I've already turned in my notice. I told them I'd stay until the end of April."

I nodded my head thoughtfully as I took a sip of coffee. "I won't miss much about this place if I get an offer from Clark Cooper, but I'll miss you."

"Same." We locked eyes conspiratorially. "You're a good friend."

My phone notified me that my lunch had arrived. I stood. "I'll keep you posted on the interview."

"You'd better."

I retrieved my salad from the front desk and decided to eat at my desk with my door shut. Looking at the clock, I winced to find it read at three o'clock. Between anticipation of my date with Ben and my growing disdain for my job, I was having trouble wanting to go fetch more billable hours for the day. When I finished my quick lunch, I forced myself down to Carbone's office to check in. As I knocked on the open door, he looked up. I said, "I wanted to check that you saw the draft complaint."

"I saw your email, but I haven't had time to review it yet."

"Hey, whatever happened on the case with the wandering cats and the dirt against the fence?"

"Ms. Vartabedian."

"Yeah, that's the one. I wrote a letter for her. Did the neighbor ever reply?"

"Haven't heard anything back from her or the neighbor, but her son tells me they're moving the fence."

Would have been nice to be kept in the loop. I guess information is on a needs-to-know basis. "Something else I should work on?"

"Check with Voorhees. I think he's got some new real estate matters."

His tone suggested he was feeling interrupted. I nodded and exited.

I repeated the procedure with Vorhees. He handed me a file. "Our client is Herman Vasquez. He's got a vineyard next to a turkey farm. He processes his grapes into raisins. You have to lay them out on paper to dry, and then the papers get rolled into what they call cigarette or flop rolls. They're only out uncovered in the sun about two weeks. Every year, our client notifies the turkey farmer next door when the grapes will be drying and asks him to make sure they don't get contaminated with turkey feathers. Every year for the past two years, the turkey farmer does a deep cleaning of his facility while the raisins are drying and blows turkey feathers, dust, and who knows what onto the drying fruit The raisin farmer then has to pay a considerable amount of money to get the raisins reprocessed and cleaned so they won't be rejected. It's happened again. We need a complaint drafted for trespass, negligence, and anything else you can come up with."

"Got it."

I took the file and went back to my office. I looked through the minimal documents, then glanced at the clock. Four o'clock. Not enough time to get the complaint done I didn't have the heart to grind at it. My date was in two hours, and I wanted to look nice for Ben. I decided to sneak out early.

As I left, purse in hand, Felicity gave me a raised-eyebrow glance. "Leaving early?"

I gave her a short nod. "See you tomorrow."

She looked like she wanted to ask something more, but she just repeated, "See you tomorrow."

When I got home, I took a long shower, then combed through my wardrobe. Half of my clothes felt like my past life as a student—mostly jeans and t-shirts. The other half was the professional wardrobe I'd acquired since arriving at the law firm. There was little that suited the present me going on a date. I finally settled on a pair of black pencil-legged pants, a beige blouse with long split-sleeves, and strappy beige sandals. I unpacked the large tote purse I took to the office and put a few essentials in a small, black shoulder bag with a gold chain.

Ben rang the doorbell promptly at six wearing black jeans and a rust-colored, light sweater with a hint of a starched white shirt underneath. From the open doorway, I caught a whiff of aftershave that hinted at oud and vetiver. He looked at me with an appreciative smile, and in his deep, smooth voice asked, "Ready?"

I was trying not to smile wildly. I grabbed my purse and nodded. Exiting, I locked the door, and we proceeded to the parking lot where the Chairo Caviar vintage truck waited. He opened the passenger door for me. "Hope you don't mind the old heap."

"I like the old girl. She suits you."

He grinned as he shut my door and went around to the driver's side. The truck started with a steady putter. As we were driving, he asked, "Have you had Ethiopian food before?"

"No. Is that where we're going tonight?"

"One of my favorite restaurants. We're actually almost there. It's pretty close to your new place."

A few minutes later, we pulled into an unassuming strip mall and parked. I'd thought perhaps we were going somewhere fancy. This was a storefront with darkened windows and dirty asphalt in the parking area. The sign outside the restaurant read "Makiberi Ethiopian Cuisine." As we walked up to the door, Ben said, "The last time I was here, the owner told me that makiberi means celebration."

"Seems fitting. It feels like we're celebrating tonight."

Ben got out of the truck, and I hesitated before seeing

him turn at the hood and head toward my side. When he opened my door for me, I looked up into his eyes as I slid from the seat. My heart did a silly little pitter-patter. We walked up to the glass door of the restaurant, and he held it open for me. As I walked in, I glanced around and was overtaken by colors everywhere.

The interior of the restaurant was indeed like a celebration. Deep terra cotta walls were accented by stone pillars and long, sheer curtains. Shallow tribal baskets in shades of brown, red, and black were hung in groupings. All along the walls were huge, Bohemian-print pouf pillows in bursts of color surrounding groupings of low tables. At the center of several occupied tables were huge ceramic platters, nearly two feet across, filled with all manner of food. Along the sides of the platters peeked ceramic patterns of red, yellow, and green. No one seemed to have an individual plate or any utensils.

Lively music played lightly in the background. I could recognize that there were traditional tribal instruments. I didn't recognize the language. It was fast-paced and jubilant like everything else about this place. A woman in a batik-print flowing dress with a brightly printed trim approached us and smiled at Ben. He held out his hands toward her. "Amhara, you look lovely as usual. How's your father?"

"He's doing well. He's here tonight. I'm sure he'll stop by to say hello." There was a twinkle in her eyes as if there was an inside joke.

Ben smiled even wider. "You know I love Bemnet's stories." He turned toward me. "Amhara, this is Skyler. We have a reservation."

She took two menus from a wooden stand near the

door. "Ah, yes. I have a table just for you." Her eyes were still twinkling. She walked toward the back corner of the restaurant, a slight saunter to her walk. We followed as she led us to one of the low tables surrounded by huge pillows. Her hand gestured gracefully. She bent into a slight plié as she set the menus on the table.

I glanced around the room, wondering if I should sit with my legs crossed or reclining to the side. There didn't seem to be a particular way. Ben offered a hand, and I took it as I tried to gracefully lower myself. He grinned as he enthusiastically plopped onto the pillows opposite me. "Bemnet owns this place. He is passionate about telling people about Ethiopian food. If he comes over, we'll have a hard time having a conversation to ourselves." I could tell by Ben's expression that he would view it as a welcome interruption.

I took up my menu with one long page of options. Each item seemed to describe one of the huge, colorful platters I had seen at the other tables. Ben looked over. "The meals here are served in a traditional Ethiopian style. There is a single platter shared by all of the dinner guests. It's lined with Injera—a kind of flat bread. On the Injera there are eight to ten different kinds of foods. There are no forks. You use the bread to scoop up the food and eat with your hands. Are you up for that?"

I was still staring at the options on the menus. "I'm always up for an adventure."

I perused the options. Nothing was familiar. I asked Ben, "What do you recommend?"

"We need to choose six entrees to go on top of our Injera. It would be good to mix some vegetarian and some meat choices. Bemnet always recommends the yellow pigeon peas cooked with onions and garlic. He'll go on and on about their health benefits." Ben gave a slight eye roll with a subtle grin. "How are you with spicy foods?"

"How spicy? I mean, that green sauce they serve with Indian food is so spicy it makes my nose run. Not a good look for our first official date night. But other than that, I can take a little heat."

He suppressed a brief, manly giggle. "No, not that hot, but some of the choices have a little bite to them. We'll choose a variety and then you can decide. The Doro Wat has small pieces of diced chicken cooked with garlic, onion, and spices like beriberi. We can order it mild or hot."

"That sounds good. Maybe mild for my first time? What's your favorite dish?"

"Hmmm…the lamb cooked with ginger, garlic, and rosemary."

"That sounds delicious. Let's get some of that."

"There's an unusual dish made with plantains mixed with green peas, carrots, potatoes and onions."

"Okay, pick one hot one if you like spicy food."

"You sure?" He looked at me quizzically and I nodded.

"Okay, then the Siga Kay Wat. It's a spicy beef. And we have all of our choices."

Ben nodded toward Amhara. She came over and took our menus and our order. As she headed toward the back, I looked around more closely. It wasn't overly crowded. I heard a low buzz of muted conversations from three other groups. The air smelled faintly of spices I couldn't identify. I looked back at Ben. "How are things going at Chairo?"

"Hey, no shop talk tonight." He raised an eyebrow at

me.

"Is it shop talk if I ask how you got into the caviar business?"

He paused with a pensive look. "I guess not. You remember meeting my sister?"

"Laurel. Sure."

"Yeah, she was at the fundraiser. She wanted to be a marine biologist. My dad was a farmer—prunes mostly. So, I was almost finished with a business degree from UC-Davis when Laurel ended up meeting that Russian guy who helped start the caviar business in California. She was in some class where she ended up doing a research project on sturgeon with him. After that, her interest shifted from the ocean to aquaculture. Dad bankrolled us with a little startup capital and Laurel and I opened up Chairo on a small scale."

"Is she still in charge of the fish?"

He chuckled. "She'd laugh at that phrasing. Funny thing is, I ended up having good instinct when it came to raising sturgeon, and she ended up being the brains behind the fundraising, marketing, and business growth. Plus, like I told you, she's the only one who would put up with me as a partner."

I smiled softly. "I don't know about that. You seem like a pretty good guy to work with to me."

The waitress came along with a couple of iced teas. Ben took a sip before asking, "What about you? How did you end up a lawyer?"

"Mmm… My aunt says I was always destined to be an attorney. She tells this story about me walking back and forth in their kitchen in my little onesie pajamas when I was only about two. I was apparently presenting an entire argument.

She says she knew right then that I should be a lawyer."

Ben smirked. "I'm visualizing that. But you didn't answer the question. That's just like an attorney."

"It sort of happened to me. I mean, you have to finish an undergraduate degree before you go to law school. Traditionally, that would be political science, but I didn't set out to go into the law. I got my degree in business. I think that's better…at least if you're going to work with business clients. When I completed my business degree, I just wasn't that thrilled with any of the jobs that were available at the time. I saw a sign-up form for the L.S.A.T.—Law School Admissions Test—and decided to sign up on a whim. I'm not sure I'll ever know why. Anyway, I took the test and scored really high. It made me rethink my career."

"I guess that aunt was right after all."

Our food arrived. The waitress set the huge, round platter on the table between us. The brightly-colored patterns on the ceramic were obscured by a thin covering of an almost greyish, bread-like substance full of tiny holes—the Injera—with scoops of our entrée choices on top around the perimeter. I looked over at Ben and he met my eyes then purposefully tore a bit of the Injera off and pinched a bite of chicken into it. Before he popped it into his mouth, he made a slight gesture toward me with his head.

I followed his example, tearing off a bit of the spongy bread and scooping a small bit of the yellow pigeon peas into it. The slightly sour and tangy taste of the spongy Injera pleasantly mixed with the starches of the pigeon peas and small bits of potato. I was ready to explore the various other meat and vegetable offerings. Ben looked at me expectantly. I smiled. "Culinary adventure approved."

We were only a few bites into our meal when a man around his fifties with dark brown skin and an engaging smile approached our table. Ben broke into a wide grin. "Bemnet, good to see you!"

Bemnet looked down at me, sitting on the low pillows, gracing me with a warm smile. "Ben, who is your charming companion?"

"This is Skyler."

Bemnet slowly nodded, still intently looking at me. "You know, he's never brought a date before."

Was that true? I felt a twinge of guilt knowing that I could be moving soon.

Ben's face scrunched in a mock scowl aimed at Bemnet. "Stop telling all my secrets! Come and sit with us. You're going to talk anyway. You might as well not be towering over us."

Bemnet didn't need a second invitation. He gracefully lowered himself onto a pillow across from both of us. "Do you like the Injera, Skyler? It's very, very healthy."

"It's my first time eating Ethiopian food, but I'm enjoying it very much."

"Do you know what it's made of?" He didn't wait for a reply. "Teff. It's a super grain with more fiber than any other grain on earth, plus many nutrients such as proteins, magnesium, iron, and calcium. It's also gluten-free and, because it's a fermented food, it's full of good gut bacteria."

Ben leaned slightly toward me, conspiratorially. "I told you he'd give you a hard sale on Ethiopian food."

Bemnet scoffed. "I'm just telling the truth. More people should eat such healthy foods."

Ben winked. "Next, he's going to tell you we need

coffee."

Bemnet turned his head in a way that made it clear he was purposefully ignoring Ben and addressed me. "On the house to celebrate your date night. You know Ethiopia is the birthplace of the coffee plant. The arabica coffee grown elsewhere can be traced back to its roots in East Africa. Ethiopian coffees are renowned for their floral notes." Amhara motioned to Bemnet. He rose effortlessly from his reclining pillow. "I must attend to a guest, but I will bring some at the end of your meal."

Ben said, "It's strong like a Turkish coffee. We'll be up all night, but you can't refuse the coffee. It would be an insult."

I was still exploring the vastly different tastes of the foods on the platter. The spicy beef was wonderful but a bit too hot on its own. I learned I could mix my bites, putting a taste of the beef together with the vegetables to make it delightful. By the time we were done eating, I was very full and wondering if I would be able to get up from the floor pillows as gracefully as Bemnet.

He appeared from the back of the restaurant bearing a large metal tray. He effortlessly lowered himself along with the tray, which he set on our table. First, he took a small bowl filled with coffee beans and passed it to me. "You must first smell the coffee beans. Drinking coffee in Ethiopia is a sensory experience and something to be shared with good friends."

I dutifully smelled the coffee beans, noticing they appeared to be warm still. I wondered if he roasted them on-site.

Next, Bemnet carefully took a small censure from the

tray and set it on the table. "As a part of the experience, we must burn incense. I could see an already hot coal at the bottom of the censure. On a fine grate on top, Bemnet added two yellowish, resinous stones. "Frankincense and Myrrh. The gifts to the baby Jesus. The smoke of the incense lifts our conversations to God."

As the resins began to emit a light, white smoke, the room began to fill with an exotic scent. Bemnet then handed us each a cup of coffee from the tray. The cups had no handles and were made from brightly painted ceramic like the serving platter for the food. The liquid inside looked as black as night. I usually took cream with my coffee, so I looked at it with trepidation before taking the tiniest sip. It was a deep, rich coffee with a floral note on the aftertaste and there were hints of sugar and a spice I didn't know. A bit like cinnamon, and yet nothing like it. I took another small sip as my brain tried to unravel the components of the experience.

Bemnet smiled. "Now you will have good conversation. Skyler, I hope you will join us again."

"Thank you, Bemnet. This has been a wonderful experience. And thank you for your personal touch, telling me all about Ethiopian food."

He bowed his head slightly as he rose and disappeared again into the back of the restaurant.

I looked at Ben, and he was softly looking back. *This is supposed to be a time of conversation. Do I tell him now that I'm interviewing with a law firm out of town? No, it would ruin the evening. But I should tell him, shouldn't I? When? Maybe after the interview, when I know if there's a chance I might move away. I can't bear doing it now.*

I was quiet on the drive back to my apartment. Ben let me be quiet. I could tell he wanted to talk more, but I loved that he gave me space. Long distance never worked out. It was better to rip the band-aid off fast and break up rather than let a relationship slowly disintegrate. If I was offered the job at Clark, Cooper & Abrams, was I ready to leave Ben? My flight left in the morning, but I just couldn't bring myself to tell him there was a possibility that our first date could be our last.

I glanced over at him, driving in the dark, the profile of his face concentrating on the road. "I should confess, I thought you would take me to some fancy French place where they served caviar."

He quickly glanced over at me, then back to the road. "Disappointed?"

"Not at all. Relieved if anything that you're not that predictable."

I could barely make out in the dimness a small, satisfied smile.

As he dropped me off and opened the truck door, he asked, "Have any plans for the Easter weekend?"

"I'm traveling and plan to see my cousin. I leave tomorrow, but I'll be back for work next week."

It wasn't quite a lie, was it?

CHAPTER 18
FAMILY-FRIENDLY

I'm not a nervous flyer, but I hate being late anywhere, so I arrived at the Sacramento International Airport an hour-and-a-half before my flight, even though I didn't expect a big line at security. After sailing through TSA's checkpoint with my carry-on bag, I looked at the clock. Still forty minutes to go before my flight boarded. *You're such a geek. Now you're stuck waiting here with nothing to do.*

The magazine and snack concessions caught my eye. Rolling my eyes at myself for not putting a book in my bag, I wandered over and selected a Romantic Vistas magazine and a high-protein bar as a substitute for a real breakfast. The bored cashier barely looked up as she checked out my purchases. I wandered back to my seat near my boarding gate to wait. Although I tried to bury myself in an article about "The Tuscan Sun: Italy in Summer," I couldn't help myself from checking my clock on my phone about every five minutes. I did pick up a few ideas for decorating my new apartment…assuming I wasn't going to be moving again soon.

They finally announced my flight was boarding—a

tiny puddle-jumper plane with seats for only about twenty passengers at full capacity. They didn't even have a jetway from the terminal to the plane door. We had to exit the terminal, walk down a set of narrow steps, walk across the misty tarmac, and up ramp stairs on wheels to enter the aircraft. As I approached the plane, an airport employee took my small carry-on and stacked it on a cart to be loaded into the underside of the plane. There was no room for onboard luggage. As I walked through the fuselage door, I realized the plane was so small that I could barely stand as I looked for my assigned seat.

I found my compact seat over a wing and surveyed my surroundings. The plane had a distinctly musty smell. Various shades of worn tan plastics outlined the window frames and seats. I wasn't sure what color the fabric of the seats was originally. It felt like an outdated school bus. *There are regulations. The airline has to go through safety checks before every flight. She looks like a relic, but she must be safe to fly.*

An older woman with graying hair took the seat across from me and immediately buckled her seatbelt. I wondered if we were going to be the only passengers. At the last minute, four twenty-something guys who looked like they belonged in a rock band noisily climbed aboard. The one who looked like the lead singer wore tight, black leather pants. Long, curly hair reached halfway down his back. The others each wore all-black clothing, sunglasses, and over-the-top accessories. The way they loudly chatted, they clearly traveled together. The bandmates took seats toward the back.

As the engines fired up, I looked out of the small

window. The twin propellers on my side of the plane rotated, first slow and then whirring. As the pilot ran the RPMs up, the engines omitted a loud whine that made it difficult to hear the rowdy rock band's chatter at the back of the fuselage. The wheels seemed to make a tiny jump as the blocks were removed, then the pilot turned the plane to taxi to our assigned runway. We waited, watching several big birds— 474s and Airbus A340s—taking flight. Finally, it was our little craft's turn. The engine's revved mightily before we launched down the runway, finally lifting off. I could feel the sensation of the wheels leaving their connection to the ground and the air catching under the wings.

I loved the rush of leaving the confines of the earth and defying gravity, so much more tangible in this tiny plane. I looked down and noticed for the first time, deep grooves in the flooring around several seats. Smiling widely, I pointed and jovially remarked to the lady in the seat across from me, "Looks like we'd better behave, or they'll open the bomb bay doors and be rid of us." She looked at me with a strange expression. Her hands sought the seat in front of her, gripping it with a blood-strangling death grip. I asked, "Are you okay?" She choked out, "Afraid of flying." I felt like a moron and turned my attention back to the window.

It was only supposed to be a thirty-to-forty-minute flight depending on headwinds, but we started to dip after about fifteen minutes. I heard the scratchy voice of the pilot over the intercom. "Ladies and Gentlemen, we're going to make a short refueling stop in Stockton."

Stockton? What the heck? No plane needs to refuel in the middle of a thirty-minute flight. That doesn't make any sense. Nevertheless, we started to descend. As we neared the "airport," what appeared to be more of a single hangar and a runway with grass growing out of cracks in the tarmac came into view from the fog. As I looked out over the wing, I saw what I thought was a burst of flame from the back of one of the engines. Then it was gone. *Did I imagine that? Is that why we're landing? At least we're not crashing. We're surely not continuing with this plane.*

It couldn't have been more surreal. I was trapped with a bunch of wanna-be rock stars and a paranoid lady in an aircraft that looked like it should be in a survivor movie. A plane that just landed on what looked to be a mostly unlit, abandoned airstrip in light, spooky fog. As my eyes peered out the window, there didn't seem to be many lights. I could make out the old-style rounded hangar, but I didn't see any movement of people, vehicles, or other planes. The pilot announced, "Ladies and Gentlemen, please remain in your seats. Our flight will resume shortly." After about ten minutes, a driver brought around something that looked remotely like a fuel truck, but at this point, it felt like it was a ruse. I had suspicions that what was going on under that wing had more to do with sparks flying from the engine than a lack of fuel to stay in the air half an hour. I thought about bolting, but where could I go? And no one offered to open the door. It was a long drop to the ground. No one else was trying to abandon ship.

After another ten minutes, the engines turned on again. The pilot turned the craft down the unusually dim runway, and we took off again. I watched the engines suspiciously for any more signs of belching smoke or fire. Another fifteen minutes and we made our approach into San Jose International Airport as if this were the most normal flight in the world.

Contemplating the weirdness of the flight as I exited the plane, back across another dark tarmac and up the stairs leading to the proper international airport, I had an epiphany about my life, however long or short it might be. I did not want to be a billing machine for an uncaring group of partners who barely acknowledged me as a human being. I caught one of the taxis circling for clients outside the airport and headed to my cheap hotel room with a newly invigored interest in tomorrow's interview.

I'd had enough of budget hotel rooms of late, but fatigue plagued me. After checking in, I checked that my interview suit, stuffed into my carry-on, was still in a reasonable state. I hung it up and set the ancient tableside alarm clock for a six o'clock alarm. It was only nine p.m., so I surfed the hotel's limited offering of channels for about twenty minutes before definitively concluding there was nothing worth watching. Instead, I changed into my pajamas and tried to make myself go to sleep. I usually don't sleep well in hotel rooms, but I guess I'd gotten better at it with all the practice I'd had eluding the Russian mob. In any case, I drifted off relatively quickly.

When the alarm went off the next morning, I woke up unusually refreshed and excited about the interview, set for nine o'clock. I had enough time to get ready leisurely. When I'd arrived last night, I'd noticed a quaint-looking coffee shop across from the hotel. I walked over. It was a mom-and-pop type of operation with a collection of small faux-wood tables that looked really old but clean. The sign at the counter read, "Seat yourself" so I found a table away from the large family with toddlers and the two older couples who were the only current customers.

The waitress approached—a fifty-something woman with mousy brown hair streaked with gray and tired brown eyes. From the atmosphere, I would have expected a uniform dress with an apron, but she wore black slacks and a forest green polo. She handed me a slightly sticky plastic-coated breakfast menu. I glanced. Way too many choices. She asked, "Coffee?"

"Sure. Creamer with it. And what do you recommend for breakfast?"

"Pancakes. We've got all kinds. I'm partial to the banana-nut pancakes with whipped cream personally, but the kids like the peanut butter and poo pancakes."

I echoed. "Peanut butter and poo?"

She gave a tired smile. "Pancakes with mini chocolate chips and spread with peanut butter instead of syrup. It's a real hit with the kids…some big kids too."

"I think I'll stick with the first recommendation. Banana nut it is."

She gave a weary nod. "Be right back with that coffee."

It arrived in a thick, plain white mug with an uncomfortable handle, but the coffee was delicious. Smooth. I sipped it appreciatively. After a half a cup of caffeine and some deep breaths, I took out my phone to check emails. Carbone wanted to know if there were any updates on the caviar case. *He can wait. I told him I was taking some personal vacation days, not interviewing. Presumptuous to be bugging me about work on my days off. Part of why I need to get away from the grind that he represents.*

My pancakes arrived, stacked four high plus whipped cream. I felt a little guilty about the sugar content but was over it at first bite. *This place is a hidden gem.* I arranged for a ride-hailing car with a pick-up time in half an hour. That would give me time to finish my pancakes and have a second cup of coffee, with my ride arriving in perfect time for the interview.

As we pulled up to the offices of Clark, Cooper & Abrams, I noted that it looked just as it had on their website. The five-story building was poised close to an idyllic, gentle river. Green grass areas surrounded the parking area. The sun reflected in the tinted glass windows as a golden glow. A fairytale castle of a law firm. Almost a small city in some respects with more than two hundred attorneys in different specialties.

I walked into the gleaming, marble lobby, toward a large reception desk manned by a lithe woman who looked like she should be a supermodel. She looked up as my heels clacked across the floor. I gave her my professional smile. "Skyler Ashford. I have an interview with Mr. Cooper at nine."

She glanced at a computer and then back at me with a bland but pleasant expression. "Yes, I see you're on calendar, Ms. Ashford. Please proceed to the third floor. Taylor will be meeting you for a tour of the firm preceding your interview."

I took a gleaming brass elevator to the third floor. Similar to many legal offices, the area just off the elevator was a waiting room with another reception desk beyond, the firm name displayed in bold, brass letters on the wall behind it. I walked up to a young man with dark hair and studious glasses, wearing a white shirt and a trendy but subtly patterned navy tie. He met my eye. "Ms. Ashford." His tone was more of a confirmation than a question. "Please take a seat. Taylor will be with you shortly."

I walked back to the seating area, well-appointed with two brown leather couches studded with brass furniture tacks, two cherrywood end tables, and two smaller Queen Ann style chairs upholstered in a subtle tan and brown print. Underneath, there was a lightly patterned cream and tan throw rug. It felt like an old-world library scene had been planted in the midst of a modernist office lobby. On the end tables were copies of the latest Wall Street Journal, Forbes magazine, and Harvard Business Review. The cover of the latter listed articles including "Six Reasonable Phobias Induced by Technology," which caught my eye. I was about to pick it up when a tall woman with deep auburn hair, wearing an impeccable deep teal suit, approached. As she neared, she extended her hand. "Good morning, Ms. Ashford. I'm Taylor Adams, an associate here at the firm. Mr. Cooper asked if I would show you around."

I stood and shook her hand. "Thank you, Taylor."

She gestured toward the back offices and began walking, looking back occasionally at me as we turned down a long hallway of attorney offices and secretarial stations not unlike my present firm's layout. "Clark, Cooper & Abrams is one of the most prestigious law firms in the area. It was founded fifty-one years ago by Mr. Abrams, who is now retired."

I would hope so.

As we continued walking, she gestured gracefully toward the attorney offices to the side like a game show hostess. "We currently have two hundred and eighteen attorneys spanning a wide range of practices, including corporate and securities law, real estate transactions, contracts, litigation, renewable energy, taxation, bankruptcy, personal injury, trusts and estates, and a wide variety of other practice areas."

She sounds like she swallowed their brochure. As we walked along, I peeked in various offices where the attorneys had their doors open. Several glanced up momentarily with a look of curiosity. *Good representation of women. A lot of younger attorneys.*

We reached the end of one hallway. She opened a door leading to flights of carpeted stairs. "The third floor primarily houses our litigation department. We're heading to the second floor, which is transactions. I hope you don't mind if we take the stairs instead of the elevator. I find it to be quicker as well as good exercise."

As we emerged onto the second floor, I asked, "What areas of law do you practice in?"

She slowed. "Corporate securities primarily, working with Mr. Holland. I also assist clients with formation of various other types of business entities and do some contracts review."

"How do you find Mr. Holland as a boss?"

She stopped and looked both ways before cheerily

replying. "Mr. Holland is a wonderful boss. I enjoy working with all of the partners in my areas of practice."

I eyed her. *Is she being truthful, or does her role as tour guide also include a cameo as a salesperson? What was that glance her checking both ways before crossing the street? Looking who's listening? Do I believe her?*

We approached a door with a large glass window on top. Taylor wore a suppressed beam of pleasure on her face. Her voice dropped to a lower tone. "This is the children's daycare. We're a family-friendly firm."

Through the window, I examined a large room occupied by an assortment of small children from infants to about four years old, all wrangled by three college-age daycare workers. Several toddlers sat at a small table with coloring books. One of the workers walked and bounced a wailing little girl in a pink polka dot onesie. The third daycare provider sat on a brightly-colored playmat playing blocks with several little ones, I judged to be about a year old. Several more children under a year of age scooted about in walkers with snacks on the trays. Taylor waved and a small, blonde boy about three years old looked up from his coloring page and waved back dutifully. "That's my son, Luis." Taylor's hand dropped, and she stepped back a half step. "There's a nap room to the side of this one with cribs and toddler beds. There's also a child-sized bathroom and a small kitchenette for snacks."

Glancing through the window, I felt like I was watching a zoo enclosure. *Is this what they mean by family-friendly?* It was as if she could sense the question even though I was sure I didn't say it out loud. She gestured and stepped to the next door over. "The firm is very family friendly. In addition to daycare, this women's restroom has a small nursing room off to the side with two rocking chairs. Do you want to see it?"

I could feel myself blush slightly. "No, I'm not married."

"But you want a family someday."

Was that a question or a pronouncement? Do I want babies? Well...yeah, kinda. But I don't want them in a zoo enclosure where I wave from the hallway...do I? What's the alternative in this kind of career? I've never really thought that through. I guess this is a pretty nice arrangement, and you could check on your kid between work assignments.

I was slightly jarred by the questions that bubbled up in me. I asked Taylor, "What kind of hours are you usually here?"

"We're a family-friendly firm, so most of our associates with children come in between eight and nine and leave by five or six." There was a pause. "Of course, we do whatever is necessary to serve the client, by way of example, when there is a trial. There are times we need to put our careers first, but the firm tries to make up for it and supports family needs as well. For instance, we have a driver who picks up older children after school to bring them back to the firm. There is a separate room across from daycare where we have an after-school tutor who comes in to help the children with their homework so moms and dads don't have to take on those concerns. Do you want to peek in?"

"That's okay. I don't need to."

We headed to the other side of the second floor, where there were more attorney offices for the transactional associates. At the far end of that corridor, we took another set of stairs down to the first floor. Taylor veered into a large room. "This is our lunchroom."

It was more like a cavernous cafeteria in gleaming shades of white linoleum with small white tables scattered throughout the center. A large bay of one-way windows offered a view of the riverbank. An enormous cafeteria-style food bar lined the back wall, presently full of empty stainless containers except for a couple that held croissants, muffins, and yogurt containers on ice. A dozen coffee pod brewers and stacks of pods, creamers, cups, and stirrers filled another counter. Only a few scattered people were present, most grabbing a coffee. Taylor said, "We have a caterer who brings in salads and entrees around the lunch hour. There are also several food trucks that regularly stop by in the parking area. If you miss the lunch hour or prefer to bring your own food, there are refrigerators in smaller break rooms on the third floor. Would you like to grab a coffee?"

"No, thank you. Do most of the attorneys have lunch here?"

"I think most do. We're a family-friendly firm, so some moms and dads take the opportunity to check their child out of daycare for a quick lunch. It's also encouraged to have lunch on campus for time efficiency. After all, while we're a family-friendly firm, there's still a billables expectation and so time efficiency is important."

She can say family-friendly as many times as she wants, but there it is…the billables expectation. "How many hours are you expected to bill?"

"That's something you should bring up in your interview."

Taylor headed back to the bay of elevators. I followed,

and she punched the button for the fourth floor. As the elevator began its ascent, she said, "The fourth floor houses our copy and print center as well as numerous partner offices. The fifth floor has additional attorney offices as well as human resources, our technology support staff, and supplies. Each floor has a large conference room and at least one smaller conference room. But we'll have to cut things short. I see it's nearly time for your meeting with Mr. Cooper."

The elevator dinged, and the doors opened on the fourth floor. This floor did not have a reception area. Instead, two large glass-walled conference rooms sat to either side, with a wide corridor in between with seating. A deposition was ongoing in one of the conference rooms with a court reporter taking notes as one attorney questioned a man in khakis and a polo shirt while a half dozen other attorneys took notes. As we passed the conference rooms, I could see an additional hallway of attorney offices beyond as on the other floors. Taylor waved cheerily to a male attorney who passed us in the hallway. We walked past a huge copy room to one side and stopped in front of a generously sized office. The nameplate outside the door read "Martin Cooper." The secretary across the hall looked up, and Taylor gave her a friendly smile. "Maggie, this is Ms. Ashford for her appointment with Mr. Cooper." The secretary went off alert. Taylor leaned in the doorway. "Mr. Cooper, I have Ms. Ashford ready for you."

She ushered me into the office. Mr. Cooper appeared to be in his mid-forties with sandy brown hair, wavy on top. His charcoal gray suit and burgundy tie presented a polished image. He stood as I entered, then walked out from behind his desk to extend a hand. I made sure to use a firm grip and look him in the eye. I noticed his hands were smooth. Not the sort of guy who did his own gardening on the weekend. He gave me a pleasant smile as his eyes told me he assessed me closely. "Good morning, Ms. Ashford." He gave a nod toward Taylor. "Thank you, Taylor." She flashed a slight smile of acknowledgement before turning and leaving.

Mr. Cooper gestured toward a guest chair in front of his desk. "Have a seat, Ms. Ashford." He retreated behind his seat behind his desk, sat, and pulled out a paper from a stack to the side. I recognized my resume. He sat back with a relaxed expression of control. "So, how did you hear about Clark, Cooper & Abrams?"

"I found it on an internet search for law firms that were looking for associates." *I wish I had a more compelling answer, but that's the truth. I won't tell him I wasn't looking in this area.*

"You're currently working with another firm?"

"Yes." *Cringe.*

"Do they know you're interviewing?"

"No." *Double cringe. I should probably say something more, but there are so many ways that could backfire.*

"I see. May I ask why you're considering a move?"

"My first case assignment. I was investigating a black-market scheme and ended up getting kidnapped by Russian mobsters who may have my current address."

He gave a hearty laugh, then he saw my face. "You're not being serious...are you?"

I was deadpan. "The D.A.'s office in Sacramento would corroborate those facts. I'm set as a material witness in a criminal trial of one of the kidnappers. The others got away."

His mouth opened at half-mast. He took a moment during which I could hear his brain doing somersaults before he collected himself. "Well, that's quite a unique reason for wanting to change law firms, Ms. Ashford." He paused. "I take it I don't need to ask if you're willing to relocate. How do you time manage your caseload with multiple client needs?"

"Honestly, my current experience has been more of a need to find enough work, but I have learned a great deal about keeping billables on track and being efficient. I've also developed my own computer spreadsheet to help me keep track of priorities and time."

He nodded. "I see. How would you deal with a client who is unhappy with how the judge ruled in his or her case?"

"Erm... I think that is something that is affected by the attorney-client relationship going into the hearing or trial. If you care about clients like family, I think they can sense how invested you are. That makes it easier for them to believe you when you explain the risks involved and what might go wrong."

He leaned back in his chair. "Do you have any questions for us?"

That was short.

"I'd like to know more about billable expectations and partner-associate assignments."

He raised his left eyebrow ever so slightly. "We expect around 1,900 hours per year, which is about 37 hours per week. We assign a managing partner to new associates, but you're free to work with other partners so long as the managing partner is kept informed. In fact, we encourage it because it helps new associates find the area of law they're most passionate about."

I took a deep breath. "Does the firm help associates learn how to bring in new business?"

He smiled. "I like the trajectory of that question. Your managing partner should be part mentor in that area, but of course, he or she has their own billables expectation, so we expect associates to be proactive on their own."

I suppressed a slight smile, keeping a straight face. "Any cases involving Russian mobsters?"

He blinked before letting out a low chuckle. "Not that I know of."

After a moment of silence, he stood, and I followed suit. He reached across the desk for a concluding handshake. "It was a pleasure meeting you, Ms. Ashford. We'll be in touch." He picked up the phone. "Maggie, Ms. Ashford has concluded her interview. Will you please make sure she knows her way back out?"

I paused before I reached the doorway. "Thank you for allowing me to fly in and plan my return flight to allow time for a visit with my cousin. It's great to have an opportunity to catch up with family in the area."

He nodded. "Family in the area is something that should be attractive should we make an offer. We take great pride in being a family-friendly law firm."

As Maggie left me at the elevator and I descended back to the first floor, my brain churned. I returned to the cafeteria to grab a coffee before heading back to my hotel. The huge space was empty except for an elegant, dark-skinned woman at a table with a little boy, around two years old, eating some crackers and slices of cheese. She wore a black skirt suit and looked like a lawyer. As I walked in, she looked up. I tenuously walked up to her table. "Hi, I'm Skyler. I'm interviewing with the firm. Are you an attorney here?"

She glanced nervously to the side, then up at me. "Yes. Shayla Nottingham. I work in the real estate division."

"Would you mind if I joined you for a moment? I'd like a perspective on the firm from someone other than the recruitment partner."

She let out an almost imperceptible sigh before nodding to a chair. I pulled it out and sat. She asked, "What kinds of questions do you have?"

I shrugged slightly. "What it's *really* like to work here?"

"*Mmm…*Well, I joined because of my son. This is Tyler." She nodded toward the toddler who now had a stream of green snot oozing from his right nostril, about to make contact with his upper lip. She made an "ugh" sound and quickly grabbed a napkin to wipe his face as he tried to wiggle away. Another soft sigh. "I'm sorry. He's sick today. That's why I'm down here now. I wanted to see for myself how he's doing and spend a few minutes with him."

I gave her an understanding smile despite my scant experience with children. "It must be hard to be a mom and have a legal career."

"You have kids?"

I shook my head.

Tyler babbled something that sounded like "*Mmmr chir.*" She asked, "You want more cheese?" As she handed him another slice of cheddar, he grabbed it with a chubby little hand and smiled appreciatively. She turned back to me. "It's something to consider carefully—your plan if you want to be both a mom and an attorney."

"You said that's why you joined the firm?"

"Correct. They make an effort to be a family-friendly firm."

"I think I've heard that about a million times today." I chortled softly.

She smiled—the tired smile of a mom. "They really are...or at least they try. The daycare is a real blessing for easy drop-off and pick-up, and I know my kids are getting quality care because I can peek in on them. The price is competitive. But the daycare is also so you can work extra hours that a normal daycare wouldn't be open and bring your kid in sick, like Tyler is today. They have a separate quarantine room just for sick kids. That sends a message."

I felt my brow pucker. "Kind of like OTC meds in the supply room where I work now?"

She let out a short, suppressed laugh. "Yeah, we have *those* too. Sometimes I don't feel like I'm the one raising my kid, but if I want this kind of career...this kind of life...I don't know what other options there are."

"What about the partners? How are they to work for?"

Her smile was genuine. "Everyone in my division has been great. Most of us have families, and there is a real sense of comradery here. We pull together when someone has a challenge. I remember a late-night working with Mr. Goodwin. We were pleased that our motion was going to put an end to a tough case. We were laughing over the copy machine at midnight. There was no 'he's a partner and I'm an associate' vibe. It's a good feeling to have a team."

Tyler babbled something unintelligible with a mouth full of cheese. Shayla repeated, "You have to go potty?" His eyes searched hers. She looked back at me. "Sorry, I need to take him back to the daycare where they have the child-size facilities. It was great meeting you, Skyler." She offered a hand to Tyler, who slid carefully from his chair, and they went off as fast as Tyler's little legs could go toward the elevators.

I placed an order for car service on my phone, then headed to the coffee bar and ordered a large coffee with a to-go lid to sip while I waited. I decided I had a lot of thinking to do.

At the hotel the following morning, I packed up my things and put on a pair of jeans and a light blue chambray shirt for the Easter party at Jessie's. I ordered another driver—it was getting expensive. While I waited, I checked out of the hotel and stood out front with my carry-on. It would only be about a twenty-minute drive toward the outside of town.

Arriving at Jessie's house, I barely got out of the car and paid the driver before Jessie was out the door. She must have been watching for me from the window. I gawked at her lumbering form. She really wasn't kidding...she was ginormous. Her face seemed a little puffy, but she had an incandescent glow about her. A small ember warmed inside me, knowing she was going to make a fabulous mother. She managed to get a third of the way down the walk before I caught up with her, trying to give her a hug over the huge beachball that was now her middle. It was strange, sort of bending over it, knowing there were not one, but two little humans inside.

I dropped my carry-on in the entryway. She immediately shuffled me into the kitchen where several of her friends buzzed about like hummingbirds dive-bombing a feeder, zooming busily, all territorial in a way that didn't make me feel safe to intrude. Clearly, they'd all brought potluck dishes. There were platters of spiral ham, green bean casserole, scalloped potatoes, layered green salad, macaroni salad, vegetable platters, and what looked like home-baked dinner rolls being uncovered and arranged on the counters.

Jessie tried to help but was getting serially shooed away. She turned toward me. "Hey, everybody, this is my cousin Skyler. Skyler, this is everybody. Over there, the gal in the red dress is Marla, my next-door neighbor. Tossing the salad is Lydia, and uncovering the macaroni is Dana, both from my church." I didn't catch the next couple of names. Jessie was the only true family there. Most of our family had scattered across multiple states. Brian and Jessie had obviously made their kind of family here. It seemed like a good one.

Uncomfortable in the crowded kitchen, I slipped toward the living room to find Brian. He talked with a group of men, a few of whom were simultaneously herding toddlers. When Brian saw me, he turned with a wide grin and walked over. "Skyler! We haven't seen you in such a long time. Did you catch a gander of Jessie? If she expands any further, we're going to need a bigger bed. I hardly have any room now." He gave a silent laugh as I grinned back at him.

Dana walked in and yelled over the din of the guys talking and two toddlers screaming in a tug-o-war over a toy, cheerily announcing, "Dinner's ready!"

As everyone moved toward the kitchen to fill plates, Brian and some of the women attempted to introduce me to a few of the men. I was trying to associate the men with their wives and kids, not entirely successfully. Someone handed me a plate. I dished, feeling both like a part of this friendly crowd and an outsider all at once. Marla directed me to the two, long, folding tables that had been set up outside on the patio. Another table to the side was filled with desserts—chocolate cake, decorated sugar cookies, and several fruit pies. I already regretted how much I'd put on my plate.

After finishing my food and getting to know a few people seated close to me, I got up and moved toward the dessert table with my eye on a pink frosted sugar cookie shaped like a bunny. Jessie grabbed my elbow. "Come inside for a minute. I want to show you something."

Empty handed, I followed her inside into the now-vacant kitchen. She abruptly grabbed my hand, placing it on her huge belly. I instinctively pulled back slightly, feeling like I was intruding on sacred space, but she held my palm gently in place. "They're having playtime. Probably something I ate." She smiled wildly.

I felt an undulation—a smooth movement of a form—then a flutter followed by what felt like a small alien trying to get comfortable. I found myself mesmerized and lost in a moment of time, feeling that tiny form being knitted together in her mother's womb.

She's creating new life. What am I creating? Mostly paper bombs with the intention they would go off in the courtroom and do damage to the opposition...or give renewed life to my clients. Some of them duds that created no momentum in my legal case. But the things I create have fleeting meaning. Nothing like what I'm feeling under my hand.

I looked into Jesse's beaming face. My voice came out soft. "That's amazing."

She laughed. "From where I'm standing, it's more like little imps using my bladder as a trampoline."

Brian walked in. "She showing you the little rascals doing their evening wrestling routine? If she snuggles up to my back at night, the twins pummel me until I can't sleep. I don't know how she does it." He looked at her with pride and love in his eyes.

Will I ever have something like that? Is this what my heart is craving? But how could I ever do a family justice with a partnership track at a law firm? Wouldn't there be major compromises? The kind that would make me question myself?

Dana burst in, interrupting my thoughts. "Do you have a server for the cake?"

Jessie busied herself with finding the utensil. Brian and I headed back toward the main party, looking for a bite of something sweet. The dads had organized an egg hunt. Toddlers rambled all across Brian and Jessie's backyard, small baskets in their hands. As I ate a pink frosting-covered bunny cookie, I watched them running, looking in the flowerbeds with an occasional squeal of delight. There was a sense of belonging and calm that was missing in my world back home. I settled into a folding chair to watch.

As the sun began to set, I set down the lemonade I'd been sipping to look at the clock on my phone. Time to call for a car to get to the airport in time for my evening flight back to Sacramento. There were also five email notifications from the office reminding me of the re-entry into the work week. Brian seemed to sense what was going on. He walked over. "When you're ready, you're not calling some taxi or something. I'll drive you to the airport."

"Oh…I couldn't take you away from the party. It's a twenty-or thirty-minute drive to drop me off." I looked around. There was still a toddler or two begging for eggs to be hidden just one more time. Most of the women had gone inside.

Brian shrugged slightly. "It's going to be breaking up soon anyway. Kids' bedtimes and all."

I hesitated. "Okay, if you insist. The rides were getting pretty expensive. I need to leave in about fifteen minutes or so."

We walked inside, and I found the women huddled back in the kitchen putting plastic wrap on leftovers and trying to figure out how to fit one more thing in the refrigerator like a strange puzzle game. The trash bin was now crammed with used paper plates. Jessie stood at the sink, washing empty casserole containers and chatting with Marla. Brian announced, "Skyler has to leave for the airport in a few."

Jessie promptly rinsed and dried her hands as the other women came over to give me hugs and say their goodbyes. When I went into the entryway to get my carry-on, Jessie grabbed me in a big hug over the expanse that was the twin girls. "I've missed seeing you, Skyler. Remember when we used to play under the orange tree? Come back in a few months, and I'll share more than a rag doll to hold."

Brian took charge of the carry-on and opened the front

door. He glanced at Jessie. "I'll be back in a flash." After a quick drive to the airport, I was on a plane bound for home, but feeling less like I knew what home meant for me. I was anxious to see Ben.

My flight didn't arrive in Sacramento until ten o'clock. When I finally arrived at my dark apartment, I didn't have the energy to unpack. I threw my carry-on in a corner of the living room and headed straight to bed, dreading tomorrow's alarm clock and my return to the office.

CHAPTER 19
RECKONING

Rude beeping from my alarm announced the commencement of another Manic Monday. I went to my closet to pick out slacks and a work blazer. This morning, everything looked dark and sterile compared to spring dresses on toddler girls and brightly painted Easter eggs. My mind replayed the cacophony of noises from the backyard as friends visited and children laughed, running around underfoot. *Do I want something like that?*

When I got to the office, the Hall of Partner Portraits seemed uncharacteristically silent, their dignified visages peering at me with unspoken questions. Felicity already sat at her desk and greeted me with a smile. "So, how was your Easter weekend?"

I hadn't told her I was interviewing, but she always had that look about her that made me wonder if she knew things. "Great. I got to spend Easter with my cousin Jessie. She's expecting twins in a few months."

Felicity nodded. "Carbone's been pacing the halls this morning."

"Something in particular?" I searched her eyes, finding

no answers there.

Her phone rang. She shrugged slightly as she picked up the receiver. "Mr. Compton's and Ms. Ashford's secretary. May I help you?" I waited a moment, but the vocal tones signaled the conversation wasn't going to be brief. I felt like I was hovering and listening in, so I proceeded to my office to drop my purse and settle in.

Logging into the computer, I found a stack of emails waited. I'd been ignoring them while I was away. One from Carbone. Petrinko had been served with the lawsuit, but immediately lawyered up. I was hoping for a default. If he just didn't do anything for thirty days, we could default him and get a judgment, but that was unlikely now he had legal counsel. I'd known it was wishful thinking. My eyes narrowed as I wondered who was paying for the lawyer. Was it Petrinko or was it Chesnokov still protecting assets from afar? I pulled up the file on the computer to look at the answer. Los Angeles firm with an address on Wilshire Boulevard on the twenty-fifth floor. Not cheap. They'd put up a fight. My jaw clenched, then I deflated.

I sat there for a moment, knowing my heart just wasn't in the game, staring at my still-empty bookcase with a profound sense of fatigue. *Is it the law? Is it just this case? Or is it this place?* I came to my senses when I heard a knock on my open door. Tellis peered in. "Skyler, can I have a word?"

I put on a professional mask with my best casual smile. "Come on in."

He took a seat in a guest chair, glancing around my office, then back at me before clearing his throat. "I assume you heard that Carly is leaving." It was more of a statement than a question, so I didn't answer. He waited a moment. "We've got some big litigation cases coming to trial in the next couple of months. I talked to Carbone about lending you out to work on them. You up to it?"

This is what every first-year associate wants—a senior litigation partner ready to take me under his wing and a big chunk of important billables. Possibly a chance to get into the courtroom. Maybe argue some motions. Why am I not doing a happy dance? This is what happens when you know too much.

"Sounds like a great opportunity." I hoped my voice didn't sound as unenthusiastic as I felt.

"The first priority is to get you up to speed on the Trenton versus Hauton, Inc. matter with Mr. Wagner. We've got depositions in a month. Most of them are babysitting jobs. I'd like you to handle them. The pleadings, prior motions, and discovery responses are scanned into the computer files. You need to familiarize yourself with them, and then we'll talk about the facts of the case from my perspective."

I answered with a curt, "Got it."

He hesitated before getting up as if he could sense there was something off about me, but didn't know me well enough to pin it down. "Let me know when you're ready for that meeting." He shot me a forced smile before walking out.

I felt odd about replacing Carly. It drove home how expendable we all were, giving me a cold feeling in my gut. The case files lived on in the computer even as I knew Carly would be leaving in a week. Another associate might be hired soon. Her office would be filled with someone else's diplomas and a small scattering of personal effects, all as if

Carly had never existed.

As I stared again at that empty bookcase I had never filled, there was a growing awareness that my world had shifted on its axis. I suddenly knew what I had to do. My lips pressed together as I stood with resolution, walking out of my office in purposeful strides. As I passed her, Felicity's head jerked up. She did a slight double-take. I gave her a curt nod without slowing.

I entered Carly's office abruptly, without a courtesy knock. Her head jerked up, eyes widening, then she leaned back with a friendly smile. "You're back. How did it go?"

I shut her office door and remained standing. "I'm leaving. Even if they don't make me an offer, I'm leaving."

She blinked slowly. "Did something happen?"

I took a step forward, lowering myself into the guest chair. "What *hasn't* already happened? But I've always been able to care...about the law...about the clients. Today, I realized I've lost that, and I don't want to become...one of *them*."

Her mouth opened slightly. Her head nodded her silent understanding. We took a moment, then a spark lit in her eyes as she gave me an intense stare. "We should leave together."

"I'm not sure it would be appropriate to give them less than two weeks' notice."

Her words spilled quickly. "I don't mean the same *time*. I mean the same destination. We should start our own law firm...together. It would give me someone to share overhead and bounce ideas off. We already know each other's strengths and weaknesses. I guess I'm inviting you to be my partner."

I took a sharp breath in. Distracted by internal thoughts in a spinning frenzy, I droned, "We don't have enough experience." Even as I said it, I felt myself begin to hyper-focus on the possibilities.

"We were both smart enough to get a position with this firm. They're as tough to crack as a top university, accepting only the top five percent of applicants. On our own, we'd likely have to accept whatever walked in the door. Little cases. A wide variety to cut our teeth on. We'd learn. It could be a difficult journey, but it would be an adventure." Her voice was bright and full of the confidence of dreams.

"You make it seem easy."

"Think on it. See if you get an offer. Just let me know when you've decided. I'm making plans. I need to know if you're in them." She gave me a soft smile.

I felt like I'd been hit with a stun gun. I nodded, numb, and rose from my seat. "I'll think on it. Let you know." Even as I left her office, I began to feel a growing sense of energy seeping in like a sunrise overcoming the dark. A feeling as if I had control of my destiny again for the first time since I'd walked in this place.

Returning to my desk, I pondered what to do about Wagner and Tellis. If I were leaving, it seemed unfair to delay notifying them. More importantly, it was unfair to the client to bill the time preparing for depositions I would never attend. *Better to let him know right away. Am I still responsible for billables on my way out? They can't dock my pay, can they?*

I felt untethered until I thought of Ben. My growing excitement collided hard with a sense of guilt...even betrayal. *Will he feel abandoned if I'm not handling the caviar case? Do I trust Carbone with it? What's my place as Ben's lawyer and...am I also Ben's girlfriend? Maybe this is exactly why the State Bar doesn't like lawyers dating clients. Nah...they're just worried about the cold liability aspects, not my sense of guilt and emotional investment.*

I'd barely been sitting a minute when I got back up. As I exited my office again with a look of determination, Felicity stared, her eyes narrowed and her head tilted, but she said nothing. Despite an internal fluttering sensation, stopping just short of nausea, I quickly walked to Carbone's office, gave Joan a curt nod, and knocked firmly on the open door.

Carbone looked up, took a second look at my face, then lowered his chin while locking with my eyes. "Yes, Ms. Ashford?"

I realized both my jaw and my fists were clenched. I felt a dread that I would lose my courage if I lost momentum. I blurted, "I'm leaving the firm. Do you need a formal two-week notice?"

He didn't blink, but his posture stiffened almost imperceptibly. "I see. Is there a particular reason?" He leaned slightly forward. "Have you interviewed elsewhere?"

I hedged, speaking firmly. "I have not received an offer from another law firm." Hearing my voice, I realized its harshness and took a deep breath. "I believe that Wagner, Tibbs, and Cobbs is not the best long-term fit for me. I have appreciated my time at the firm and your mentorship. I have learned a good deal, but I believe my time here is complete."

He leaned back. Hands forming a steeple, he rubbed them slowly together as he regarded me with a cold, hard stare. There was a practiced politeness in his voice when he spoke. "Thank you for letting me know. We won't need any formal letter."

My hands fell limp to my sides. I squeezed my eyes shut and momentarily glanced out the window before looking back at him. "I'm sorry to be so abrupt. Mr. Tellis approached me about litigation support. I felt it would be unfair to the client…uh, unfair to the firm…to delay making this decision. I hope that you will give me a good letter of recommendation."

He looked at me unblinking. For a moment, I imagined something reptilian, then he made a sound in the back of his throat. "Again, thank you for your consideration. I'll notify those that need to know, including Mr. Tellis and human resources."

I could sense he was waiting for me to leave. I was no longer part of his concerns. *Did I hope for something more?* I shook the thought from my head and left with a curt head nod.

Joan looked up as I left his office—a stare like a predator who could sense blood in the air…or rather gossip. I knew it wouldn't be long before the news spread.

Returning to my office, I stopped at Felicity's desk. She deserved to know before the firm rumors fired up. As I stopped at her desk, Felicity lifted her face with a slight sigh as if she already knew what I was going to say. I gave her a crooked smile. She pursed her lips. Her voice came out soft. "You're leaving us."

I nodded gently. "You've seen us—associates—come and go. It seems you could tell."

One eyebrow raised as she stood and placed a hand on my shoulder. "I've sensed your unrest. I knew you didn't fit the mold."

"The mold?" I unintentionally flinched.

She sighed, dropping her hand. "My dear, you still have a sense of humor and a heart. And I suspect you might even be the type to want a family. In some ways, you have to sell your soul to the firm to fit the mold. I'm quite glad you realized that's not what you wanted sooner rather than years from now."

"But you knew…?" My voice softly rose in pitch before trailing off.

"From the day I met you." She flashed a motherly smile with regret behind her eyes.

I looked toward my office door, shoulders slightly slumped. "I gave them two weeks. Tellis wanted me to work on some depositions for Wagner, but I suppose I need to talk to him. He probably won't want me doing that work now. I'll have to ask around."

Felicity was silent as I shuffled back into my office.

I'd barely seated myself and was looking down at my desktop when I caught the peripheral forms of three men in suits abruptly entering my door. My head jerked up. My spine bristled. Carbone, Tellis, and Voorhees. *The Three Horsemen of my Apocalypse? This can't be good!*

Tellis spoke first, his tone cold. "There will be no need to give a two-week notice. We've reviewed the files you're currently working on. There's nothing of importance pending."

Carbone joined as if completing the thought. "We'd like you to gather your things and leave immediately."

They needed to come in as a group? Like I was going to do something wrong? Cause a commotion? They feel like they need witnesses? What were they thinking? The air was leaving the room as the emotional assault took up all of the available space.

Tellis continued. "One of us will wait and escort you out of the building. Your final paycheck will be mailed."

My vision closed in, a narrow halo of yellow. *Was I hearing this right? Escorting me out of the office like they were some bomb disposal unit? I hadn't even gotten to tell Carly yet!* I felt the blood leaving my face. I couldn't find words. I just blinked.

Voorhees offered, "Felicity can help you gather your diplomas and..." He looked around the room—the bareness of it, the lack of any personal detail. "...whatever else personal you may have."

Tellis cleared his throat. "You've already been locked out of the computer system. There should only be the firm's property on the computer and no personal emails."

He's stating it like a fact. Damned efficient takedown. Good thing I kept personal emails separate from business communications.

They all stared at me like I was some criminal or alien misfit. I felt like I needed to say something, if just to get them to leave. My voice came out as a soft croak. "I understand."

Tellis and Carbone performed what looked like a military-precision turn, leaving in lockstep. Voorhees remained. Now that the other two were gone, his face softened. "I'm sorry, Skyler."

My head snapped toward him, eyes glaring and voice suddenly cold. "I was the one who quit. I'm being treated like I was fired."

He remained silent.

Felicity peered in the doorway. "May I be of assistance with anything?" Her tone soft, she shot me a sad, knowing smile. Still stunned, I suspect I looked baffled because, without a further word, she squeezed past Voorhees and began removing my diplomas from the walls. Stacking them neatly on my desk, she whispered, "I'll get a box from the supply room."

I looked over at her, my face feeling drawn, a metallic taste in my mouth. "No need. It's all I have here. My diplomas and my purse."

Felicity gave me a warm embrace. "I'll miss you, hon."

I sunk a bit into her hug. "Me too."

As she stepped back and moved toward the door, Voorhees picked up the diplomas. "The least I can do is carry these for you."

I wanted to say no—tell him he shouldn't even touch my things after the way I'd been treated—but I saw his eyes. Voorhees wasn't the enemy. I picked up my purse and followed him out of the office. We took the back route and down the stairs, discreetly away from the peering eyes of the receptionist. It would be as if I disappeared from the office without explanation. Better yet, as if I'd never existed.

I arrived home with a melting pot of emotions all swirling together. Relief, anger, frustration, guilt, a lightness of spirit, and a heaviness of heart. They all tried to play King of the Mountain until they were exhausted and felt like they might have a migraine headache, even though I didn't get one. It was only two in the afternoon, but I hadn't had lunch. I told myself I should be hungry. The thought of food sounded repelling.

I was full of "shoulds" like I should call Ben, I should call Carly, I should eat, and I should...I didn't even know how to define the rest of the "shoulds." Taking care of myself seemed best served by completely shutting down, so I gave in to it. I pulled off my business suit, discarding it crumpled on the floor in a corner of the bedroom. Turning off the lights and trying to ignore the sunshine trying to seep in through the drapes, I lay on my cozy bed and pulled the covers up to my ears, thinking the exhaustion would take over and let me sleep. I hoped for a reboot and reset, but my brain had other ideas. All of the suppressed emotions bubbled their way up and overflowed into quiet, hot tears. *I quit. I quit. I'm the one in control! Why does it feel like I just got fired? What have I done? The monkey always grabs the next vine before letting go of the one in his hands. I'm such a stupid, stupid money. Am I really committed to venturing out on my own? With what money? These things take time...take planning.* My brain continued to berate me for a good hour while I tried to make the world shrink to that small, warm, and dark place under the covers where I could be in control and get my bearings.

When I woke, the setting sun cast dim shadows on the wall. I checked the bedside clock. Six o'clock. *Did I just dream this day? No. I'm really unemployed of my own doing.*

I dragged myself out from under the covers, still in just my underwear and bra, now a little chilled as cool air hit my skin. Pulling on sweats, I wandered to the living room and found my computer. I needed to notify the people important to me about what had just gone down.

First, I texted Carly. I didn't want to telephone the firm to talk to her. *I didn't know they'd shuffle me out so fast. I wonder why they didn't do it to her. She must have had work they needed her to finish.* A dark part of me wondered if the firm had also blocked all incoming emails from me, but I shook off the nonsense of that thought. I just typed, "Need to talk." She'd already know the firm no longer employed me. I didn't want to communicate any details on the law firm's email system.

Next, I dialed Ben's number. He answered after two rings with an exuberant voice. "Skyler, you're back. How was your Easter weekend?"

My voice came out meek. "I quit my job."

"You did what?" I could hear the disbelief over the phone line.

"It's confidential, but Carly and I are both leaving and going into private practice together. Uh…well, maybe. Or…I did interview with another law firm, and I might get an offer, but it's out of the area. I…uh…anyway, I quit this morning, and they shuffled me out of there by the afternoon."

His voice felt stern. "I'm coming over." I heard the phone disconnect before I could reply.

I looked around. Nothing out of place. I looked down at what I was wearing. Acceptable, but I could still feel a crust of saltiness on my cheeks. I went into the bathroom.

Smeared but not unredeemable. I washed my face and lightly applied fresh makeup before heading to the kitchen, where I frantically opened the cabinets and the refrigerator door, inventorying my supplies. A couple of oranges, a can of soup, some past-its-date milk, a container of yogurt, and a Styrofoam takeout plate way in the back of the refrigerator that I was afraid to open.

Why do I feel the need to make snacks? Some weird, ingrained "hostessing" thing? He's probably coming over to lecture me about what a bonehead move that was to quit my job. Or maybe he's upset about his case. Or...or...maybe he's going to try to convince me to go back. What kind of snack do you make for that? I realized I was still in a tailspin.

I went back to the couch to wait for Ben. I figured I didn't have time to shower. I sat there, wondering how long I was going to have to feel like I was waiting outside the principal's office (not that I'd ever been that kid). I acutely heard every car that drove past, every door that slammed, and every cricket that chirped for what seemed like a long time before the doorbell finally rang. When it did, I rose slowly and walked with trepidation to the door. Peering through the peephole confirmed it was Ben. *What is he holding?*

I opened the door. Ben broke into a wild grin and held out a bottle of champagne. "Sorry it took me so long. Had to make a stop along the way."

My brows creased as I took hold of the outstretched, offered bottle, trying to make sense of it. "I...uh...come in." *He's excited I quit?*

Ben looked carefully at me. "I assumed it was a celebration. Did I get it wrong?"

"Yes. No. No. I don't know yet."

He took me by the hand and led me to the couch, gesturing for me to sit. Then, taking hold of the champagne bottle, he took it to the refrigerator. "This can stay chilled until we decide."

I liked the sound of that "we." Returning to the living room, he sat down gently beside me. "Spill the whole story."

Where do I start? I ducked my head. "This last weekend, I interviewed with another law firm out of town."

His eyes flashed, but his face remained calm. "You weren't just visiting your cousin? You're planning on moving?"

I quickly shook my head. "I haven't made that decision. I've been unhappy. Carly is leaving. I knew I had to do something, so I explored my options and also visited my cousin Jessie. With Russian mobsters here and family there, I thought maybe it was the answer."

"Thought?"

My voice lowered. "But then…I kept thinking about you. Plus, I haven't heard back. I don't know if I'll get an offer." The words rushed out.

His brow crinkled. "But you quit? You were thinking of me?"

"I got back to the office this morning, and I just couldn't do it anymore. Before I could talk myself out of it, I marched straight to Carbone's office to put in my notice. But then they ushered me out within the next hour." I willed my eyes not to brim with tears. *They didn't listen.* I looked toward the ceiling trying to keep them from spilling over.

His face still registered confusion, so I tried to explain more clearly. "I quit, but the minute they knew I was leaving, they wanted me out. Immediately. Locked me out of the computers and my office email. Even had Voorhees escort me out the back."

I saw his hand clench. "That's not how you handle people...treating you like a criminal."

"No. I understood. Security and all. There's a lot of private information at a law firm." *Why was I defending them?*

His voice was full of indignation. "Well, *I* don't understand!" His eyes softened, registering pain, and his voice oozed disappointment. "So now, if the other firm makes an offer, you have to take the job out of town." His shoulders slumped.

"No. *Erm.* Well, I haven't decided, but Carly is going to open her own office and wants me to join her."

His eyebrows raised, his eyes widening with hope. "And..."

"I'm thinking about it...Probably." *I know he wants me to stay. Why can't I just promise? Why am I so afraid that if I commit, I could be abandoned? Has the distrust from the firm leeched into other areas of my life?*

He exhaled, forcing a smile I knew was for my benefit. "Then I say we open the champagne. Celebrate getting away from that pack of vultures. We can always get another bottle when you decide what's next."

I felt myself relax for the first time since breakfast. "I don't have any champagne flutes, but I'll hunt for some kind of glasses." I went to the kitchen to rummage through clean glasses. As I pulled out two short, simple water glasses, I heard the pop of the champagne cork from the living room.

He poured a small amount of chilled champagne into

the oversized receptacles. We raised our glasses, touching them awkwardly in a toast with a *clunk* rather than the clink of fine crystal. Tasting the dry, bubbly liquid, I recognized that he'd picked a decent champagne, but never having developed a taste for it, the gesture meant everything, and the experience was just a ritual—a physical representation of my decision to celebrate new potentials.

Ben set his glass down. "I feel like we should have a proper celebration. Want to change out of those sweats and go to dinner?"

I glanced self-consciously down at my informal attire. "It's been a long day. Would you compromise? Maybe stream a movie and order in Chinese food?"

He grinned, settling himself into the couch and patting the cushion next to him. "I'll pull out my phone and get a delivery order started. You want to pick the movie?"

As I sat next to him, he put his free arm around me. The weight of it felt comforting and warm. The world was less lonely and far less scary having someone like Ben to share it with. We perused movie channels as we waited for dinner to arrive, Ben trying to convince me we should watch an action movie and me pointing out the RomCom options. We finally agreed on an epic adventure film just before the doorbell rang.

Ben jumped up. "I'll get it."

"I'll get plates and forks from the kitchen."

He raised an eyebrow at me. "They give you chopsticks, you know."

"Yup. That's why I'm getting a fork."

As he was accepting the food delivery, my phone notification chimed. The lock screen showed there was an email from Clark, Cooper & Abrams, LLP.

Ben headed toward the kitchen. "Where do you want this?"

"Uh…coffee table is fine." *Liar, you just want to have time to check that email without Ben seeing.* "Go ahead and get comfortable. I'll bring the plates. What do you want to drink? There's water or soda…or more champagne."

"Waters fine. You sure you don't want a hand?"

"*No.*" It came out hasty. *Could he hear the strain in my voice?*

I quietly unlocked my phone to bring up the full text of the email. *What do I want it to say? I'll feel insulted if they don't offer me a position. But that would make deciding to stay easy. If they offer me the job, it would be a great career move. More pay. Family friendly. Near family. Just not near Ben.* There it was on the screen in undeniable reality. I had the position if I wanted it.

Ben called out, "Don't forget a few serving spoons."

I set my phone down roughly like it was poisonous. Quickly gathering the plates, utensils, and a couple of bottles of water, I returned to the living room. Ben was rustling through cartons, opening them, full of smiles.

I decided not to tell him…yet. I needed to sort myself out first. As I watched him, I felt a profound sense of loss that didn't compute. After we ate, I fell asleep, content with Ben's warm arm around me, only halfway through watching some movie I would never remember. But I would always remember the feeling of Ben's embrace. He left sometime in the night.

CHAPTER 20
NEW HORIZONS

I found myself tucked in with a blanket on the couch late the next morning. A loud knock sounded at the door. My frazzled brain registered the sound without decoding it, but the pounding wouldn't stop. I groggily made my way to the front door and turned the knob. Carly, in a fresh, professional business suit. Me, in last night's sweats, hair cattywampus, wondering if I'd drooled when I slept. I rubbed my eyes. "Carly."

She pushed through the door. "Where have you been? The firm just says you've 'left.' What the hell does that mean? They made it sound like you'd been raptured. They fired you?" As she verbally rapid-fired, she stomped to the couch, nearly knocking over a leftover Chinese food carton as she plopped down, arms crossed and back straight.

I followed, standing groggily, arms limp at my sides. "I quit."

She looked at me incredulously. "You quit?"

"Well, either we're starting a law firm, or I'm accepting that offer and moving out of town, so yeah. I told you I was done. I didn't think it would go down the way it did."

Her brow creased. "So, you got an offer? Boy have I been out of the loop."

"Not really. They emailed me last night. But, yeah, I got the offer."

I heard a heavy sigh as she reclined from her on-alert posture. "Okay, I'm not tracking. You quit *before* you got the offer?"

"I decided I was leaving no matter what."

Her eyes closed then slowly reopened. "So, when did you give them your two-week notice? You didn't tell me when we talked yesterday morning."

"No, no. I've been straightforward with you. I offered a two-week notice. An hour later I was being whisked out the back door like I never existed."

Her lips pursed with her deep frown. "Heinous." Her eyes widened as they flicked over me. "They don't know about my plans...our conversation...do they?"

"Not from me. Not unless they have your office bugged." There was sarcasm in my voice. I began to pick up the Chinese food cartons to take them to the kitchen trash. "Can I get you something? Coffee? Water?"

She ran her fingers through her hair, shaking her head. "Looks like quite a party last night."

I grabbed the last carton and threw it away. "Ben."

Her head jerked toward me with a fleeting smile. "Ben, huh."

"I called to tell him. Thought it was only fair. He came right over. I thought at first he was upset, but he arrived with champagne." I paused. "I would have called you too, but I didn't have your personal number."

"The email was cryptic. When I got in this morning and

heard the rumors, I wasn't sure if you were okay. Especially after your recent adventures. I made an excuse and headed over."

I moved the throw blanket Ben had covered me with before he left and down next to her on the couch. She smoothed her jacket. "So, you got an offer, huh? Was it a good one?" Her eyes asked the question she wasn't saying.

"Yeah. Attractive. But I think I'm done with big firms."

She sat further upright. "So, are we doing this thing? I'm looking at an office space to rent on my lunch hour today."

It was faster than I wanted to make the decision. I'd thought last night that I'd give it the week, but there she was, staring at me. It felt like the right time to make a leap of faith. "If we're doing this thing, you'd better give me the address so I can assess the place."

Her face broke into a smile. "Alright."

My smile wavered, and I looked down. "Carly, I don't have a lot of money saved up. I don't know what you expect, but we'd need to talk it all through. Maybe this weekend? I've got the offer as a fallback position, so if you're not comfortable with what I can offer, I wouldn't hold it against you, and you'd know I had a soft place to land." I looked up through my lashes, searching her face.

Her voice was soft. "This weekend then, but today, we'll let ourselves dream about the possibilities and check out some office spaces." For the first time, I noticed dark circles under her eyes. She shifted, turning slightly toward me. "I've been working through the tough details myself. Maybe you'll want the assurance of a big firm once you hear the shoestring budget I've got." I heard a hint of worry in her voice.

I stood. "But not this afternoon. Today, we'll dream about the possibilities. You'd better get to the office before they ask too many questions or don't want you taking that long lunch."

She rose, lips pursing slightly. "See you this afternoon. I got your number from Felicity. I'll text you a few addresses."

After letting Carly out, I headed to a hot shower. It felt odd to get ready so leisurely and to put on jeans on a weekday. I hardly knew what to do with myself until noon. I went in to tidy the bedroom and picked up my discarded suit from yesterday. I took pity on it, having been thrown away with disregard, reminding me of how I had been treated yesterday. I gently smoothed the fabric and hung it up until I could make a trip to the dry cleaners.

Wandering to the kitchen, I spooned some yogurt in a bowl and poured a small portion of granola on top. I opened the outdated carton of milk and took a whiff. It was going to be black coffee this morning. I definitely needed to hit the grocery store for a resupply on my way home.

Law firm start-up costs. What would they be? Rent of course. I'll find out more about that number in about an hour. I doubt we can afford any staff. Calendaring software? Malpractice coverage? Will we be able to budget for legal research software? Where we can't skimp is advertising. We'd have to get clients in the door—fast.

Taking my laptop to the kitchen table along with my breakfast, I began creating a spreadsheet between sips of coffee. My phone beeped. A text from Carly with the addresses. She had three offices lined up to see with brokers. It was almost time to leave.

Driving up to the first proposed office space, I felt optimistic. It was in a three-story large office complex for professionals. The clean, white design of the building told that story. Carly stood out front with a man in his early forties wearing a suit. I suddenly felt underdressed as I walked up to them. Carly turned. "Skyler, this is Mark Stine. Commercial real estate broker."

Mark smiled a congenial smile. "Skyler, great to meet you. I was telling Carly, the smallest space we have available is around 1,800 square feet on the first floor. It has two executive offices off of an ample lobby that can be divided into smaller spaces."

We made our way into the building, and he opened the glass door to the space. It smelled of fresh paint and new carpeting—a subtly checkered beige print. The "lobby" was cavernous. Carly immediately headed into one of the two smaller offices with Mark on her heels. He gestured toward the window. "View of the central fountain feature. Very relaxing." Carly shot me a slight eye roll through the doorway at the sales pitch.

She rejoined me, still staring at the size of the lobby. Mark caught my questioning look, remarking, "A few tenant improvements would create additional smaller offices and perhaps a copy room."

I flinched inside. *Tenant improvements. That would*

add substantially to the start-up costs. Oh, and I hadn't thought about it, but we would definitely need computers and a copier. The numbers were adding up in my head quickly, making me feel a little dizzy.

Carly asked, "What's the price per square foot here and the term?"

Mark gave her a broad smile. "Only $22.50 per square foot and the term is negotiable."

I did the math in my head. Over three thousand a month, and a lease meant that we were locked in for at least a year. The seriousness of the commitment hit me hard, and I felt my stomach roll. Carly was still smiling at Mark like we had all the money in the world. "Thanks, Mark. We'll let you know soon."

Mark followed us like a used car salesman as we left, clear out to Carly's car. "That space can fit up to five attorneys." Carly nodded but didn't say anything further. When it became awkward, he finally retreated. I looked hard into Carly's face. "Is this the average cost?"

She seemed so calm. "I wanted to start with what I'd like, and we'll work our way down to what we can afford."

I nodded, "Which one is next on the list?"

"There's a brick building out on Fortner Avenue. If you want, leave your car here and we can drive together."

I nodded and got in. She tuned into some smooth jazz on the radio and chatted as we drove. "The next one is smaller. The freeway access isn't as good. Could be annoying if we have a lot of court appearances at the downtown courthouse." I nodded, still processing.

As we drove up to the property, I noted it was small, one-story brick box building with only four tenant spaces, but it was surrounded by a small strip of green grass with two willow trees crowded out front. Not unpleasant. Another version of Mark waited for us in his real estate broker suit. As we got out, he rushed toward us, hand extended. "Hi, I'm Zack. You must be Carly…" He looked back and forth between us, suddenly unsure. Carly extended her hand. "Yes. And this is Skyler, my partner."

Partner It had an unfamiliar ring to it.

We entered the office space. It was older but well-kept with reasonably new, multi-colored industrial carpeting and unmarred light gray paint. The reception area was welcoming if small. There appeared to be two doors off the main area. Zack gave us his sales smile. "There are two offices and, down this short hallway, a break room. The hallway is wide enough for file cabinets." He looked pleased with himself.

We glanced through the two executive office doors. One larger and one much smaller. *Which one of us would take the small office? The one who could pay less for start-up costs? That would probably be me.*

Carly's head turned, generally perusing the place. She looked Zach in the eye. "What about restrooms and a copy room?"

Zach kept his smile steady. "Public restrooms are just outside. This large office can be divided if you would like another room for a copy machine or other function, but I'd recommend using it as a conference room."

So much for the big office. And that's more tenant improvements or… Rats, I'd forgotten we'd probably need a conference room. Common restrooms with an outside entrance were less secure and could be unpleasant if it rained.

Zach had been largely ignoring me, addressing all of his attention toward Carly. *Probably because I wore my jeans, and she looked the part.* I intercepted Zach with my best professional tone. "And the lease price and terms?"

He looked at me like I'd just materialized. "Economical. $18.50 per square foot, so only about eighteen hundred a month. The lease term is negotiable, but the landlord would prefer a tenant offering three years."

Three-year commitment. It rattled in my head.

As we drove away, Carly's voice was bright. "So, about a thousand a month each when you include cleaning fees and utilities."

Cleaning service. Utilities. My head hurt. Janitorial was another line item I'd forgotten in the budget. We'd be committing to thousands of dollars a month that we'd get sued for if we didn't pay, and we didn't have our first client. That big firm offer was beginning to look more attractive, but I didn't want to back out on Carly.

The last office was much smaller at only 806 square feet, but it was part of a professional three-story office building in a good part of town. It didn't shout attorney like the first building and housed a variety of businesses, but a law firm would fit in the mix just fine. The restrooms were down the hall instead of outside, and there were two small partner offices as well as a small, combined break room and copier room. There was also a large conference room shared by the entire building that could be reserved. It was down to $1,200 per month. That would have sounded like a lot at the beginning of this long lunch, but it was sounding pretty reasonable to me now. We asked the Mark-Zach lookalike named Phil to send us a copy of the lease to review.

Carly dropped me back at the first office building. Before getting out of the car, she remarked, "You were quiet today."

"Taking it all in. I haven't had as much time as you to get a feel for the expenses. It took my breath away."

She nodded, thoughtfully. "We'll talk budget this weekend. I'm confident we can make it work. We'll have to put in the hours and pull in the clients."

I got out of the car. *It's all beginning to sound like the big firm—kill what you eat, billables, putting in hours. Not exactly family-friendly? But then again, it was Carly. I had a lot to think on. We had to set clear expectations so we would remain friends and run a successful business if we were going to do this thing.*

I stopped by the grocery store on the way home to get the basics. I added ingredients for Lemon-Garlic Salmon, asparagus with hollandaise, and herbed baby potatoes. After all, I didn't have to work this afternoon. Maybe I could at least make a nice dinner for Ben to thank him for his support last night.

After unpacking the groceries, I texted Ben to invite him for dinner. We set plans for six thirty. After that, I went back to my computer and the budget spreadsheet, adding the low number for rent and lines for copier rental, computers, cleaning service, and office supplies. I stared at them, procrastinating on the research it would take to fill in the numbers. I decided to take a break before a headache set in. I wasn't ready to face the projected total.

By the time I'd done some light cleaning and had the salmon put together to pop in the oven, it was time to get ready for Ben. What I was wearing was okay, but I wanted to look nice. I thumbed through my closet, finally settling on a pink print blouse. Ben had seen me in enough somber suits. I wanted to show him a feminine side. I refreshed my makeup and added a spritz of peach-honeysuckle perfume.

When the salmon was nearly done, I quickly put together the hollandaise sauce, covered it, and set it aside while I put the asparagus in the microwave. Nothing was left but setting the table. I did that quickly, wishing I had special dishes, but my simple white plates were classic I decided.

The timer dinged for the salmon. I took it out, wondering if I should cover it to keep it warm, but then the doorbell rang. When I opened the door, Ben had a bashful look and a bouquet of pink alstroemeria blooms. He casually held them out to me. I took them and stood aside for him to walk in. He gave me an appreciative glance. "Anything I can help with?"

"No, I've got everything under control. Just have a seat." I caught myself smoothing my hair. Taking the flowers to the kitchen, I looked for something that would do as a vase. Not finding anything suitable, I used a large drinking glass and cut the stems to fit before placing the impromptu arrangement at the center of the table. As I quickly dished the salmon, asparagus, and potatoes and set them out, Ben looked appreciatively at my efforts. "It looks delicious, Skyler. Thank you for doing this."

I chuckled. "Least I could do after the sympathy and tuck-in service last night."

"You snore, by the way." His lips were pursed in mirth, and his eyes twinkled.

"Do not!" I feigned shock although I suspected the

same. *I just hope I didn't drool on him. I was so exhausted and overwrought last night.*

His voice relaxed. "It was a ladylike, little snore."

I raised my fork and an eyebrow. "Shall we eat?"

As we dined, I asked, "Any news on your case?"

He put his fork down, a slight worry line forming on his brow. "Not yet, but they tell me Nick Petrinko hasn't answered the lawsuit yet. Another week and they can default him. He had that expensive Beverly Hills law firm, but they seem to have backed out. Probably haven't been paid. It's feeling like his brotherhood has abandoned him."

"If so, you could foreclose on the real estate in collections. Although the loan would have to be paid off, that's still nearly a million available to pay a judgment."

"Exactly. Well, less Carbone's fees, which haven't been cheap. But more importantly, have you talked to Carly?"

I set down my fork, smiling. "Tomorrow is her last day at Wagner, Tibbs, and Cobbs. We took a long lunch today…to look at office spaces."

"And?"

My smile faded. "I found out how much they cost! We have a meeting this weekend to go over a proposed budget. But, Ben, I don't have that much in savings, and we'll be committing to a pretty significant monthly overhead. Honestly, it's got me a little spooked. We'd have to reel in clients quickly and keep up a brisk pace of business. Maybe it's not so different from a big firm with the work hours and stresses." I looked down at my plate, my appetite waning.

"Listen here, it's very different. You'd be your own boss. That can be scary—I know from running my own business—but it could be really satisfying too. As long as you and Carly are on the same page about how to run things, you'll do just fine."

"That's one of the things I want to talk to her about this weekend—being of the same mind about management and life goals."

"Life goals. I like the sound of that. It's not a term you'd hear at Wagner, Tibbs, and Cobbs, that's for sure." He took a casual bite of potato. "So…what are these 'life goals'?"

I blushed. I could feel the heat in my cheeks and lowered my head. "Um. I'm thinking those through."

When I looked up, he had a satisfied smile on his face. "I could help with that, you know. Maybe even with those professional goals."

I wondered what was in his mind at that moment, but it felt too awkward to ask. Instead, we continued chatting about likes and dislikes and favorites like a couple casually getting to know one another. When it was time to clear the dishes, he followed me into the kitchen, trying to make himself useful, but mostly being underfoot in the small space. But I once again thought that I could get used to this.

CHAPTER 21
REV YOUR ENGINES

Things moved rapidly after my weekend meeting with Carly. We hashed out our expectations—pushed like mad to make things work but support life goals—and agreed on a scary budget. Carly was going to invest in the least-cost copier rental that would serve our requirements. We decided to use our laptops until we could afford a more impressive computer system. We signed the lease at the cheapest office space. I agreed to figure out how to get the best results within our advertising budget.

The State Bar has so many restrictions on lawyer advertising that I decided the best route was to use an assortment of the various web-based services that provide case leads. We had about a thousand dollars a month allocated for that purpose. In my mind, I was translating every dollar into billable time that I had to earn before I could earn money to put gas in my car or a loaf of bread in my cupboard. Like the commercial real estate brokers, every service we needed had salespeople trying to get our business. Working through what was sales hype and what would actually work was almost harder than working a legal case.

I finally signed us up with two lead-generation services that would help get our website noticed and assigned each an initial $500/month maximum spend. It all needed to be put together on a shoestring budget, and we could adjust between the services as we saw how they performed. We just needed a phone number and a website to direct traffic to. Thankfully, Carly had a nephew in high school who wanted to study web design. He put together something that looked professional enough to do the job, highlighting the types of legal work we hoped would come through the door. We wanted business cases, not personal injury, estates, or criminal law.

Problem was, we couldn't afford a receptionist. I'd found a web service that would create a phone number we could use as our office number, but the software would route the calls to either my mobile phone or Carly's. So, when a client used the advertising website to call us, the phone-routing software would ring one of us and charge us for the lead. *Cha-ching*—every time our phone rang, it represented advertising dollars leaving our bank account. Every missed call would potentially be a missed opportunity.

It felt like it was only minutes before the service went live that my phone rang. "This is Skyler."

"You the attorney?" The voice was male, husky with a slight accent I couldn't place.

"Yes, you're speaking to an attorney."

"Uh, well, I have this legal matter. You do civil, right?"

"Yes, but civil law describes a broad range of case types. May I get your name?"

"Uh." There was hesitation on the line. *Why is he hesitating?*

"I need it for a conflict check. The Rules of Professional Responsibility require that I make sure who I'm talking to and that I'm not talking to someone who is suing one of my clients."

"Oh, yeah. *Erm.* Bryan *Mashilesihdhil.*" He said it quick and unintelligibly.

"Can I get you to spell that last name? Slowly."

"M-A-Y-S-V-I-L-L-E."

"Got it. We don't have a conflicts problem. Now, Mr. Maysville, what type of problem are you calling about?"

"My car."

"Yes?"

"We put it in my ex-girlfriend's name 'cause I couldn't qualify for a loan at the time. I made all the payments. Now she's mad at me and gone psycho. She took the car and won't give it back. Trying to say it's hers, but I made all the payments."

"I see. But title is in her name?"

"Yeah, but isn't there some paper you could file somewhere that makes her give it back to me?"

His tone indicated that he was under a serious misperception that attorneys could simply write something on a piece of paper and make magic happen in a day. "We could file a lawsuit, but those take time."

"Yeah, yeah. Could you do that?"

I could tell by his voice he didn't have money for lawyers. "Well, what's the car worth?" I could hope it was an expensive sports car worth more than the twenty-five thousand dollars minimum for damages to file in the Superior Court, but I already knew that wasn't the answer I was going to get.

"Yeah, I paid like ten thousand in payments."

"And is there more owed on the loan?"

"Yeah, like another thousand."

"It sounds like a small claims court matter. Attorneys can't appear in small claims court, Mr. Maysville. Also, if you're no longer with your girlfriend, she's probably going to want you to pay off the car, so she doesn't have any liability anymore before she gives it back to you." I wanted to try to salvage the call. "I could write a letter to her and help write a settlement agreement. Sometimes a letter on attorney's letterhead makes a difference."

"Small claims court, huh? Okay, I'll do that."

He hung up abruptly before I could ask any more questions. Shaking my head, I realized that, *cha-ching*, that call had just cost me thirty-five dollars for the lead.

It also dawned on me that Carly and I hadn't discussed our billing rates. I texted her. After a quick reply, we settled on fifty dollars an hour less than we'd been billed out at while at Wagner, Tibbs, and Cobbs. A little competitive edge but high enough to make headway on that overhead.

Carly and I had pooled our funds and opened a joint bank account that would serve as the operating account for the firm. I felt guilty that she put in so much more than I had, but she had just smiled and inferred that we'd consider it a business loan. If it was a client, I would have made them sign a loan agreement with specific terms, but that's not how Carly was operating with me. I shook off the hypocrisy. It still wasn't enough initial capital to give much comfort about the operating budget, but it would at least cover some startup costs. I grabbed my keys from my purse, about to head out to the office supply store to look for a desk for my new workspace, when my phone rang again.

"This is Skyler Ashford."

"Hello, dear. You have to help me. My son and daughter-in-law are just completely incompetent parents and now they're going through a divorce. She's a druggie. I'm sure of it. Smokes that *weeeeed*. Who knows what else? My son can't hold down a job for more than six months at a time. He's probably going to need to move out of state to get something. I think I can get some hair samples from her without her knowing. I've heard about grandparent rights. I want custody. Cody and Jennifer. Five and eight. And..."

"Hang on. Slow down."

"Yes, dear?"

Busybody. She wasn't going to get custody from what I could tell, and I really didn't want to know more details. "That sounds like a family law case. We don't take those kinds of cases, but I have a friend, Sylvia, who does. Would you like her number?"

"Oh, yes, dear. You've been so kind."

I gave her Sylvia's number and hung up, realizing another *cha-ching* had just hit my bank account. *Now I'm paying to get other lawyers' leads?*

I called Carly and got a text back: "On a call. I'll call you back." A few minutes later, my phone rang with Carly's ID. "Skyler, you must have activated the advertising. I just got a call. That's why I couldn't take yours."

"Did we get a new client?"

There was exasperation in her voice. "Some woman who wanted to know if I knew where she could sign up for classes to become a notary public. We didn't get charged for that, did we?"

Sheepishly. "Yeah, every time we take a call. I'll see if I can put in some additional negative key words to help filter what kind of calls we get, but I think we're going to have to sort through a lot of junk."

I could hear her gently clear her throat. "At least the phone's ringing."

"There's that."

"You get any calls yet?"

"Two. They took up my time and wanted legal advice, but they weren't the kinds of clients we could take in."

"It's okay, Skyler. We'll get there."

After we hung up, I gathered my keys up again and headed to the store to pick out furniture for my office. Once there, I walked the line between something I would have for a long time and something that seemed affordable. The one place I didn't want to skimp was a chair I'd be sitting in all day long. I remembered the chair at Wagner, Tibbs, and Cobbs. I still believed they'd just pulled it from an old conference table. I wanted a chair that said I was a partner. I needed to feel...and act...like a partner.

A text came through from Ben. "Chairo is having another dinner event tonight. Can you join?"

I texted back: "What time?"

"Six-thirty."

"I'll be there."

I'd paid extra for the office supply store to deliver the furniture the same afternoon. I headed to our new office to scope things out until it arrived, imagining in my head where I'd position my desk, client chairs, bookcase, and file cabinet I'd purchased. Carly was already there with a hefty man in black work trousers and a short-sleeved blue shirt with a sweat stain. He was muscling a large multi-function copier into what would be our copy and supply room. I waved and walked toward them, standing in the wide hallway.

Carly, uncharacteristically dressed in jeans and a black long-sleeved tee, waved back distractedly. The man gave a final shove, and the behemoth piece of equipment settled into place with barely enough room for his ample frame to maneuver around it in the compact room. He handed Carly a well-worn electronic notepad. "Sign here, ma'am." She scribbled a signature with her finger, and he handed her a thin booklet. "Instructions. And you call the number on the back if you have any problems. Pleasure doin' business with ya."

He headed toward the front door, the odor of sweat wafting past me as he gave a nod. "Ma'am."

Carly nodded toward the machine. "On lease. Copies, staples, hole punches, scans, faxes, and even Bates stamps."

I looked appreciatively at the resource, wondering how much it cost per month, but then again, we had agreed on a budget, and we would (hopefully) need it. "I've got office furniture arriving in about an hour."

She waved toward her office door. "Mines already in. Do you want to see?"

I followed her in.

It suited Carly perfectly. She'd put wallpaper on one wall—tones of light grey and misty blue. The desk was a gently whitewashed wood, and she had chosen a cream-toned leather executive chair. An expansive, dusty blue and cream throw rug graced the space under her desk and the client area. On the far side, two guest chairs in dusty blue. On the wall across from her desk, a large, gray-washed wooden clock, and on the wall behind, her diplomas, hung in the now-familiar frames provided by our former employer. The final wall had large windows, open to the street and a view of the willow trees. It was light and airy with touches of femininity that didn't overpower its professional air. Perfect. *Why hadn't I thought of a rug?*

She wore a pleased smile that was contagious. "Carly, it's perfect. It suits you."

"You think?" Her eyes searched for further approval.

"A great space." She seemed satisfied and sat down at her desk.

"I'm bringing some framed artwork from home and then it should be finished. Oh, and I had the internet connections set up this morning so our laptops will work." She pulled out a small piece of paper and jotted something down before handing it to me. "The internet connection information and password."

She'd been busy. I was impressed. "Thank you for all the hard work."

She stood suddenly. "We need to open as soon as possible, but I'm famished. Been here since before breakfast and had to wait on all the deliveries and installers. I'm going to grab something to eat. Want to join?"

"My turn to wait on deliveries. After that, I have dinner out at Chairo with Ben. Probably another fundraiser."

She nodded and headed toward the door. "Be sure to bring some of the new business cards. That could be a great place to network. They're on the countertop in the break room."

I was curious, so I found the two boxes and opened one up. Classy design. Very Carly and also suited me. *Should I really take them to the Chairo dinner? That seems wrong. I don't want to network at Ben's event. But she's right that I should always carry some with me. After all, if someone asks...well, that would be different.* I tucked a generous stack into my wallet as a precaution. *I'll get a proper business card holder soon.*

I headed to my office. I'd brought my laptop, but there wasn't anywhere to sit. I plugged in and sat on the floor like I was back in kindergarten during reading time. The office furniture wouldn't arrive for another half hour at least. I figured I could use the time to get a few more things. I texted Carly: "Ordering a few things online at the office store. Did you already get supplies?" There was a quick reply: "No. All yours."

I'd opted for a black leather executive chair with lumbar support and a black desk with a glass top—a design more like a table than a desk as I hated those little keyhole spaces most desk designs had for my long legs to fit. I decided to see if they could add a matching credenza to the order at the last minute. If it didn't arrive until tomorrow, that would have to be okay. I also added a large gray and cream throw rug to tie in the gray wooden bookcase that would arrive soon. After that, I went to the supplies section of the website. After all, we had a copier, but no paper. I added copier paper, staplers, staples, legal notepads, pens, paper clips, binder clips, Redwell expanding file folders, telephone memo pads, a coffee machine with pods and creamers, disposable coffee cups, bottled water, a document shredder, wastepaper baskets, and some clipboards. I figured that was a good start, and it added up quickly.

I heard a truck outside and got up, my legs protesting at having sat kiddie-style for so long. Looking out of the window, I recognized the office supply store's logo on the side of the truck and went out to greet the delivery person. *Guess that credenza will be on tomorrow's delivery.* Turned out to be two guys. I pointed out my new office, and they quickly hauled in several large, heavy boxes. Looking at them leaning against my office walls, I realized I should have also opted for assembly. I opened the first container, struggling to extract the heavy pieces of my bookcase, and found a set of confusing instructions written in several languages. Several tools would be required. Ones I didn't have. I put in another order for a basic toolbox. It wouldn't be delivered until tomorrow either, so assembly would all have to wait. I needed to get ready for the Chairo dinner anyway.

At home, I took a shower and extra time with my hair and makeup. I dressed in dark gray palazzo pants with a silky black blouse and paired the outfit with black, open-toed pumps. At the last minute, I slipped the stack of business cards in my silver clutch. The drive out to Chairo seemed a little surreal since the last time I was there had been on law firm business and gotten kidnapped. So much had transpired that it seemed like a lifetime ago, yet vaguely déjà vu. I parked and walked back to the entertainment space behind the offices, following the sounds of a smooth jazz live band. Similar to the fundraiser I'd attended previously, the evening was lit by a myriad of strung lights and professional chefs manned the bar-b-ques along with black-and-white-clad servers passing around various hors d'oeuvres featuring Chairo caviar. I snagged a blini and a glass of champagne before my eyes searched for Ben.

I spotted him chatting with his sister, Laurel, and another gentleman in a business suit with a bright, mustard yellow turban on his head. Ben smiled broadly as he noticed me walking toward him. "Skyler, you remember Laurel. And this is Ravi Singh. He is the CFO of Accelogistic Transport, Inc., headquartered here in the Delta. They run a fleet of over five hundred trucks, including the reefers we use for transport of Chairo's caviar."

I involuntarily shivered, recalling my last encounter with a big rig, but held out my hand to Mr. Singh. "It's a pleasure to meet you, Mr. Singh."

Ben continued in his polished, professional tone. "Mr. Singh is also a supporter of the River Conservancy." Mr. Singh nodded, taking a sip of champagne. Ben waved over one of the servers, who offered Mr. Singh another blini before she moved on toward other guests. Ben gave me a knowing glance. "Ravi, I recall you mentioning that you were having some issues with some trucking claims involving brokers. Skyler just opened a new law firm specializing in business law. She might be an excellent connection for you."

I was sure a look of surprise went over my face before I could suppress it. "Uh...yes, I formerly worked for

Wagner, Tibbs, and Cobbs."

Laurel nodded toward my clutch purse. "Do you have any business cards on you?"

I blinked before opening my purse. *Thank goodness Carly had prioritized the printing.* "Sure." I handed a card to Mr. Singh, who looked at it for a moment before tucking it into his coat jacket's inner pocket. "Thank you, Skyler. I'll check out your website when I'm back at the office."

Laurel, dressed this evening in an elegant teal dress with a high-low hem, continued to talk to Mr. Singh as Ben steered me toward the seating area. "We're about to be seated. Let's get you settled before the announcement." We approached a table, full except for two seats. He pulled out a chair for me. I sat, and he gestured to the couple to my left. "I'd like you to join me at my table with Mr. Jacques Baudelair and his wife Avril, owners of Rusal Caviar, Inc. They've heard about my case and how much assistance you've been to my company." He gave a slight head tilt toward Jacques. "Skyler's got business cards for her new firm if you're interested." He looked back at me and then to the couple to my right. "Next, Tawny Gavin and her husband Joel, owners of Gavin Farms. They farm extensive holdings in almonds and plums. Across the way, there are Conrad and Vivienne Almasel. Conrad is CEO of Arkitechton, LLC, a local construction company that specializes in large commercial builds. Vivienne is an C.P.A."

Ben was still standing. "Pardon me for a moment while I check on the food service for a moment." *Why did I feel like this had been set up just for me? Surely not, and yet that would be so like Ben.*

Conrad looked at me with curiosity. "Are you the

lawyer Ben said was kidnapped by Russian mobsters in order to investigate a break in his case?"

I forced myself not to lower my gaze. "I was kidnapped, and the firm was handling a large case for Ben that ended up leading to criminal activity, but I can't talk about it too much as the court case is still open."

Vivienne looked toward her husband. "Now that's a brave and tenacious woman. Skyler, I think we might need one of those business cards."

The other couples followed suit, and I dealt out business cards like a round of poker. Ben was at the bandstand, grabbing a microphone. I turned my head as I heard his amplified voice. "Ladies and Gentlemen, we're about to start serving. Please find your tables. And…Skyler would you please come up here?" He looked at me as I froze with a look of surprise for a moment before standing and joining him, trying not to allow my face to express my embarrassment and shock. "Ladies and Gentlemen, I have the pleasure of introducing Ms. Skyler Ashford to you this evening. Many of you know about the legal challenges Chairo Caviar has faced in the past few months and how the interruption of the Russian mob's black-market caviar sales has benefited the entire industry here in the Delta. Ms. Ashford has been instrumental in achieving those results, and now she's opening up her own law practice. She would never approve of the promotion, but I'm so proud of her, both as a friend and now a bit more. She has business cards available tonight. Please consider her for any legal needs. And now our wait staff will begin serving. Thank you all so much for joining us this evening."

As we shuffled back to the table, I hissed, "You could

have warned me," followed by a softer, "and that was amazing." Ben just grinned.

We took our seats as the servers began making their rounds. Ben looked toward the Gavins. "How are almond prices this year?"

Mr. Gavin's face fell slightly. "They're killing us on the pool prices. I'm also getting hit with a lot of extra charges that I don't agree should apply." He glanced toward me. "Would you want to take a look at the contracts?"

I gently nodded once. "That's exactly the type of business my partner and I are hoping to bring to our new firm. I'd be delighted. Why don't you send a copy of the document to me via email, and I'll call you tomorrow."

"I think I'll do that."

Before we could converse further, our table's food began to be served. Conversation paused as everyone dug into several gourmet dishes, all featuring sturgeon, of course.

Avril Baudelair leaned toward Ben, speaking with a baritone voice for a woman, dripping with a smoky French accent. "You're dating this lovely creature?"

A low blush rose on Ben's cheeks. "You've found us out."

She laughed low, even this gentle expression somehow having a tinge of French accent. "Then you mustn't let her go. She is quite exceptional." She looked toward me as a heat rose up my neck.

Ben looked sweetly at me. "I don't plan to, Avril. You give very good advice."

"Jacques and I found each other in the restaurant business before we bought the aquaculture farm. He has never failed to both challenge and entertain me. We say we will always make each other laugh, even into old age. I think that is a blessing. It is one thing to find someone you feel amorous about, but a double blessing to find someone who is also your match."

The band began playing some danceable music. Laurel took the microphone. "Ladies and Gentlemen, please take this opportunity while dinner is cleared to dance and mingle. Dessert will be served shortly."

As Ben and I looked at each other, still quietly taking in Avril's words, Laurel walked to our table. "Skyler, come join me. I have some friends I'd like you to meet." As a few couples began to dance, Laurel took me from table to table, introducing me to various local businesspersons. Now I knew this was a plot. A very sweet plot to help spread the word about the new law firm.

Servers began placing dessert on the tables—a decadent, three-layer rustic apple chunk and walnut cake with crème fraiche filling and a generous caramel drizzle on top. Laurel returned with me to the table with Ben. With a sly wink to her brother, Laurel walked away. Everyone at our table had finished dessert and was sitting back slightly, looking as if they had just experienced a pleasant torture. The couples began making the noises and "politenesses" that come at the end of a lovely evening. The band had stopped playing and were packing up, as were the chefs.

In the quietness of the evening, we lingered after the other couples had wandered toward home. I turned with questioning eyes to Ben. "I never heard any request for fundraising. This wasn't a River Conservancy event?"

"No."

My eyes darted around. "I would be paranoid and self-centered to think this event was to promote the law firm, but you and Laurel were sweet to introduce me to so many important people in the business community."

He looked away into the distance. "It's good to have an event like this every once in a while. Keeps Chairo fresh on people's minds. Thanks some of our most important vendors."

It would be narcissistic not to believe him, but the jury is still out on the purpose for this dinner.

Ben walked me out to my car. He leaned forward, planting a gentle kiss on my forehead. "Good night, Counselor."

I wanted to lean in for a kiss, but I remembered out prior conversation about taking it slow. Instead, I raised my hand, gently caressing his cheek, leaning close. "Thank you for this wonderful evening, Ben."

When I got home, it was late, but I rang Carly anyway to fill her in. I woke her. She groggily instructed, "Be at the office at eight tomorrow, Party Girl."

Okay, okay, I was there before nine a.m. After all, we didn't have office hours...yet. Carly typed away on her computer when I walked into her office to say good morning. She looked up. "You're going to marry Ben... Right?"

It was too early in the morning, even at 8:46 a.m. for that conversation. "We're still taking it slow, and he hasn't asked me."

"It wasn't really a question." She kept typing.

My phone rang, rescuing me from further "engagement" on that topic. "Good morning. This is Skyler."

"You guys do real estate law?"

"Yes."

"I gotta problem with my neighbor and her animals."

A vision flashed in my memory of Ms. Vartabedian wanting me to herd cats and complaining about dirt being piled next to her fence.

The whiny voice continued. "She's gone and done it again. Her dogs are on my property. I got back from the grocery store and the big one had me trapped in my car for thirty minutes, growling and snapping while my milk and hamburger were spoiling in the trunk."

"I see."

"And they killed a neighborhood cat too. And then there's the fences. And she's playin' that loud music in the morning. And…"

Why did they always want to rapidly spill out a long, drawn-out story that wasn't a clear statement of a legal problem? And why does it always go from cats and dogs to fences?

I cut her off. "What about the fences?"

"Well, they're on my property by about five feet. And then there's the way she drives her car…"

"How do you know the fences are on your property? Have you had a survey done?"

"Well, no, but I know it. I been at this property for thirty-five years, since my daddy gave it to me, and he always said the fences was all wrong."

"And do you want make your neighbor fix that now?"

"Well, yes, and get her to keep her dog in the yard, and not play loud music, and turn off her porch light after ten at night, and drive her car slower, and…"

"I think I've got the picture. We could try writing a letter to address the fence problem, but the other issues may be more difficult to demonstrate damages or get a restraining order."

"Oh, a letter would never do. I want you to sue her. You understand? Haven't you been hearing me?"

"We could do that. Our initial retainer for litigation is Fifteen Thousand Dollars."

She cut me off, her voice indignant. "Why, that's highway robbery!"

"You'd be surprised how much money court can cost. First, there are the hours of preparing a complaint, then you have a first appearance fee and service of process. Before that, you'd need a survey done to make sure your father was correct about where the property line is actually located. That alone could be a few thousand dollars."

"Now yer insulting my daddy? Well, I think I just need to call a few other lawyers."

She hung up without a further word. Could it have been a business opportunity? Instead, I felt like I'd just dodged a bullet. I'd barely recovered when my phone rang again. I took a deep breath and put on a cheery, professional tone. "Skyler Ashford."

A calm, male voice, perhaps older but I wasn't sure. "Skyler. This is Dane Walker. I've got a little business deal I'm hoping you can help me with. My associate and I started up a venture about twenty years ago." *Definitely older.* "We manufacture a specialized type of coating for roofing.

Doesn't sound glamorous, but we have a strong patent. We're ready to move on and have a bigger company that wants to buy us out, including the patent. We need someone to draft up the documents and work with the buyer's attorney to get this deal closed."

"We'd be happy to help if we can, but I need to enter names for our conflict check."

"Yes, yes, totally understand. Our business is Roofing Synergies, Inc. and the other shareholder is Ned Traynor. The buyer is Global Roofing Solutions, Inc. and its CEO is Vance Whitlow."

"Great, I don't recognize any of those names. Where is this deal taking place?"

"Global Roofing has their main headquarters in Wyoming and we're a California company."

Oh, I was liking this potential client. Was Wyoming going to be a problem? "My license is under California law. If the buyer wants the contract to be pursuant to Wyoming law, you will need to consult with someone in that state." *I cringed as I waited for the response.*

"We're the seller and in control. I want this deal to be under California laws. Can you draft it?"

"I'd love to. We have to get an attorney-client fee letter signed by you and a retainer." I was scrambling to estimate the necessary hours. "How does two thousand dollars sound?" *Would that be a sufficient retainer to ensure our payment without scaring him off?*

"That's fine. I've got your email from your website. I'll email the deal points. Send me the fee agreement and a retainer invoice. I'll overnight a check."

After we hung up, I realized that I didn't have any

contact information for the new client. Rookie mistake, but I could see the phone number in my phone's call log. I booted up our new law office management software and created a new contact, then I ran into Carly's office. "I just got our first client!" My voice registered my excitement. She stopped what she was doing. "That's great. What kind?"

"Business transaction. A sale."

She grinned. "We're official."

I froze. "I asked for a retainer. Did you open a trust account?"

"Attorney's IOLTA account. Yes. It's all set up in the software too. When you send the retainer request, it will route payment to the IOLTA."

"He's sending in a check."

"Yeah, that works too. We don't get hit with credit card processing fees. It's illegal for attorneys to pass those on to clients in California, you know."

I was still glowing when the front door chimed, announcing someone had entered. I went to the lobby to see who. It was my credenza and office supplies delivery, including the tools I needed to assemble my office furniture.

Reluctantly, I trudged back to my office to face the job. Not my favorite thing, and some of the parts were heavy and awkward. I was beating myself up for not arranging for help when Carly walked in. "You're going to strip the screw if you keep trying to do it that way." She walked over and helped brace the side of the bookcase so I could get a better angle.

"Thanks, Carly."

"Part of the job. We're a team, remember?"

We worked together for a couple of hours before things

were put together and Carly wandered back to her office. I finally had a desk and chair where I could work and a place that felt tidy and an expression of my personality. I set my laptop on the newly assembled desk and logged into my email. Not only an email from Dane Walker on the business transaction, but also inquiries from Ravi about his trucking broker case, as well as a request for a contract review from one of the business leaders that Laurel had introduced me to last night. It was beginning to feel like this was real.

Carly popped into my office a half hour later sipping a cup of coffee. "Thanks for getting all the office supplies—especially the caffeine fix. I got a call from one of my dad's contacts. He's a contractor. He was asked to do a custom build for a graphics design firm. They're claiming that the inability to open the windows to get fresh air is interfering with their ability to create."

"That's the goofiest thing I've ever heard of. Heck, they're not lacking any creativity to come up with that nonsense. How do you even plead that in a complaint?"

"I'm not sure, but he's going to send the complaint to us later this afternoon. Anybody can sue anyone for anything, and you still have to defend. They asked for two million in damages, so he can't ignore it, and the response is due in two weeks."

"Well, graphic arts is a creative business, and this lawsuit certainly is creative."

"Agreed. I'd like to get his attorney fees back for him, but we'll have to see what claims are in the lawsuit. I asked for a hefty retainer. I also got another new client—a farmer who claims he was delivered defective bee hives."

"How can a bee be defective?" I squinted slightly.

"The farmer explained that hive strength is measured in part by the number of frames in the boxes that are put in the orchard. He claims he contracted for five frames but, when he snuck a peek inside the bee box, there were only four frames. Additionally, many of the pollinators seemed diseased. Because the crop wasn't well pollinated, his production of almonds was down by nearly twenty percent. That translates to a really big number. This could be a great lawsuit for us."

"Or a nightmare to prove. Did he take pictures of the frames in the hives?"

She frowned. "No, but his farm manager was also there when it was opened." She raised an eyebrow. "And he's a paying client with legitimate and significant damages."

I felt my mouth open, and my eyes widen. "I didn't mean to sound doubtful. It's just strange—the kinds of cases that people bring us."

She gave a low chuckle. "If they were easy, they wouldn't need us."

"Maybe we can find other farmers who had the same problem as witnesses to help prove the client's case. They might also want to sue."

"Exactly what I was thinking."

I heard my phone ringing. I'd left it on my desk. I rushed back to get it before I lost the call, answering without looking at the caller ID. "Law firm. This is Skyler Ashford."

I heard a soft snigger. "Just me, Counselor."

"Ben. Sorry. How are you?"

His voice was cheerful. "Pretty good. Mr. Carbone just called to let me know that they got a default judgment against Nick Petrinko. They are going to proceed on collection and feel hopeful that they can foreclose on the real estate."

"On, Ben, that's great news!"

"We should celebrate."

I laughed. "We've been doing a lot of celebrating lately."

"Nothing wrong with that. Laurel and I are going out to dinner. I know she'd love for you to join us. I'll pick you up at seven."

I heard the front door chime just as Ben and I hung up from our call. As I walked out to the lobby, I was shocked to see Victoria. As usual, she wore sky-high stilettos with a flowy business suit, this time in a vibrant red. Standing in a relaxed posture, her eyes glowed when she saw me. "Love the new space, Skyler."

"What are you doing here? How did you find me?"

She chuckled. "I *am* a private investigator after all. I wanted to track you down to give you some news. Bob at Fish and Game has been keeping in contact with the authorities in London. They intercepted Serge Chesnokov with a large amount of contraband caviar. They're pressing charges. It looks like Serge will be out of business and likely behind bars."

I snorted, not quite convinced. "I hope it sticks."

She clasped her hands behind her back, a pensive expression on her face. "It should. At least we know he's not operating in the United States anymore. I also heard Nick Petrinko was defaulted in the civil case. It looks like Serge has enough problems of his own that he's abandoned Nick. After we testify in the kidnapping case, Nick will be incarcerated also."

I blew out a hard breath. "It was a heck of an

introduction to law firms for me." My mouth puckered as if I'd just tasted something acidic.

Victoria's face wore a sad smile. "I can't believe you were a first-year associate and navigated all of this. You should be so proud of all you've accomplished." Her eyes roamed around the office. "And all of this now...you're going to do great things."

I strode forward and gave her a warm hug, my voice full of emotion. "We went through a lot together. How are you?"

She waved a hand dismissively. "All part of the job. Speaking of which, I'll leave a business card. You never know when you could use a good investigator." The sleuth looked hard into my eyes as she handed it over. "I thought you should know there was one more name that surfaced when I was investigating the firm. A lawyer involved on the inside helping Sergei."

My eyes searched hers for a long second. "Carbone?"

Her eyes widened slightly. "Tommy? No." The sides of her mouth rose almost imperceptibly. "Oh, he's got his secrets, but corruption against the firm isn't one of them. Hard on green associates, his motivations lie in his profit margin as a senior partner and dreaming of the retirement he'll never take. He'll be in one of those legacy portraits in the hallway of the firm."

Exasperation creeped into my voice. "Then who?"

"Gerald Cobbs."

Carly gasped. "The tax lawyer?"

Vicky nodded. "He was involved with the Czar Alexander bankruptcy case when he worked for another firm, prior to joining Wagner, Tibbs, and Cobbs. That's where he met Sergei and got involved with the creation of World's Finest Caviar and restructuring Sergei's other assets. Someone with some financial sophistication had to be involved with the bank loan in Montana and laundering the proceeds through fictional vendors. He was a high-level lateral transfer when he joined what was then just Wagner and Tibbs. He fast-tracked into a named partner position, so this is going to be a big blow to the firm if it gets out. And I don't see how they can keep it quiet. He's facing serious jail time in addition to losing his license to practice law."

My mind reeled as I considered what my time at Wagner, Tibbs, and Cobbs had cost me...and what I had gained—an unbelievable story, experience, and courage, Ben, a law partner, and new friends. Was it worth it? I certainly wouldn't have signed up for the wild ride of legal insanity if I'd known. I was still a little paranoid about Russian mobsters. But life is an adventure. I was about to start a new one.